D-DAY

APOCALYPSE

BOOK 1:
DESTINATIONS

JT WHITE

NEWMAN SPRINGS PUBLISHING
320 Broad Street
Red Bank, NJ 07701

First originally published by Newman Springs Publishing 2024

ISBN 979-8-89308-769-7 (Paperback)
ISBN 979-8-89308-770-3 (Digital)

Printed in the United States of America

For my family and friends, I hope you believe your support has always been recognized and will never be forgotten.

Our actions may be impeded...but there can be no impeding our intentions or dispositions. Because we can accommodate and adapt. The mind adapts and converts to its own purposes the obstacle to our acting. The impediment to action advances action. What stands in the way becomes the way.

—Marcus Aurelius

FOREWORD

A RIVETING POSTAPOCALYPTIC JOURNEY

WHITE TAKES READERS ON A SUSPENSEFUL AND harrowing journey through a devastated landscape. Set in the aftermath of national and global catastrophes, the story follows a group of survivors as they travel from Georgia to Tennessee. Led by a dynamic Army veteran, they face danger, deceit, and unexpected adversity along the way.

White weaves a plot filled with twists and turns that keep readers hooked. The real-time unfolding of events adds to the sense of urgency, while moments of heart-pounding action heighten the stakes.

The characters' personalities and interactions play a crucial role. As strangers brought together by circumstance, they influence the group's sociology. White skillfully portrays their development—both individually and in relation to one another—amid the challenges they face.

While *D-Day Apocalypse* is fiction, it raises questions about our own responses in dire situations. The realistic portrayal of events prompts readers to consider their own choices and resilience.

Overall, J. T. White's novel combines suspense, character-driven storytelling, and a dose of realism. It invites readers to ponder the what-ifs and reflect on their own capacity for survival.

B. G. Sanders
Former Marine Corps Sniper / Private Security Contractor

PROLOGUE

JUNE 6, 2024

THE DAY STARTED LIKE ANY SUMMER DAY in Georgia, muggy and hot. The usual things that accompanied Monday mornings were gridlocked traffic and everyone hurrying to get to work. Vehicles whirred by in the express lane that drivers paid to use. The other six lanes crawled along at a snail's pace.

The greater Atlanta area was home to extensive industry and commerce. On a daily basis, 75 percent of the outer-lying area's population made their way into the city for it. Among all of this was Hartsfield-Jackson International Airport, the busiest airport in the world. Each day around 2,700 flights and 275,000 passengers came and went.

When the coronal mass ejections occurred, the effects lasted for twenty-eight hours until the entire globe's electrical grid was wiped out by the electromagnetic pulses that were a result of the CMEs.

Almost all grocery stores were cleaned out before the end of the week. It started very civilized; cards couldn't be used, so stores only took cash and coins. Most people conducted transactions with cards and phones and didn't carry much cash. Those people panicked and flooded to the banks. Without armored trucks, currency wasn't resupplied, and that ran out. Most looting was contained in small areas but grew out of control when word of mouth spread that all banking institutions had been ordered to close until further notice.

The collapse of the global market was inevitable as stocks and commodities were no longer being traded. Those who had cash were better off using it to start a fire than trying to exchange it for goods.

The new currencies were tangible goods like fuel, salt, sugar, coffee, flour, medicines, and guns and ammunition. In some cases, people began to trade pure gold and silver. Regardless, paper currency was now worthless like Deutschmarks post–World War I. It was recorded history that German citizens lined the walls of their homes with the diminished banknotes. History had repeated itself but on a much larger scale.

Those who were generally in good health and possessed skills passed down from elders or developed on their own survived. The old, obese, diabetic, and generally anyone needing medicine on a regular basis were the first to die in the months to come. They estimated in later years that close to a million people died that first day from flights alone that crashed. In the coming weeks, that figure doubled from people who were in hospitals. That factor doubled again the following week from those that required specialized medications and medical treatments such as dialysis. The numbers continued to pile up in the following months as illnesses and contagions like flu and the new, hyperaggressive COVID strains went unchecked. By the end of 2024, it was estimated that of the world's 8 billion population, only 45 million remained worldwide, and 1.3 million remained of the original 339,122,888 estimates in the United States.

AM radio communications were present with battery-powered radios after the first day, but they soon became fewer and fewer. It started off with the Emergency Broadcast System telling people to stay indoors due to the outbreak of flu and the COVID strains. They were combined with conflicting instructions of where to get local medical attention, then food.

The last presidential announcement came ironically on 9/11 via AM radio. It was announced as if it was the State of the Union Address. As it was radio, of course, the fanfare didn't follow through with the pomp and circumstance associated with the normal televised proceedings. There was nothing inspirational in his words; it was like a priest giving last rites to an atheist. No hope was given. He said that a new America existed and that where the absence of law thrived, we as a nation should choose the highest moral character whenever possible. He ended it by saying, "God bless us all and pray for things to get better." We would find out later that he'd contracted one of the COVID strains and died a week later. Most of the leaders in Capitol Hill had already perished or abandoned their offices by then. The new government as it existed then was being led by a handful of military leaders and the Department of Homeland Security. Several weeks later, another would step in as POTUS.

In July, there were rumors over old CB radios, sporadic ham traffic, and occasionally pirated AM broadcasts of a collection of outlaws simply called the Group that had banded together and was wreaking havoc in South Dakota. One broadcast said they'd managed to take over a National Guard Armory in Sioux Falls, South Dakota. All attempts to thwart them had been met with devastating failure. Prisons were soon emptied either by inmate revolt or mass escape. These newly freed criminals found refuge in the Group. The Group's numbers were being enhanced on a daily basis. Since the military was concentrating on potential invasions from foreign enemies, they left them alone as the lesser of two evils. Nearly all law enforcement agencies were crippled and ill-equipped to handle such a daunting challenge, and as it was a remote problem, the surviving people of South Dakota were left to fend for themselves.

A southern exodus began as fall drew nearer. From the north, many survivors either joined them or suffered in silence. Many who fled were already victims of the Group. Men who didn't join them were executed, and their women were taken as personal sex slaves or used to serve the group in any fashion that was required. By the end of November, new rumors were told that South Dakota, North Dakota, Minnesota, Southern Manitoba, and Southern Saskatchewan were also being governed by the Group.

At the same time, it was also rumored that other bands of outlaws had copied the Group's methodology, and as many as fifteen large criminal gangs were spread out across the country. Largely, the remainder of the southeastern states were unaware of their existence.

PRESENT DAY

DECEMBER 17, 2024

THE DAY WAS COLD AS USUAL; IT had been cold the day before and the day before that. Most days were cold; they had been chilly or freezing for the last two months. What was usually a mild winter in northern middle Georgia had been uncharacteristically colder than in previous years or decades before. The sun was barely covered by a few wispy clouds, but it did nothing to warm the day.

Two lonely figures stumbled along 985 North. The road was littered with leaves, scattered vegetation, and abandoned vehicles of all shapes and sizes. The smaller of the two grasped her throat, desperate with thirst. Stooping, she grabbed a handful of snow and greedily crammed it into her mouth. The snow melted slowly, and while it satiated her thirst, it chilled her even more. She then tripped over a desiccated animal that might have been a raccoon. Beth gripped her companion's arm and looked up at him apologetically.

"Tell me when you need to drink. Eating snow drops your core temperature. We need to melt snow and not eat it." Robert smiled at her grimly and restored her balance.

They approached an exit as they moved northeast from Atlanta. There were no signs for food, gas, or hotels. "Let's see what's here, there might be a house we can camp out in." Beth nodded in agreement, and they marched right into the exit. It was a small town named Flowery Branch.

As they exited the ramp, they were greeted with a fire station and a cemetery immediately to its right. They moved on past a small business and ventured into the first subdivision they came to on Warren Road.

Beth let her mind wander back to normal life as they entered the subdivision. She spotted a small home that couldn't have been more than a two-bedroom house. The landscape was now overgrown, but from the hedges and the carefully manicured gravel path to the door, you could imagine that the owner took great care and pride in their home. She began to let her mind wander when a shrill voice came out.

As Beth and Robert inched past the once-proud home, they approached another home. While similar in style, it could never have been cared for in the same way. On the doorstep of this home stood an elderly woman holding a gun that was long and mean. A pipe hung from her mouth that made her speech even more pronounced in a southern drawl.

"What y'all doing here? Ain't nothing for ya?" she asked and demanded at the same time. She leveled the shotgun at them as she spoke.

Robert put his hand in front of Beth to halt her progress. He eyed the old woman in genuine fear, then spoke. "Ma'am, we're tired, thirsty, and hungry. More than anything else, we just want to rest for the night. If there is anywhere we can do that near here, we would be very thankful to know." Robert queried in his most polite voice.

The pipe bobbed up and down in the woman's mouth as she worried the stem between her teeth. Her weathered face softened a bit as she eyed Beth and Robert pathetically. "Where you two from?" she asked, lowering the shotgun slightly but still ready.

"Northeast Tennessee, ma'am, but we were at Georgia Tech when everything went south. We've been hunkered down with a fellow student in Buckhead the last three months. Our classmate left the house one day, a day turned to a week. We ran out of food and left. We found his body three miles from the house. He'd been beaten to death and stripped naked. They even took his underwear and socks," Robert confessed.

Beth stared at the ground as tears fell, remembering the body of their friend and his brutal treatment.

Robert went on. "We found a map and are planning on heading back to Tennessee." Robert pulled a folded map from his backpack and unfolded it. He held it and pointed to it, then flipped it over for the woman to see a highlighted route. "We're taking 985 North until it turns into Highway 23, it runs all the way into Kingsport, where we're from." He folded the map and returned it to his backpack. "We're not looking for trouble, ma'am, we're just passing through."

The old woman lowered the gun and motioned for them to follow her. "Y'all come on in for a bit."

The old woman turned her back to them and opened the door, stepping inside. Beth and Robert walked up the gravel path. Their feet made audible crunches with each step. They ascended two steps and wiped their feet on a floor mat that read in block letters, "Don't knock, you'll piss me off."

As they entered, the woman pointed at a faded, threadbare otto-man and a straight-back chair that probably belonged to the kitchen table. They were close to a small fireplace where flames were consuming what looked like deadfall from trees in her yard. "Warm your-selves. I'll be back in a bit," she echoed from a nearby kitchen.

Beth sat on the ottoman and rubbed her hands together vigor-ously, then held them palms out toward the fire. Robert stood with his back to the fire, letting it warm his legs.

Moments later, the woman returned with an old camp percola-tor. She approached, and Robert stepped out of the way as she moved closer. She pulled back a steel ember curtain and set the pot on a thin layer of embers. Beth's eyes widened, and the old woman noticed. "Don't get too excited, it's just pine needle tea. The coffee and real tea ran out a month ago. Saw a survivalist do it on a TV show and thought I'd try it. Not bad. I do have a little sugar left, so I threw some in. It's about gone too, though. I heard that the grocery store at the square has some food left, but I can't drive, and that's too far for me to walk. I got some food left, but I really can't spare it," she said with a matter-of-fact tone, without malice.

"You two boyfriend and girlfriend?" she asked, easing herself into a fake leather armchair. Pieces were missing where her hands

3

rested, revealing stained fabric underneath. Smoke tendrils from her pipe floated upward as she waited for an answer.

Robert noticed that she was much smaller than she previously appeared. She was wearing a plaid housecoat that no longer disguised her thin body sitting down. "No, ma'am, we're not. Beth and I were at Tech on academic scholarships. It's just a coincidence that we were from the same area. She went to a high school in a neighboring town, Churchill. I went to a high school in the neighboring city. I was wearing a ball cap with the mascot from my school, and she was wearing a hoodie with her school mascot. Our schools played each other in all the sports. We passed each other going to class one day, and we've been friends ever since."

Beth sucked in her lower lip at the mention of friends; the old woman noticed but said nothing.

"Call me Myrtle, like the beach," she said flatly. "You can stay here tonight, but you'll need to go tomorrow."

Steam began to escape from the spout of the pot. Myrtle stood up slowly and made her way to the fireplace. She picked up the pot with the hem of her housecoat to protect her wrinkled hand. She took a ceramic cup from the mantle, filled it, and handed it to Beth, then repeated the process for Robert. Beth lifted the cup to her lips; it had a slight citrus aroma. The tea was warm, and the sugar barely disguised the fact it was warm water, but she was thirsty, and it felt good warming her throat and belly.

"Thank you, Myrtle," Beth said sheepishly. Robert repeated Beth's sentiment. He sipped the cup and finally sat in the kitchen chair.

"There're two single beds in the back room. My grandkids stayed with me time to time." She sniffled and wiped a tear from one eye before continuing. "I don't even know if'n they're alive." She paused and stared out the window, her face hardening. She didn't speak for nearly a minute.

"That I know of, there ain't but a couple folks still living in this neighborhood now. The batteries in my radio died a few days ago, last thing I heard was a recorded announcement on a loop. Lady said emergency rations were being delivered to the largest cities and that smaller ones would need to fend for themselves. Reason I'm telling you this is about the biggest city on the way is Asheville, and that's a long walk in itself. And I ain't seen a car go by in days, even then, it was a sheriff cruiser that they used in the parades, I think it was an old '54 Ford. My Subaru wouldn't start after those flare things hit us," she rambled.

"Where was I? Oh yeah, ain't too many people around here now. My nephew is a deputy with Hall County. They came in 'bout a month ago. They put Xs on the doors where people were dead and took a census of the living. There's one family living down the street and a friend of mine living in the back off another road. He came to see me a week ago and left me some food. He was supposed to come see me today. He's a nice man but keeps to himself. I'm kinda worried about him. He wasn't looking very healthy the last time, so I'm thinking that might be why he hasn't come." She paused again and stared out the window at the darkening sky.

"Myrtle, would you like me to check on him?" Robert offered.

"Yes, I would. Could you go in the morning?" Myrtle pleaded.

Beth looked at Robert, lifting her cup to her lips. She then set her cup on the hearth. "We can do that," Beth said with a hint of a smile.

Myrtle stared at Beth's shoes. "Not before I get you something decent to put on your feet."

Myrtle rose from her chair and disappeared into what must have been her bedroom. She returned a few moments later and handed Beth a shoe box. "You look to be the same size as my daughter-in-law. Was going to give these to her for her birthday. That's come and gone, they live in Utah. Just don't know if I'll see them again. They always flew in a couple times a year." Myrtle's lower lip quivered slightly.

Beth opened the box and removed a new pair of green and brown Merrell Moab waterproof all-terrain hiking boots. "They are my size!" she exclaimed with a huge smile on her face.

"You should wear them tomorrow and break them in before you two start traipsing all over Georgia. You don't, you'll be wearing blisters all over them feet," she advised.

"We'll go first thing in the morning," Robert suggested.

"Thank you for the shoes, Myrtle. Oh look!" Beth held up two pairs of wool socks for Robert to see. He smiled back at her.

"Mandy liked hiking, and I just bought them on Amazon when I ordered the shoes," Myrtle explained.

"Well, thank you. Are you sure you want to give me these? You might be able to trade them for something," Beth said.

"I just did, you're going to check on my friend," Myrtle said, waving her hand at her like she was shooing away a fly.

Over the next two hours, they all exchanged varying stories of events that took place on June 6. It was now referred to by those who survived in the following months as D-Day due to the significance of the WWII event. On that day, a series of solar flares and the resulting EMPs impacted the earth, wiping out, as far as reported, every energy grid worldwide. Nearly all modern vehicles were manufactured utilizing electronic fuel injection, thus becoming inoperable. With this issue, food, medicine, and nearly everything else that was being transported disappeared, and services like law enforcement, firefighters, and rescue became inert.

Myrtle talked about her nephew; he was one of maybe two dozen deputy sheriffs left. He offered to bring her food, but she lied to him, telling him she was well-prepared, not wanting to take food out of the mouths of the four kids he had at home. He was the only relative she had who lived close to her.

Beth talked about how she was worried about her mother, father, and younger sister. Her sister was the chief concern as she was wheelchair-bound, having suffered a spinal cord injury. Robert leaned over and squeezed her hand gently, drawing a smile from Beth and Myrtle. Myrtle then winked at Beth, going unnoticed by Robert.

Finally, after exhausting all conversation, Myrtle showed them to their beds and retired to her own room. Robert noticed an audible click as she locked her door. He didn't blame her; she had only known them for a few hours, and she had given them shelter. Beth set her new shoes by the foot of the bed and took off her sneakers and set them down. She took off her coat and lifted her arm, sniffing at her armpit. She wrinkled her nose. Robert grinned, knowing he probably smelled worse. They went to bed wearing their clothes, as the fireplace's warmth didn't extend into the rear room.

Less than a minute later, Robert could hear a soft snore escaping from Beth. Robert started to reflect on the last few hours but was soon snoring himself after shutting his eyes.

DECEMBER 18, 2024

Robert woke to sunlight peeking through the closed curtains. He rose and stretched his six-foot frame, then put on his shoes, ignoring the smell. On D-Day, he weighed 240 pounds; now he was likely around 200. He was chubby back then but worked out and was considerably stronger than the average guy his age. At 22, he was fortunate enough to obtain his degree before the catastrophic event in June. He chuckled to himself, realizing his bachelor's in international affairs was completely useless.

He spread the curtains allowing the light to fill the room. Looking into Myrtle's backyard, he noticed the grass was overgrown but noticeably more managed than the other lawns they'd seen entering the subdivision.

"What's funny?" came a weary voice. Beth rolled back the covers and stretched while yawning. She set her feet on the floor, rubbing sleep from her eyes.

"What?" Robert asked, running his fingers through his shoulder-length curly blonde hair.

"I heard you chuckle. What's funny?" Beth insisted.

"Oh, I was thinking my higher education is now completely useless," he told her.

"Ah, well, my cybersecurity degree isn't exactly putting food on the table either," Beth offered and snickered in return. She rose from the bed and stretched further. Beth pulled a hairbrush from Robert's pack and started to run it through her black hair, which now hung below her shoulders. After returning the brush, she took out a hair tie from a pocket in her jeans and quickly put her hair into a ponytail.

She took the new shoes and a pair of new socks, putting the spare pair into a pocket in the backpack. She peeled off the soiled tube socks and wrinkled her nose again. Donning the new wool socks, she carefully put on the new shoes and laced them until they were secure. Standing up, she walked around the room, testing the fit. Beth had lost weight too; on D-Day, she weighed 135 pounds, which suited her five and a half feet in height. She wasn't an athlete per se but did take to yoga and cardio kickboxing twice a week, accentuating that by running three miles every Saturday morning. Now she was probably around 120.

Robert watched Beth prance lightly around the room and found himself staring at her as carnal instinct reared its inquisitive head. His eyes lingered on her chest and then quickly averted to her behind. She spun around, and he quickly averted his eyes to her feet.

"So?" he asked, watching her flex her feet.

"They fit! Better than I thought. If I wasn't wearing these thick socks, they might be a bit loose. Overall, I'm not complaining. We should be on the lookout for some new shoes for you too," she said, pointing at his cross trainers.

Robert dropped his chin and eyed his shoes. She was right. They were already well over a year old on D-Day. Now the threads were coming loose at the tread. "Yeah, I hope we come across something. Last time we tried using cash, it only brought laughter. Remember the guy selling bottled water?" he reminded her.

Beth merely nodded in agreement.

They exited the bedroom to a noticeably warmer temperature and the aroma of baked bread. The percolator was sitting further away from a larger fire than the one they were greeted with yesterday evening. Near the fire was a plate filled with biscuits and a small jar of blackberry preserves.

Myrtle had exchanged her housecoat for flannel-lined blue jeans and an Atlanta Falcons sweatshirt. She was also wearing rubber boots. She wiped her hands on a dish towel. "Had some powdered milk and flour tucked away. Help yourself, I've had my fill." She gestured toward the plate and walked to the front door, raising a blade in the blinds to look out.

Robert and Beth looked at each other as their bellies beckoned them to stop the hunger.

"Go on, I've got enough flour and powdered milk for a bit. It's the few things I have that I can spare," she said without looking at them, continuing to stare through the door blinds.

Without further direction, they resumed their seats from the previous evening. Robert took a biscuit, spread a spoonful of preserves on it, and handed it to Beth. She immediately bit into it, almost moaning with pleasure. Before Robert could bite into his own, Beth shoved the last bite of hers into her mouth. Beth poured them cups of pine needle tea, and over the course of perhaps ten minutes, they ate all but four biscuits, which Robert put into a pocket on his pack.

Myrtle was now seated in her chair. "How long it been since y'all ate?"

"Two days," Beth answered. "It took us six days to get here. We had a few candy bars and packs of peanut butter crackers. Our water ran out the day before we got here."

Robert put on his coat and shrugged his pack over his shoulders. "We had to hide quite a bit. We'd make a few miles and then have to hide from thugs and gangs. We had some trouble in Suwanee before we got on 985. When we got close to the exit, a couple of guys jumped out of a van on the interstate. They rushed us and tried to take my pack. There wasn't anything in it except for a couple of changes of clothes for Beth and me. But it took a nasty turn when the bigger of the two pulled a knife. I used my pack as a shield, and when he came at me, he stabbed my pack. I told Beth to run. I fell over a truck wheel, that's when I found a lug wrench. When he came back to me, I swung for the bleachers. I hit him in the head, and the other guy picked up his knife and ran away."

Myrtle just nodded in understanding.

"We stayed off the main roads after that, hugging the tree line once we got on 985," Beth added. "People just turned nasty, seems like overnight," Beth said to her.

"Naw, people always been nasty, sweety. It just took something like this to bring out the worst in them," she said flatly.

Robert helped Beth into her coat and moved toward the door. Myrtle stood up using her arms to aid her. "Make sure you steer clear of the house with the rail fence. You'll know it when you see it. They got dogs and animals. They were mean before D-Day, now they're downright unpleasant," she cautioned.

Myrtle wrote the address and handed them a post-it. In neat, elegant cursive, it read,

Lane Stone 6814 Falcon Crest Dr.

As the door closed behind them, Beth and Robert turned to each other. In unison, they said, "I need to pee." Five minutes later, they walked behind one of the houses with a big red X spray-painted on the front door. Robert fished in the pocket of his pack and handed her a small roll of tissue in a ziplock bag.

Robert stood watch and peed against a tree while Beth stooped behind a bush. When he finished, he fished out the lug wrench he had hidden and put his pack back on. Beth walked up and stuck the tissue back in his pack. As they walked, the red Xs became more prevalent. All the houses were abandoned, and the quiet here was even more haunting.

"I keep expecting zombies to come moaning around the corner, you know, like *The Walking Dead*...decayed with ripped and torn clothes and dragging a leg...maybe one clawed, weathered hand stretched out in front of him...or her," Beth joked.

"Let's not set any further expectations that don't involve cheeseburgers and beer," Robert grumbled.

Soon they approached a curve in the road, and the wood rail fence came into view. As they got closer, they noticed a skinned animal hanging from a tree. A tall, thin man was butchering the carcass, a pistol hanging on his hip in a quick-release holster like the ones police carried. Steam rose into the air from the entrails below the dead animal, masking the man's expression. Robert could see a small herd of goats grazing further away in a neighboring yard. In the same yard, he saw a chicken coop and several hens pecking at the ground. Noticing Robert and Beth, the man stopped his work and watched them as they passed by. Two large Anatolian shepherds sat quietly at his heels, also watching their steps. A small whistle escaped the man's lips, and the two exploded from their position and ran toward the goats, jumping over a three-foot-high chain-link fence with an ease that would have humbled Olympic hurdlers. The dogs immediately resumed their sitting position. No words were exchanged. Only when they were out of sight did the man return to his work.

"Crap on a cracker! I thought they were coming after us!" Beth whispered harshly.

"So did I!" Robert exhaled. He then realized he was squeezing the lug wrench, making his knuckles turn white. He relaxed his grip and quickened his pace. Beth matched it in response.

It took them another fifteen minutes before they found the mailbox they were looking for. It stood at the bottom of a severely steep driveway. Halfway up the driveway, their breaths plumed out of their mouths. A No Trespassing sign was nailed to a large oak tree on the right. Once they got to the top of the driveway, they took in their surroundings. There were no vehicles in the driveway. The yard was slightly less overgrown than Myrtle's; a tire swing hung from the limb of a tall oak tree. In the backyard, two cords of split firewood were stacked between elm trees, and a metal patio table was covered in leaves beneath a crape myrtle. A yellow Tonka dump truck and a Radio Flyer red wagon sat empty, parked by the garage door with several plastic toys lying beneath them. Stacks of firewood sat in neat rows on the front deck that led to the front door.

Robert nudged Beth and pointed to the chimney. "No smoke."

They ascended three steps and stood in front of the door. Without hesitation, Robert knocked three times. "Mr. Stone, Myrtle sent us to check on you." He waited for a minute, then knocked again. "Hello, Mr. Lane Stone? Your friend Myrtle sent us to check on you. She's worried about you."

Another minute passed, and then finally, a deep voice could be heard somewhere inside the split-level home. "Hold on!" Another minute passed before they heard locks disengaging and the door opened.

Standing before them was a man roughly the same height as Robert. This man was much larger, though. He looked them up and down, then spoke, holding a shotgun with a collapsed stock at his side. "Only reason I answered is I didn't want Myrtle trying to walk back here. Tell her I'm fine. Hold on and stay there." He shut the door behind him. A few minutes later, he returned, swinging open the door at them carrying a plastic bag. "It's enough food to carry her a week. Tell her I'll be around in another week to check on her. Would have been there yesterday, but I threw out my back splitting wood."

Robert then noticed that the man reminded him of his father. His beard was almost completely white save for his mustache and a matching V-shaped red patch below his lip. Those matched his bushy hair sticking out the bottom of a black knit hat. His chest was broad, and his shoulders were rounded, indicating the muscle beneath, no doubt from the chopping of all the wood. His expression was hard and strained. It was hurting him to stand. He handed them the bag and started to close the door. He stopped abruptly and returned his gaze to them. "Have you eaten?"

"Yes, sir, Myrtle made us biscuits this morning," Beth answered.

Lane Stone chuckled without smiling. "That woman has got more flour than any one person I ever knew." He then noticed the lug wrench Robert was hiding ineffectively behind his back. "You planning on using that, son?" he asked, pointing to Robert's right side.

"Oh, sorry, sir. Just being cautious," Robert quickly said, looking embarrassed. He removed his pack, shoved the lug wrench into it, and returned the pack to his back. He quickly told Lane about their journey and ambush on the interstate. Lane nodded, his face contorting in pain.

Lane eyed them suspiciously, then stood back away from the door. "Better come in and warm up. Didn't feel like starting a fire last night. Paying for it now. You'll need to start it. Kindling and dryer lint by the fireplace."

Lane collapsed into a brown cloth recliner, grimacing, still holding the shotgun in a defensive posture. Beth sat down on a couch that was beginning to show signs of wear. The cushions were compressed, obviously due in part to the large man's size. He slept there often, she assumed. Robert got to work using a small axe to split the kindling into smaller sticks. He used these to build a small pile, on top of which he placed several pieces of kindling. He then tore a small piece of dryer lint, placed it next to the small sticks, and struck a match to the lint. The lint immediately caught flame; Robert blew at the flame gently, pushing the flames further into the sticks. The sticks quickly caught and started burning the kindling. He then placed three large split logs on a cast iron cradle. A few minutes later, the flames caught the larger pieces and grew larger. Robert stood and then took a seat next to Beth.

"Young lady, in the kitchen above the stove, there's aspirin. Please bring me two and a glass of water," Lane pleaded. "You two are going to get killed walking around here with nothing but that lug wrench," he cautioned, pointing at Robert's pack sitting on the floor.

"I get what you're saying, but Beth and I were students stranded at Tech. And they won't allow students to keep guns inside student housing," Robert said flatly.

"You mean to tell me you been stranded at Tech this whole time?" Lane asked, raising his eyebrows.

"Not exactly. We were staying at a friend's house in Buckhead," Robert said. He retold their story in abbreviated details and their plans to walk home.

"That's one heck of a long way to go hoofing it. There're some bad hombres lurking here and there. The worst of them showed up in the last few weeks. I don't worry about Myrtle too much, her nephew keeps a pretty good eye on her. But I had some visitors. Reckon they saw the smoke from the chimney and decided there might be a few prizes inside. Thing of it is, they tripped a solar laser, and I knew they were coming."

Beth interrupted him, handing him the aspirin and water. He thanked her, and she sat back down next to Robert.

"That was their first mistake. The second mistake was not seeing the cameras in the trees." Lane's face hardened abruptly, stopping himself from speaking further.

Robert and Beth looked at each other but said nothing. When they returned their gaze to Lane, he began again.

"Anyhow, those bad hombres would be delighted to see your girlfriend undefended," Lane warned.

Robert's face flushed. "Mr. Stone, Beth and I are just frie—" Before he could finish his sentence, an audible ping sounded through the entire house. It was a sound like a phone-text alert but much louder.

Lane stood quickly, grimacing, and grabbed a remote control from the coffee table that separated them. He quickly pointed it at a flat-screen TV on a small kitchen table. The TV blinked to life, displaying six frames, each giving varying views to the outside. At the top left of the displays, three figures could be seen slowly making progress up the steep driveway. Lane clicked the remote, and that screen blew up to fill the entire screen. Two were Latino; the other was white. Lane pointed the remote at the screen, and a circle appeared. He moved the circle over the middle torso of one of the men. As the display was about to lose sight of them, a hand reached behind the man's back and returned to his side, holding a semiautomatic pistol.

"You two, back room to the right. Lock yourselves in. Go to the bathroom and lock yourselves in. Push against both sides of the medicine cabinet and arm yourself. Go now!" Lane Stone grumbled in a stern voice.

"Sir, I can..." Before he could finish, Lane said in a low whisper, "Now!"

Robert took Beth by the hand, pushed her to the rear of the house, and entered a bedroom that had clearly been occupied by a woman with its furnishings. Robert quickly turned and shut the door. It was much heavier than he realized when first opening it. It was heavy metal painted to look like wood. After shutting it, he realized there were three deadbolts and a bar sitting upright in a cradle, ready to be dropped. He dropped the bar into another cradle, allowing it to create another barrier lock. Robert ushered Beth into the bathroom and shut the door. Inside, he engaged two more deadbolts and quickly found the medicine cabinet. He did as instructed until he heard a click. Somewhere, a spring responded, and the cabinet came back to a resting position, with the left side parting from the wall slightly. The whole cabinet swung away to reveal two handguns. The larger was a Beretta M9 with two spare magazines. The other was a Smith & Wesson, hammerless snub-nosed .357 with two quick-release drum loaders. At the bottom were two boxes of ammunition for each pistol. Robert took the Beretta and handed the snub nose to Beth.

"It's real easy. Point and squeeze the trigger." He demonstrated to her by pointing the pistol and mimicking a finger squeeze with his index finger outside of the trigger guard.

Beth nodded and told him, "Got it. My uncle took me to a range once. It was a revolver too."

Robert looked at her in surprise. It was at that moment he realized that, for the last four years, he really hadn't gotten to know Beth as real friends should. When they'd first met, it was ecstatic joy at finding someone from your community in a world full of strangers. They later began to get to know each other by spending time devouring pizza at Mellow Mushroom. Then it was playing frisbee golf, which transpired to binge-watching *The Walking Dead* and *Peaky Blinders* on Netflix. In all that time, Robert had always admired how beautiful Beth was. He was attracted to her, and he figured that Beth knew this from all the times she caught him checking out her ass or catching him avert his eyes quickly during swimming trips, eyeing her bikini top. There were also several times she caught him staring at her, hypnotized or being caught speechless by things she would say or do. Secretly, he had always wanted something to happen, but one unfortunate day, he had accidentally eavesdropped on a conversation between Beth and one of her classmates.

"Are you and Robert a thing?" Luminita asked in her thick Romanian accent.

"No, we're just friends. Shoot your shot. I'm sure he'd like you," Beth offered. She had instantly regretted it, unbeknownst to Robert. She just felt that she needed to concentrate on her studies. And after school, would he really want to take home a girl from the trailer white trash that was her family?

Robert snapped back to reality when he heard three quick gunshots, then a fourth. He ejected the magazine from the pistol and checked to see if it was loaded. It was. He looked at the ammo; they were hollow points. He quickly snatched the pistol back from Beth and popped open the drum of the pistol. It, too, was loaded with hollow points. She snatched it back just as fast, eyeing him with disdain, popping the drum back in place.

"I checked it already!" she said with venom in her voice.

"Okay, okay!" he exclaimed, clearly dismayed by her reaction.

He slid back the action and saw that a round was already chambered. He clicked the safety off, staring at Beth. He'd already known he was going to protect her at all costs, but the independence she suddenly displayed unnerved and excited him at the same time.

They were startled when they heard a door slam. Minutes went by, and then they heard two quick knocks followed by Lane's deep voice. "You can come out now! Grab the first aid bag from under the sink on your way out!"

Robert retrieved the bag and opened the bathroom, exiting with Beth behind him on his heels. Robert quickly raised the barrier from its cradle and disengaged the deadbolts. Opening the door, they noticed a trail of blood droplets leading into the living room. They found Lane in his chair, holding a blood-soaked dish towel to his left shoulder. Robert went to the window and saw three bodies lying still on the ground.

"Put that kit on the table and open it, please," Lane directed Robert. "Don't suppose either of you know any first aid?"

"Actually, I do, sir. One of the last badges I got before I made Eagle Scout," Robert said.

Lane's eyes widened in surprise. "Didn't think there were any more Boy Scouts left," Lane exclaimed, clearly impressed.

Robert put the pistol in the waistband of his jeans in the small of his back, then put on a pair of purple neoprene gloves from the kit and quickly inventoried its contents. Robert pulled Lane forward gingerly and examined the rear of the shoulder—no exit wound. He then lifted Lane's bloodied hand and towel to examine the wound. From the look of it, it was a small caliber bullet, but it was still inside him. Robert shrugged off his coat, as did Beth, with the housewarming from its growing fire.

"Lane, do you have anything for pain besides aspirin?" Robert asked him.

Lane looked at Beth. "Young lady, if you would be so kind again, there is another bottle back where you got the party favors. Inside the actual cabinet, there's a bottle of Percocet." Lane noticed Robert quickly eyeing him and then averted his eyes. "Relax, guys. I had hernia surgery a year ago. I didn't take all of them. I don't like pills unless I really need them." With the explanation, Beth disappeared.

When Beth returned, Robert whispered to her, and she dug into her pocket and reluctantly handed him a small package. Robert took a small antiseptic wipe and rubbed it around the wound. He then took the package, removed the plastic, and pulled out a tampon. Robert grabbed a Bic lighter and put it between Lane's teeth. "Bite down!" With that, Robert plunged the tampon into the wound. Blood immediately soaked the sanitary absorbent and controlled the bleeding.

Beth returned to the small kitchen and filled a glass with water. She started to take the water back when she spotted a bottle of Jack Daniels that hadn't been opened. She cracked the label and poured a couple of shots into the glass. She shook out two pills and returned to Lane. Lane took the pills with his right hand and quickly shoved them in his mouth, chewing the capsules and wincing at the alien taste. She quickly handed him the liquor, which he gulped down.

"Thank you, young lady," Lane told her but inhaled sharply, expecting the glass to hold water.

"Let's give it a few minutes to let the meds take effect. I need to take that bullet out. Beth, help me get Lane on the floor," Robert told her.

Robert grabbed the coffee table by himself and carried it away, a couple of magazines falling to the floor as he moved it. He helped Lane to his feet and eased him to the floor. Beth helped steady Lane, and he was soon lying on the floor. Beth took a small couch pillow and gently placed it under his head.

"Do you have a clock?" Robert asked Lane.

"No," Lane said in a strained voice.

Beth put a blanket over his lower torso. Robert looked out the window and tried to gauge the time by the sun's position. He guessed it was somewhere between nine and ten o'clock. His mind wandered to a cup filled with pens and pencils. He quickly snatched a number 2 Ticonderoga pencil and found a small cactus plant on the windowsill. He grabbed the arm sleeve protector from Lane's chair and used it to pluck the cactus from the planter. He placed the cactus on the windowsill and tapped the soil into a firmer surface. Once he completed that, he plunged the pencil into the soil and grabbed the planter in one hand.

"Paper plates?" Robert asked Lane.

"Cabinet beside the trash can," Lane grunted.

Robert took off and quickly returned with a paper plate. He burrowed a hole in it until he could drop it over the pencil and onto the top of the small planter. He then held the planter next to the frame of the window and measured the squareness of the vertical pencil and the horizontal planter against the frame. After adjusting the pencil, he determined a true angle and set the planter back in the window frame. Robert examined the shadow from the pencil and marked it with another pencil from the cup. He counted off five minutes to himself, extending his index finger from his clenched fist, and started over. He did this two more times, counting on his fingers at his hip. He took the pencil and made another mark on the shadow's new position, measuring the distance between the marks and making enough to span an hour.

After thirty minutes, he approached Lane and saw that he was asleep. Rummaging through the kit, he laid out bandages and surgical tape. Robert disappeared and quickly returned with a disposable razor. With Beth's help, he removed Lane's shirt and then shaved the area around the wound, taking extra care not to worsen it. Beth pulled the blanket up until it covered his abdomen. Robert took a pair of hemostats from a sterile package and got to work. He removed the tampon with a little effort as the material had expanded, absorbing the blood. When it came free, it made a sound that reminded him strangely of biting into a watermelon. He popped the lid on a one-use saline bottle and cleaned the wound. Lane moaned in his sleep but didn't move.

"Raise the blinds all the way, I need more light."

Beth jumped up and filled the room with more light, allowing the sunlight to fall on Lane.

Robert closed his eyes briefly and said a quick prayer for Lane, asking God to make his hands accurate. "Clean your hands with a couple of those antiseptic wipes, and put on a pair of those gloves. Once you've done that, grab that suture pack and be ready to open it," Robert directed Beth, pointing at the small pack with a small, curved needle. It was then that he noticed the bag was military issue.

Beth sat patiently, watching Robert as he gently probed the wound for what seemed like an eternity. He poked gently until he found the bullet. He examined the instrument's depth, noting a small trademark stamped into the metal. He squeezed the pincers together and started to pull upward. Lane's brow furrowed, and he sucked air through clenched teeth.

Robert continued his effort until finally the instrument cleared, and he held it triumphantly in the air like a trophy. He quickly laid down the clamp, letting the slug fall free. He then took another one-use saline bottle and cleaned the wound, then cleaned the blood from around it. He extended his hand to Beth and took the suture. He leaned over the wound, getting closer to observe his task. He stopped and handed the suture back to Beth, rummaged through the bag, and then donned a surgical mask. He extended his hand to Beth, and she handed back the needle. Before the needle touched the skin, Lane woke up.

"You ever done that before?" he asked, his eyes still shut.

"Just on an orange. The stitches were good, though," Robert said and briefly smiled.

Lane grunted once, then quieted. Robert methodically sewed until there was a small puckered cross-stitch that looked like a butthole. Robert cleaned the skin again and changed his gloves, noticing that one more pair remained. Robert covered the butthole with antibiotic ointment and then bandaged it with gauze and tape. He then taped another bandage over that one to keep it clean. Robert asked Beth to get another pillow. She escaped to another room and returned with two bed pillows, then helped raise Lane gently, elevating his head and shoulders higher.

"Those guys probably got friends—friends that will probably come looking for them," Lane whispered.

"Where do you want them?" Robert asked, anticipating his request.

"There's a drop-off in the backyard, drops about ten feet into the forest. There's a wheelbarrow at the back of the house. That ought to make it a bit easier." Lane cracked a smile and went on. "They won't be alone."

Robert eyed him suspiciously. He grabbed his coat, and Beth started cleaning up the soiled items from the emergency operation. Exiting the house, Robert took in his surroundings. It wasn't the first time he'd seen a dead body, but somehow this seemed different. He averted his gaze from the bodies and went to the rear of the house. He quickly located the wheelbarrow and returned to the bodies. Loading the first body proved to be a more difficult task than he imagined. After several attempts and turning the wheelbarrow over, he stood back, caught his breath, and thought about the task. An idea sprung to life. He flipped the body over on its back, then grabbed the man's hands and pulled him up until he was bent over at the waist. He let the arms go, and the body stayed in position. He quickly maneuvered the wheelbarrow behind and tipped it over until the front was wedged under the man's buttocks. Robert returned to the front, grasped the man's shoulders, and shoved them forward until the wheelbarrow tipped over with the man's legs hanging over the front. He grabbed the handles and guided the single wheel with relative ease due to the hardness of the ground. Once at the drop-off, he dipped the nose, feeling the weight and gravity take over as the body slid out and fell to the forest floor. He looked to see where the body fell and noticed two more bodies sprawled out no more than a few feet away. Now he knew what Lane had meant. He shook off the macabre sight and went back to work. The last two bodies were much easier now that he had a method.

Ten minutes later, he walked back through the front door. Lane was sitting in his chair now, wearing a flannel shirt. Beth stood and brought Robert a cup of coffee. He thanked her and took a seat on the couch.

Robert sipped at the steaming cup slowly, careful not to burn his mouth. "Who were they?"

"Don't know, really. Two of 'em showed up day before yesterday. I met them at the front door. Not knowing what they wanted, I had my shotgun," Lane said, pointing at the Mossberg 12-gauge leaning by the fireplace. He took a deep breath and went on. "The one that did all the talking said they needed food and water. I told them I didn't have anything to spare. Then he said they just have a look for themselves. I said no. They moved toward the door. I raised the shotgun, and they backed off. I watched them leave and went back inside. About an hour passed, and one of my lasers pinged," Lane explained.

Robert silently wondered how many lasers Lane had set up out there.

"They were sneaking up from the neighbor's yard. I met them in the backyard. This time, they were carrying pistols. They started to draw on me, and I dropped them both. That's the company I was telling you about. That's how I really threw my back out. Gimme a minute, I need to think for a sec." Lane touched the area of the wound and winced.

Robert retrieved his coffee and let it warm his hands. He sipped it, then handed it to Beth. She wrinkled her nose; she preferred creamer and sugar, but she said nothing. They both sat stoically as Lane sat in silence, though his face betrayed deep thought. Robert looked at the floor and noticed the magazines that had fallen from the coffee table. He picked up *American Hunter*. The cover displayed an expensive hunting lodge, the tagline at the bottom read, "Exotic Game on American Soil." He thumbed through the pages and saw what he believed to be a white-collar executive dressed in safari attire, holding a hunting rifle. He assumed it was a place for people with disposable income and an opportunity to bag animals like Cape buffalo, gazelles, or kudus.

The other magazine was *Popular Mechanics*. He didn't understand the technical language on the cover. Eyeing the magazines more closely, he noticed they were both dated May 2024. He checked it to memory, then noticed for the first time that the air held a faint odor of marijuana. He discreetly swept the room but found no evidence of paraphernalia that suggested its use. He quickly shook off the thought, as it would be hypocritical to judge someone for something he'd experimented with himself. He'd enjoyed those experiences, watching the *Chappelle's Show* and playing video games. It was a momentary escape from the continuous stress that came from the rigorous curriculum and performance that professors and instructors at Georgia Tech demanded. He'd never bought it or sought out to get more. It was just around.

Lane stood and retreated to the same room that he and Beth had taken refuge in earlier. They heard the locks engage and then… nothing. Minutes turned into hours.

"Robert, it's getting darker. I'm thinking we're here for the night?" she asked more than declared.

"You're right. Lane seems to be an okay guy, but…" Before Robert could finish, Lane emerged from the rear room. Lane wearily strolled back to his chair. He flopped into his chair more than sitting.

Robert got up and examined Lane's wound. There was minor bleeding, proving he had, for now, decently treated the gunshot. He gently pulled back the tape and reapplied two new strips. He retrieved a bottle of water from a plastic twenty-four-pack that sat neatly in five stacks in the corner of his kitchen. He opened the bottle and placed it in Lane's good hand. Lane brought the bottle to his lips and sipped it slowly and methodically until it was empty.

Lane drew in a deep breath and spoke. "Listen, I'm not staying here. I was planning on leaving when spring came. Those gunshots were heard by somebody, I guarantee you that. Where'd you say you were trying to get to?" Lane asked.

"As close to the Tri-Cities as possible," Beth answered quickly.

"Well, fate's a funny thing," Lane said, winking at Beth.

Beth shifted uncomfortably on the couch and unconsciously inched closer to Robert.

"Relax, young lady. My late mother—that was her room in back—she died last year before D-Day. Guess it was a mercy, to be truthful. She wouldn't have lasted without her medications. Anyhow, she left me her vacation cabin in Banner Elk, North Carolina. I reckon that'd get you two a lot closer and a lot quicker, wouldn't it?" he asked, eyeing them both.

"You mean you could get us there?" Beth asked, wearing a hopeful expression.

"Wait, how? You have a running vehicle?" Robert asked in amazement.

"Follow me," Lane said, pushing himself from the chair and holding his left arm to his chest.

"Hold on a sec," Beth said, and she retrieved something from the first aid kit.

A minute later, she helped Lane's left arm into a sling and adjusted the fit until his arm was secure.

"I should have thought about that," Robert said, admonishing himself.

With Lane's arm secured, he motioned for them to follow him. He took the stairs to the foyer, then followed another set of stairs downward. He turned left and opened the door to his garage.

An audible click sounded in the darkness before light filled the garage with two battery-powered LED lamps hung from the ceiling. Robert and Beth looked at the enclosure with genuine surprise.

Things were stacked from floor to ceiling but what was most impressive was the black Ford F-150 4×4 crew cab truck and the 5×8 foot trailer sitting beside it, also a matching black. The bed of the truck was empty, but the trailer was already loaded with a 4×3 poly container secured with a padlock. There was barely walking room to move around, but Lane maneuvered through the spaces easily.

Lane ran though the inventory with a voice and expressions of pride. He started off by explaining that the whole garage was a Faraday cage built at great expense, motioning with his arm in a circular motion. Built with aircraft aluminum and steel, he explained. He went on to describe extra measures that Robert had no understanding of. Beth, however, just nodded and appreciated his understanding. Lane continued the explanation with Beth, and she offered rebuttals. They conferred back and forth for almost twenty minutes.

Robert was completely confused with their technical speech and grew frustrated.

"What else?" Robert asked, his arms crossed.

"Oh, sorry. I get carried away a bit," Lane apologized.

He motioned to the right corner of the garage. "There're fifty 20-liter containers of potable water. That's 264 gallons, we're taking half of that because of weight. Next to that, starting at the bottom, two poly containers are 400 pounds of rice, we're taking half of it because of weight. Above those, the next three cardboard boxes each contain thirty meals ready to eat, or MREs, those all go. Next to that, the bottom poly box contains a four-man tent, a two-man tent, and a one-man tent, those all go. Above that are vacuum-sealed freeze-dried beef and chicken, 150 pounds combined, that all goes. The next two polys are pasta and beans, above that are various spices. That all goes. The next row of polys is filled with salt, that all goes. Each one holds fifty pounds. The next row is all seeds, they all go."

The next twenty minutes, Lane continued with the inventory. He checked off a camping stove and thirty miniature bottles of propane, cooking gear, utensils, pots, an iron skillet, plates, and bowls. He then checked off six overstuffed ziplock bags filled with dryer lint, ten 5-gallon jerry gas cans, wool blankets, and finally tools and spare parts that included oil for the truck, belts, hoses, and a kit with variations of every hand tool that a mechanic would drool over. Lane did a twirl, viewing the garage. The last item he added was a Husqvarna chainsaw in a plastic box with two small fuel cans sitting on top of it.

"So you're a prepper?" Roger asked.

"Hello, have you been paying attention?" Lane asked in irritation.

Robert took in the surroundings again and said in a flat voice but with a praising expression, clapping his hands like he was on a golf course, "Well done, sir."

"You're damn right!" Lane exclaimed, putting his right hand on his hip in a half-hearted Superman pose, puffing out his chest. "I haven't showed you the best part yet." Lane turned and motioned for them to follow him.

They exited the garage and passed the stairs to another door. They followed him through to find another bedroom that suited a man of his age. A king-sized bed sat to the right with a 42-inch flat-screen hung on the wall directly opposite. Beneath was a multi-shelf holding a DVD player, a VCR, and below that, surprisingly, an Xbox with the controller sitting atop. Directly to the side was a DVD holder filled with movies and video games. Below that sat a small camp chair, a duffel occupying the seat. Beside the right side of the bed sat an antique night table with a framed photo of three kids at an aquarium with their backs to the camera, watching a beluga whale. In the bottom right corner was the Georgia Aquarium logo. On the left side, a wicker night table stood. On top of that wicker, a stuffed animal puppy sat that could have come from any carnival, but it was stitched together as if it had been torn apart. Lane now took a position in front of another door that Beth and Robert believed was a closet. Lane waited until they were both looking at him and beck-oned again with his index finger flicking back and forth to follow.

"Trust me. This is important," he whispered, opening the door and walking through.

A light flicked on inside as Robert and Beth followed Lane. It was indeed a walk-in closet. Lane's clothes hung from the wall on a long rod, and several baskets mounted beneath held his socks and underwear. At the end of the closet was an old dresser.

"Can you carry that dresser into the room? It's not heavy," Lane asked and advised.

Lane moved out of the way and retreated to the room. Robert and Beth lifted each end, and as Lane said, it was quite light consid-ering its size. Robert could have carried it himself if the space weren't so confined. Once they had set the dresser in front of the bed, Lane returned to the space the dresser had occupied. Using the wall to steady himself, Lane lowered himself into a kneeling position. He removed a Gerber spring-assisted lock blade tanto and deftly popped it open with his thumb, making a *schwick* sound. Lane promptly wedged the tip beneath the molding until he exposed a corner of the old shag carpet. He closed the knife with one hand and returned it to his pocket.

Robert and Beth looked on in curiosity. Beth looked at Robert, and he shrugged with a look on his face that said, "How am I supposed to know?"

Lane began to pull back the carpet and padding, shuffling backward on his knees as he went. Finally, he stood and stepped to the side, revealing a 3×3-foot trap door. There was no lock, only a depression for fingers. Lane bent over to open it and almost fell. Robert quickly caught him by his good shoulder and steadied him.

"Would you like me to?" Robert asked sheepishly, thinking Lane wanted to unveil the surprise. Lane used his right hand to steady himself against the wall and backed away, allowing Robert to move past him. Beth patted the man's shoulder and guided him to his bed. "Rest for a minute. You don't want to fall and reopen that wound."

"There's one of them stick-on battery lights you push on, stuck to the inside wall when you open it. Just start taking things out and bring them to the bed," Lane ordered.

Robert reached down and pulled at the door. It was heavy, but once it opened, two lift supports hissed and lifted it slowly until it rested against the wall. He reached into the dark and found the light, pressing it in. The domed light clicked and filled the space with a soft white glow. Its contents further increased his impression of Lane Stone.

The first thing he noticed was a tub of desiccant on the floor to absorb humidity seven feet down. Then he saw a homemade but well-constructed wooden ladder that faced the wall. He stepped to the side and used the edge of the door to balance himself so he could descend the ladder.

"Unload it all!" Lane bellowed from the bedroom.

Robert expected to find guns, and he wasn't disappointed. All the guns were enclosed in thick vacuum-sealed bags. The transparent plastic hugged their outlines, betraying their identities. The first he handed up to Beth was an open-sight Ruger 10/22. It wasn't loaded, but enclosed in the plastic were two 50-round banana mags along with the original 10-round magazine that came with the rifle. On the other hand, he lifted a single-barrel 12 gauge. He couldn't make out the model, but he guessed it was a much older Winchester.

27

Beth turned on her heel and walked away. She returned seconds later as he took the third long gun out and examined it. It was a blacked-out Savage .270 with a scope covered with a black smock and three factory 5-round magazines. He handed it to her, and she disappeared. He then grabbed two identical rifles that could only be AR types, chambered for .556. They were unloaded without mags. They both had rails, top and bottom, for various attachments. He briefly saw Colt stamped on one of them. Sitting atop both were halogen dot sights, and enclosed in their wrappings were detached forward grips and miniaturized cleaning kits but no mags. He handed them both to Beth, and she retreated. The next long gun confused him; it was longer than the others. It was heavy but vaguely familiar. He'd seen the barrel and mechanics before, but it didn't fit the shape. It dawned on him then that it was a Browning automatic rifle, known as a BAR during WWII. This particular gun had been modified; it was blacked out as well. There were no wooden stocks but had been replaced with carbon and plastic furniture. Three original mags, along with a detached scope, were enclosed in the wrapping.

He handed this weapon up slowly until Beth could feel its weight and wouldn't drop it. From the bedroom, he heard Lane say in an excited voice, "There's my baby!" He also heard Beth giggle, and it pleased him. Next in line was a Mossberg 940 covered in camouflage woodland, with an empty bandolier as its only attachment. Beth took the gun and disappeared. That did it for the long guns. He turned to the inside wall and grabbed two pistols he couldn't be sure of their identity, but they were seated in thigh holsters, which were also vacuum-sealed. Each pistol had four extra mags enclosed in their wrappings. He handed these up as Beth returned. The next pistol was unmistakable; it too was seated in a thigh holster with three extra mags. He pivoted and held the pistol to the light, confirming what it was. A blacked .44 Magnum Research Desert Eagle stared back at him. He felt the weight and appreciated it, wishing he could hold it free of its plastic prison. As he admired it, a voice asked him with repeated giggles, "Would you two like to be alone?"

Embarrassed, he handed it up to Beth. Beneath the hanger were two identical Walther compact .380s. They were enclosed in the wrapping and contained four extra mags. Beneath those were two more identical Berettas wrapped like the Walthers together with six extra mags and two suppressors in their wrappings. He lifted all four pistols to Beth, who had been patiently waiting. The last pack of pistols was Sig Sauer P250 .45s, which had three extra mags per pistol. The last wall was stacked from top to bottom with ammo cans. He didn't bother examining them, just started handing them up and stacking them until Beth made room for him to continue.

Five minutes later, the ammo cans were gone, and Robert could feel a small tightness in the small of his back. The cans were heavy, and he was sure his back would pay for it later despite his youth. Then up went four small pelican boxes without markings, two blacked Kabar knives with what appeared to be plastic sheaths sealed in wrapping, two machetes in olive drab sheaths, and lastly two 90s-era full Army Ranger rucks and a North Face hiker's backpack also full, that had been painted by hand in camo.

Robert climbed out of the hole, pressed the light off, and closed the door. He wiped his sleeve across his forehead, absorbing beads of perspiration. Emerging into the room, Lane was running his finger back and forth over a piece of paper that had been unfolded. "There's two more. Go back and shove the hanging clothes from the far left. Grab that case," Lane instructed.

Once more, Robert retreated to the closet. He did as instructed and swept back the hanging clothes to discover a misshapen rounded bundle over two feet in length and another poly case that was over three feet long. He took them from a shelf hidden by the hanging garments and carried them back to Lane.

"Did you get a badge in archery?" Lane asked Robert.

"I did," Robert answered.

"Then this is yours. For the bullet removal," Lane said and gestured for him to open the case.

Robert opened the case to find a break-down recurve, quiver, tools, extra strings, and arrowheads varying from target to broadhead. He opened the nylon bundle to find four dozen graphite arrows with rigid plastic fletching.

"That's a Hoyt Satori. I'm not an archer myself, I took it on trade. Fella owed me some money about two years ago. He couldn't pay me back, so he gave this to me instead. Was supposed to have been the best recurve on the market for what it is. Aluminum and carbon," Lane explained, stroking the limbs admiringly.

"It's dark now," Beth said as she motioned to the window.

"Guess we ought to get some sleep. Gonna be a long day tomorrow. There's some extra pillows and blankets in the closet at the end of the hall. Beth, you can take my mother's old room. Robert, there's a sleeper sofa in the middle room," Lane told them.

They left the room and went upstairs. Robert placed a couple of logs on the fire, and Lane took up position on the couch. Robert surveyed the middle room, which turned out to be a home office. Firelight bounced off the hallway and provided a small glow that enhanced the shadows around the office. Robert fumbled with the cushions and managed to unfold the bed. He found Beth in the closet. She spun on her heel and handed him two quilts and a pillow. She fumbled around and found the same for herself. From the next room, raspy snores echoed into the hall.

"I don't want to sleep alone," Beth said in a whisper.

"Are you sure? I smell pretty bad," Robert reminded her.

"So do I," she squeaked.

"Okay, fine. No jokes," Robert warned her.

They made the bed in Lane's mother's room. The room had a faint odor of lavender, and the bed smelled of blended perfumes. The quilts were heavy and did a good job keeping them warm.

During the night, Beth migrated closer until she was inches away from Robert. They both smelled like stale sweat and wood smoke, but Robert was keenly aware of how close she was to him, and the stink did nothing to quell the hormonal stirrings when her ass pressed up against his groin. He played back an old TV show in his mind, *Northern Exposure*, until the memory veered into a different direction when the scene unfolded as the characters communed at the Brick, the local bar. Then he thought of cheeseburgers, fries, and draft beer. As his stomach grumbled, he drifted off into a restless sleep.

DECEMBER 19, 2024

ROBERT WOKE TO THE SOUND OF LANE moving around the house. The footfalls were accompanied by creaks on the floor. As he blinked sleep from his eyes, he realized he was still sleeping on his side, and Beth was spooned into him, her ass still against his groin, and his hand was on her hip. His groin ached from an erection that pressed against his jeans. He inched away from her and did his best to reposition the bulge. He peeled the covers from his frame and got out of bed as quietly as possible.

He found Lane in the kitchen, staring out the window and sipping coffee. "Coffee's on by the fire," Lane said without turning. Robert found a camp percolator by the fireplace identical to Myrtle's. He wondered if Lane had given her an identical one.

"Have a seat. I need to change that bandage," Robert said to Lane's back.

Lane took his chair and flopped into it with a grunt. Robert unfastened the sling and unbuttoned Lane's shirt. He took an antiseptic wipe from the kit and wiped it over the tape edges, hoping to loosen the adhesive. Moments later, he peeled the tape back and observed the wound. There was minimal spotting on the bandage, but the tissue around the stitches was puffy and red. He cleaned the wound, applied more antibiotic ointment, and then rebandaged it.

"I did my best, but I think it's getting infected," Robert said with a sour look on his face.

"I figured as much. I took Ciprofloxacin when I woke up. It's a pretty strong antibiotic, and I should have enough to get healed. It was left over from a kingsnake bite I got a couple of years ago. They aren't poisonous, but they carry enough bacteria to rot your hand

31

off. Luckily, it's at the end of its shelf life. You get about twenty-four months, then it just loses its potency," Lane said as Robert rebuttoned his shirt and reslung his arm.

Beth walked into the room, stretching and yawning. Robert refilled his cup and handed it to her.

"Thank you," she said, rubbing the sleep from her eyes and taking the cup. She blew into the cup and sipped tentatively.

Lane sniffed the air. "Ya know, if you two would like to clean up, I've got a gravity tank run to the hot water heater, and there's enough propane to heat it at least one tank full. There's an egg timer in the bathroom downstairs. If you can hold it to five minutes, there'll be enough for all of us to have a shower before we get on the road."

Beth's eyes brightened. "Really? Me first!" she said excitedly.

"Let's get everything loaded first. There're some energy bars in the cupboard. Grab yourselves some food, and we'll get started."

They all ate, and with Lane supervising, they loaded the pickup and then the trailer. Lane directed them to load everything but the ARs and an ammo can filled with 30-round magazines already filled with shiny brass. Lane quickly gave a tutorial on how to load the magazines, popping a round out and expertly popping it back in place. He instructed Robert to pull back the charging handle and slam a round in the chamber. He had him put one in the front and one in the rear of the cab. Robert and Beth protected everything, tying tarps over the truck bed and trailer and securing them with braided nylon cord. He walked them through the house and stopped in his office. Robert quickly folded the bed back into the sofa and replaced the cushions, having forgotten last night.

In the light, Robert and Beth quickly surveyed the walls. There were pictures of what appeared to be Lane's children in various stages of childhood, Lane, and a woman who must have been his wife. There were a lot of pictures of Lane as a much younger and thinner man, all of which showed him wearing woodland Army fatigues. There were several pictures of airborne troops dropping by parachute and another where they were rappelling from Blackhawk helicopters. There was one of him on the ground clearly yelling at another soldier, his face decorated in camo paint, gathering his canopy by the cords while others did the same, and some were still dropping to the earth. The last one showed him in his dress greens, wearing a maroon beret. Robert's father and uncle were in the Army, and he recognized the significance of the badges. Lane had a blue braided cord that hung from his right shoulder, indicating he'd graduated from the infantry school at Fort Benning. On his sleeve were three gold chevrons and one rocker; he was a staff sergeant. He had jump wings, of course, an expert infantry badge, and had qualified as an expert in marksmanship. There was no crest around the EIB, and there were very few ribbons; he had not served in combat.

Lane watched Robert scan his picture. On the opposite wall was a framed *USA Today*. The headline read in bold print above the fold:

82nd Airborne Patrol the Sands of Iraq

Below the headline was a picture of a platoon of soldiers in desert camo moving across an endless desert.

"Screwed my knee up on a jump. The Eighty-Second deployed without me," Lane said, hanging his head low. He clearly felt remorse. "Robert, can you grab that fire safe? Be careful, it's heavy. Just load it in the back of the cab. Beth, could you load some clean towels, blankets, and pillows?" Lane asked them.

Robert lugged the heavy 14×12-inch fire safe down the stairs with considerable effort, and Beth retrieved the items Lane asked for and loaded those as well. Meanwhile, Lane went into a desk drawer and removed two holsters. He went and plopped into his chair. When they returned, he tossed the holsters to Robert and Beth one at a time.

"Might as well have something to hold those pistols in. A lot better than your waistband or pocket. You need to be able to get to them fast when you need them," he said, staring out the window. The sun was up, probably close to eight o'clock.

"When are we leaving?" Beth asked as she fitted the revolver into a leather clip-on belt holster and placed it on her belt.

"Yeah, Mr. Stone, I was wondering that myself," Robert said as he unbuckled his belt and threaded it into a nylon holster with a mag pouch.

"Look, until my wing is up to snuff, I'm going to depend on both of you. I'm guessing those guys will get back over here soon and not be real happy about their friends drawing flies. I'm going to drive us out of here at least until we get to Tallulah Gorge. Reckon I'll pull over there and let you drive, Robert. If we don't run into any trouble, it's only about three and a half hours to the cabin. Figure we'd unload the truck and trailer, spend the night, and drive you home the next afternoon. Beth, I want you to keep an eye on the road, scanning ahead, behind, and on both sides of the highway. Unload a set of binoculars, and one of those pelican cases has a night-vision monocular just in case. I've got a ham radio in the glovebox; I'm going to scan as we go. I do hate leaving this place for them. I know they're just going to trash it. So I'm going to beat 'em to the punch. Beth, if you don't mind, I'd like your help grabbing a few other things. Robert, if you would, please open the garage. There's a 2×4 to the right of the garage door, you're going to need that to prop the door open. And you both should be calling me Lane from now on."

Lane and Beth went into his office. He directed her to take family pictures down and put them in a box. Lane added an old Bible, a photo album, and a 35mm camera with a telescoping lens. Its bandolier had holsters for five extra rolls of film. Beth lifted the box and headed to the stairs.

Robert backed the truck out of the garage, swung it around, and backed it up until it was close enough to hook up the trailer. Robert lifted the trailer and walked it in, setting it on the ball. A padlock was locked around a steel rod. He retrieved the truck keys and quickly found the right key. He then pulled the truck into the driveway and set the emergency brake. Beth walked out and loaded the box into the cab.

Beth slipped out of her clothes and stepped into the shower. The chill she felt being naked quickly disappeared as the hot water splashed over her skin. She quickly lathered her hair and rinsed it out. She filled shower gel into a washcloth and cleaned herself as quickly as possible. She would have liked to shave her legs and armpits, but there was no razor to be seen. She finished by washing her feet. She let water hit her face as the timer went off. She took a towel from the rack and dried off. She felt somewhat normal as she put on clean clothes from the pack. She spied unscented antiperspirant spray and used it quickly, sticking the can under her shirt.

Robert was sitting on the bed as she emerged, drying her hair with a towel, steam billowing out from behind. She handed the pack to Robert and pulled her brush out before he went in and shut the door behind him.

Robert peeled off his clothes, feeling the dirt stripping away like candle wax. He set the water until it was hot to the touch and stepped in. He went through the motions and was soon drying himself when the timer dinged. He too found the spray and applied it generously.

Lane was waiting, much like Robert had been, holding a stack of folded clothes in one arm. He stood as Robert emerged. They said nothing as they passed, and Lane shut the door. Lane allowed himself to exhaust the remains of the hot water by design as he went last in the shower queue. He brushed his mop of red hair and trimmed his beard and mustache with scissors. He applied spray to the right armpit but ran dry on the second. He grinned, realizing why. He found baby powder and tried to compensate by rubbing a small handful into the neglected pit vigorously. He dressed without putting on his shirt.

As he emerged from the bathroom, Robert was waiting with the first aid kit.

"Have a seat," Robert ordered as he began extracting supplies to redress Lane's wound.

Robert put his skills to work, and within minutes, he was helping Lane into a red and black plaid flannel shirt. He helped him back into his sling and pulled him to his feet. When they stood, Lane stepped back a foot and eyed Robert. Robert caught his gaze and wrinkled his brow.

"What?" Robert asked blankly.

Lane held his gaze for five seconds. "You remind me of my son. Not just physically but your courage, intelligence, and your ability to take charge."

"Thank you, sir. I don't know about all of those compliments. I'm just somebody trying to survive," he said, feeling embarrassed.

"No, you're being a bit modest. Not only have you kept yourself alive but that girl too. You've been doing a man's job," Lane said, patting him on the shoulder and wincing from the pain it triggered.

"Go ahead and stack the best you can all the remaining water and dry food. We'll drop it off with Myrtle."

Robert went into the garage and started stacking the remaining food and water. Lane appeared a few minutes later. He went into the corner of the garage and slipped out of the sling. He handed the sling to Beth and told Robert to keep the truck running. He picked up a shovel and returned inside.

He walked around the house, allowing warm and pleasant memories to return, his children playing, Thanksgiving, and Christmas. A fleeting memory of more romantic events. He quickly accepted the knowledge that he would never return and plunged the shovel into the fireplace. He walked into his mother's room and dumped burning coals on the mattress. By the time he returned to the sleeper sofa, smoke was rolling from the other room. He dumped coals in his office and did so again on the couch in the living room, and once more reluctantly to his favorite chair. Smoke was quickly starting to build; an orange glow could be seen from his mother's room. He turned and descended the stairs for the last time.

"I never liked this house anyway, Mary wanted it," he mumbled to himself under his breath as he descended the stairs and left his house for the last time.

Lane picked up the Tonka truck and threw it in the back seat, then climbed into the driver's seat. Beth and Robert got in, shutting their doors. Lane disengaged the emergency brake and slowly descended the steep driveway. Moments later, they drove by the rail fence. The tall, thin man was on his porch, swaying back and forth on a porch swing. The dogs sat sentry-like statues beside him. His gaze followed them as they passed.

"Can't stand that guy," Lane mumbled. "Well, won't have to set eyes on him again." He chuckled.

They parked in front of Myrtle's on the road. He walked to the front door with Robert and Beth in tow, carrying boxes of dry goods, foods, and coffee. Robert carried the extra water and food inside her house. Lane tried to talk Myrtle into coming with them, but she refused. Lane and Myrtle hugged, and they all said their goodbyes. Walking to the truck, they could see a pillar of black smoke filling the cold morning air.

The road was clear as they headed east on Falcon Parkway and soon rolled into the small city of Oakwood. Lane slowed his truck as he approached the Publix shopping center. There were dozens of vehicles still sitting where they'd died on D-Day. The old Ford police car that Myrtle described sat with a '70s model Jeep CJ-7 and an old Blue Bird school bus. The Jeep and the school bus had Hall County Sheriff's Department stenciled in black letters on the side. Three deputies stood in front of the Jeep smoking. They had abandoned full uniforms and now wore blue jeans and winter coats issued by the department. They all turned in unison and watched Lane drive by. Lane went through the intersection, passing the Walgreens, and drove by the old barbecue joint.

Beth turned and watched them. "Two of them are getting in that old Jeep," she announced.

Lane took the exit to 985. He was just about to get on the highway when he spotted the Jeep in the rearview mirror. Lane accelerated, and as the speedometer touched sixty, a blue light came from the dash of the Jeep. Lane didn't bother to pull over to the side of the road; there was no traffic. He slowed to a stop as the Jeep rolled up behind the trailer, and both deputies stepped out and approached.

"You two don't say anything unless they ask, and be careful with your words. I know one of these guys," Lane said as he rolled his window down.

"Morning, Lane. Where you headed to?" asked Jesse Brooks, a short slender man in his thirties. His cheeks and nose were flushed from the cold, giving him the appearance of wearing makeup.

"Morning, Jesse. I'm taking my niece and nephew home to West Virginia," Lane lied.

The other deputy took position by the passenger door and motioned with his finger to lower the window. Robert lowered the window. The deputy's eyes immediately went to the AR that was hidden from Jesse by Lane and the console.

"They got an AR!" the deputy said cautiously through the window.

"Jesse, tell me what you need. I need to make miles," Lane said, shifting uncomfortably in his seat.

"Lane, not gonna lie. Sheriff ordered us to stop every vehicle and confiscate any firearms and any excess fuel beyond the need of local travel," he said with a tinge of guilt in his voice.

"How long you known me, Jesse, fifteen years? I'm not giving you my guns. And you can't have my fuel. I'm leaving, and if you try to take anything, we're going to have a problem," Lane said in a low growl.

"Get out of the car now!" the other deputy yelled. He drew his gun at the low ready.

Robert tensed but didn't move. The last thing he wanted to do was get into a gunfight with cops.

"Mark, holster your gun!" Deputy Jesse yelled.

Deputy Mark didn't holster his pistol immediately, but when Jesse yelled at him again, he finally acquiesced but left his hand on the grip.

Jesse winked at Lane and gently cut his eyes and motioned to the left with his head. It went unnoticed by everyone else. Lane said nothing and left the engine running as he slowly got out of the truck, rolling up the window and shutting the door behind him. Jesse walked about twenty feet away and turned to stand in front of Lane and spoke in a low voice.

"Lane, Sheriff Campbell died. Word got to the state, and this fella from Homeland Security showed up and took over. I wasn't going to take anything from you. I was starting to warn you. But... anyhow, this new guy is all Fed, calls himself Agent Bass. The National Guard and our active-duty forces have been put on high alert in case of a foreign invasion, and all local guard and reserve that were still alive got rounded up and sent to Fort Benning and Bragg. They're suspicious of an attack on the eastern and western shores, specifically Norfolk and somewhere in Alaska. And some kinda mega gang is growing in the northern states around the Dakotas. This new guy Bass says we need to collect guns and fuel in case a local militia needs to be formed. Says he doesn't have faith that locals could form an effective defense." Jesse looked down the highway at nothing, not wanting to look Lane in the eye.

"Yankee?" Lane asked.

"Yep, New Hampshire, I think." He was still staring down the highway. He paused for a second before continuing. "The major highways are being blockaded by deputized state troopers. The real state troopers have the interstates locked down. With the weaponry you have and all the gear, you're likely to get stopped and have this stuff taken away. Knowing you, I imagine you have quite a few things they'll want." He suggested and asked which route he was taking.

Lane eyed him suspiciously for two seconds, then remembered the young teenager he'd taught proper tackling technique on weekends when the deputy was a freshman in high school. He allowed that memory in and responded. "Was planning on going up 985 until 23 hit I-40 into Asheville and jumping back on 23," he said in a muted voice.

"I think your best choice is to go through Helen and the national forest. Take Highway 75 and stay on the back roads. I know it's going to take longer, but head up to Hiawassee, shoot over to Clayton, and up through Dillard. Here, take this." Jesse withdrew a folded sheet of paper and handed it to Lane discreetly.

"What's this?" he asked.

"It's an authorization for traveling commerce. It gives you the authority to conduct commerce by obtaining and trading goods for Hall County. It's the only way you'll get through any roadblocks. Anyway, it's not a hundred percent guarantee. Give me a few rounds of 5.56, and I'll give that to Bass. If they try to radio for verification, he'll be more apt to vouch for you." Jesse took the paper back and printed Lane's name at the top in a blank space. He handed it back to

Lane. He noticed at the bottom in print was the name Patrick Bass, State Authority Agent, Department of Homeland Security; beneath that was a signature in black ink that would have embarrassed a doctor. Lane folded it up and put it in his pocket, wincing at the soreness.

Lane turned on his heel and marched back to the truck, opening the door. "Pop out that AR mag and give it to me," he directed Robert. Robert eyed the deputy from the corner of his eye. Slowly he reached over to the AR and depressed the mag release. He pulled the magazine free and handed it to Lane.

Lane shut the door and walked back to Jesse, handing him the loaded magazine. "What about your deputy back there? What's he gonna do?"

"Oh, he's okay. I was his training officer before D-Day. He's still wet behind the ears, but he's a good man. Fact of it is, we're all only doing the bare minimum to keep this Bass fella happy. There's one storage room in the department. Truthfully, we've been collecting guns from the gangs. We keep what we want for ourselves and occasionally put a few guns and trinkets in the storage room. He seems to be placated, but he's got one lackey that follows him around like a puppy. He keeps inventory and keeps hounding that we need to confiscate more. But the rest of us are pretty much doing what we think is best. We don't bother law-abiding folks. It's our community, not his. Like I said, the gangs… We've had to put down a lot of gang activity. That's another reason you'll want to be careful on those back roads. Thing of it is, fuel is scarce, and there aren't many vehicles running that aren't military. So that's why we've got the bus running. We just load up and go where the gangs are. Which brings me to your truck. Why is it running?" he asked incredulously.

"Turned my whole garage into a Faraday cage," Lane said blankly.

"A what?" Jesse asked, dumbfounded.

"Jesse, I don't have time to explain. I need to get on the road."

"Okay, good luck and be careful. Watch out for the bad guys. I'll keep an eye on your place for you," he offered.

"Don't worry yourself about it," Lane said, pointing at the distant plume of black smoke curling in the breeze.

"You do that?" Jesse asked.

Lane nodded and got in the truck. Jesse twirled his finger in the air and told his partner they were leaving.

"Lane, one more thing. If the military sees that young man, they'll most likely take him. Their numbers are pretty bad." Lane nodded in understanding and got in the truck.

He put the truck in gear and sped away. Beth handed Robert another magazine over the seat. He replaced the mag and sat back as the speedometer hit 65.

Five minutes later, Lane pulled off of 985, took the road to the hospital, then quickly turned right at the Kroger's and began to make his way to Helen. After Robert and Beth both asked what they were doing, he quickly explained the exchange between him and Jesse.

The drive took another twenty-five minutes before they entered the little tourist town of Helen. Just before entering the tourist trappings, Lane pulled into a small strip mall. Most of the storefronts were boarded up. The only two that weren't were a cigar shop and a store that catered to hikers. The only vehicles in the parking lot were a Porsche Cayenne and a Subaru Forester, both of which hadn't moved since D-Day. He pulled up alongside the curb outside the hiker's storefront. At the top of the door, in gold leaf letters, read Appalachian Gold Outfitter. Beneath it was a handwritten sign in black marker.

> Headed back home to family, don't think I'll be back.
> Take what you need but be respectful.
> Take care of what you take.
> I don't think replacements are coming anytime soon.
>
> God bless,
> Nell

Robert and Beth looked at each other, then at Lane, with puzzled expressions.

"Beth said you needed shoes," Lane said dryly, glancing at Robert's feet.

They all got out of the truck and went inside. A cowbell rattled over the door, startling them. The store was dark; the windows were painted with mountain scenes, blotting out the light. The light filtering through the door cast stingy beams at their backs, creating elongated shadows from the trio. Lane fished out a small LED flashlight and moved forward. The shelves and displays were largely unmolested. A few things were littered on the floor: empty shoeboxes, plastic wrappers of indistinguishable origins, and, oddly, a wedding dress. Lane cast the light around and was surprised that a lot of the store's stock remained. Lane spread his light on the checkout counter; beside the cash register was a cardboard display with LED keychain flashlights. He picked one up and depressed a rubber button on the bottom. It immediately lit up and spread a comparable beam to his own. He repeated the process and handed them to Robert and Beth. They all set off in different directions while Lane kept moving to the door to keep an eye on the truck.

Robert immediately spied the shoe rack against the wall that ran the length of the store. He quickly scanned the inventory until he found a pair of brown leather Timberlands. He found a bench and tried them on, walking around in them to test their fit. They felt tight, so he removed them and went up a half size. He tested these, moving around, and the fit was comfortable. He wondered to himself if his feet had gotten bigger.

"The rain has stopped, the flood has gone. How come you still got those high waters on?" Beth sang a school rhyme as she lit up Robert's ankles with her flashlight.

"Huh?" Robert replied.

"Your jeans. I hadn't noticed until now, but your jeans are too short. You must have grown in the last few months."

Robert walked to the front door; there was a height sticker affixed to the frame of the door. The sticker was used to help measure the height of potential robbers. Robert stood against the door and placed his hand on his head against the sticker. He realized that it must be the boots. He took the boots off and repeated the process.

He stood back, leaving his hand against the sticker. According to the sticker, he was over an inch taller. Staring at his feet, the cuff of his tattered jeans did appear a little higher on his ankles. He noticed a display with folded pants and investigated.

Beth selected several sports bras and elastic leggings. She found a shopping basket and deposited her finds along with five more pairs of wool socks. She collected other treasures and was soon standing by the counter as if she were waiting to pay.

Robert backed into an out-of-sight corner and tried on two pairs of Redhead hiking pants and a pair of Carhartt black denim jeans. He stuffed his items into a basket as Beth had and added wool socks and a pack of underwear. He stuffed a green balaclava, black mechanic gloves, and an olive drab booney hat in his basket to complete his haul. He joined Beth at the counter and noticed there were eleven flashlights on the display. He searched behind the counter and found on the lower counter a frame that held plastic bags for customer purchases. He handed one to Beth and started stuffing his things in another and dumped the rest of the flashlights in. Beth stuffed a handful of ChapSticks in her bag as an afterthought. Robert emptied a display of beef jerky in his bag along with three bags of peanut M&Ms.

Meanwhile, Lane shined his light in the corner to a Columbia display holding winter coats. He quickly selected three hooded-style Gore-Tex coats in gray and black woodland camo patterns. He walked back to the front of the store and handed them the coats.

"Try these on," he ordered, handing them each a coat and shrugging into the one he selected for himself. Lane had made accurate selections for them all. They admired the new coats briefly, collected their haul, and exited the store. The cowbell clunked again, echoing into the parking lot.

Remarkably, as they crossed the bridge, there were a few people milling about. A charcoal grill was smoking on the patio of the Troll Tavern while a man tended it; two women stood by. A couple hand-in-hand were strolling along a side road; they both had scoped rifles slung over their shoulders. An older man pushed a wheelbarrow in front of the quilt shop filled with firewood. Behind him, further up the street, a white draft horse pulled a flatbed wagon, a single man holding the reins from a bench. Lane recognized the horse; it was Millie, and the man holding the reins was Harold. He remembered taking the family on coach rides around Christmas. They now noticed that everyone had turned in their direction as Lane slowly rolled to a stop after he crossed the bridge.

"I'll be right back," Lane said as he got out of the truck, shutting the door behind him, and approached the old man. The old man watched him shrewdly as he got closer. His brow furrowed, then relaxed as he smiled at the visitor.

"Lane Stone, sure hope you didn't drive all this way for fudge and funnel cakes," the old man cackled, clearly amused by his own humor.

"Benjamin, you look good all things considered," Lane told him sincerely.

"And you're a bad liar. On to business, young man. What can the mayor of Helen do for you?" the old man asked.

"Information would be a good start. Are there any troop movements coming and going, and are they forcibly enlisting soldiers?"

"Oh, they're coming and going alright. Can't tell you what I don't know though. But I can tell you this. On D-Day, I hired the tubing fellas to round up everybody and get 'em out of here in that old school bus of theirs. It cost me a bit of money, which in hindsight was worth a lot more than the $3,000 in cash I gave them. I had them dropped off at the sheriff's department because that's where they all voted to go. Anyhow, we've been protected, you might say. When all the bad folks started misbehaving, I had all the roads blocked with them derelict vehicles and had all our police people step up patrols. The point is, there's close to thirty-six young men of fighting age here. One day, the Humvees showed up and had a talk with me. They've been through here a dozen or so times since. They had every opportunity to wrangle our boys up, and they never so much as did a double-take at any of them. They might eventually start conscripting, but it hasn't happened here yet."

"Thanks, Benjamin. I guess we'll push on through then. We've got a bit of a drive ahead of us." Lane sighed.

"Don't know if I'd do that if I were you. Temperature is dropping, and the humidity is up. Almanac says we're due. And those nimbostratus clouds coming in from the west pretty much seal the deal," he said, pointing to the west. There were clear skies almost as far as the eye could see, but at the edge of the horizon, tall columns of nimbostratus clouds lined the sky from north to south.

"Any place the three of us can hold up for a few days?"

"Yup, 'fraid I can't just let you have it for free though." Lane started to interrupt, but Benjamin held his hand up to keep him silent. "Hear me out first. Every single person here made their living off tourist dollars, that's gone now. What we need now is salt or gold and silver. Folks 'round here always been good 'bout keeping gardens and hunting, but what we don't have is salt. Sugar we can do without, but canning vegetables and putting up meat and fish, well…you get the picture. There's a place I can put you up for a week. It's stocked with food. Nobody but a handful know about it, and those folks contributed to stock it. We can buy salt, but we need…"

"Five ounces of silver bullion," Lane offered.

"That'll do," Benjamin replied with a smile.

Lane's back was turned to them as he spoke to the old man. He set the wheelbarrow down, and the old man stuck his hands in his pockets. They couldn't hear the exchange, but a few minutes later, Lane opened the rear driver-side door. "Turn the truck off, and hand me the keys."

Robert did as directed and handed him the keys. Beth looked on with curiosity as Lane selected a small key and set aside his pictures to uncover the lid of his fire safe. He unlocked and lifted the lid, its contents unseen to Robert and Beth. He removed something and quickly shoved it in his pocket. He locked the lid again and put the box of pictures back in place. He walked back over to the man and removed something from his pocket and handed it to him. The man examined it, smiled, and stuck it in his pocket. They shook hands, and the man pointed up the street and returned to his wheelbarrow.

Lane returned to the truck and started the engine. He put it in gear and slowly pulled away.

"What are we doing?" Beth asked quizzically, wrinkling her brow.

"Be patient," Lane said, looking in the rearview mirror. He wasn't looking at her; he was watching the road behind them.

A low rumble suddenly filled the quiet, growing louder, and a motorcycle pulled out in front of them. The driver raised his hand and motioned for them to follow.

"That's our guide," Lane said. Robert started to speak, but Lane held up his hand for him to wait.

They made their way through town on the road that led into the Chattahoochee National Forest. They had gone a little more than six miles when the motorcycle slowed to a stop next to a gravel road. Lane pulled up beside him at the entrance.

A young man in his twenties removed a full helmet with a Georgia Bulldog collegiate sticker on the side. He shook loose a mane of slicked-back brown hair and smiled.

"This is one of the forestry roads. It basically loops around this side and comes back out to the main road in about thirty miles. Nine miles in is the ranger station. The last ranger left four months ago. There's an open-ended steel hut that you can back your truck in. It's long enough, you won't have to unhook your trailer. The key to the station is under a flowerpot on the porch. If it snows like Benjamin says, you should have enough wood for a couple of weeks," he said, lifting his nose and sniffing the air.

"We won't be here that long, but thanks for telling me. Tell Benjamin this is much appreciated."

"There's enough food up there for a month. The solar panels should have the bank fully charged. It's got well water. Nobody's stayed here since the ranger left. Sam had it stocked up for emergencies, not sure why though. If anything happens, I'll ride up and let you know. Anyway, just lock up after you leave and put the key back." The young man finished by extending his hand to Lane, who took his hand and firmly shook it. Then the old Indian motorcycle roared off, speeding down the road.

Lane rolled his window up, shifted into neutral, and turned a switch engaging the four-wheel drive. He pulled onto the gravel and started down the road painted in splotches of sunlight streaking through the conifer-lined road. The drive was uneventful, and the only sounds were from the truck's engine. Their bodies jostled from side to side as the wheels found occasional ruts and holes in the road. The only noise came from the truck's suspension and the heater gently whirring.

The last few miles, Lane asked Robert and Beth to get out and walk in front of the truck to remove deadfall from the trees hanging over the road. He watched them working in unison. Robert would grab the largest ones, tossing them away into the pine needles. Beth followed suit with the smaller ones Robert left untended. It made slow progress, but after an hour, the ranger station came into view.

A few minutes later, the truck and trailer were safe and secure under the steel shelter. Beth found the key under the flowerpot just as described and opened the front door to the station. She flicked a switch, and an overhead LED lamp filled the interior with bright light. She went around from room to room, sliding open olive-drab curtains and surveying the furnishings. A small desk sat by the front window with a straight-back aluminum chair. A spiral notebook and a desk lamp were its only occupants. An overstuffed armchair sat near the fireplace; it was covered in fabric that reminded her of Navajo blankets. A futon sofa sat against the wall with a small bookcase filled with books. In the center of the room was a small desk with a closed laptop. On the wall in front of it were two 42-inch flat-screen monitors. She guessed these had been used for displays connected to cameras somewhere in the forest. Behind her were framed photos of rangers, three men and two women. She scanned over them and moved on. She moved on to a smaller room; it contained double, identical furnishings: a single institutional-style steel bed with a nightstand with a drawer stood against each wall. The walls were bare except for a single poster of Smokey Bear, emblazoned at the bottom with a banner in red letters that declared, "DON'T START FOREST FIRES." She moved into the next room; it contained a set of bunk beds of the same institutional style constructed from steel, another single bed, and a set of steel lockers that could have come from any school or YMCA. Next was a bathroom that contained a sink, toilet, and shower. She moved into the last room, the kitchen.

The first cupboard was filled with spices of the normal varieties. Below it were large assortments of food containers with lids, many filled like Russian Matryoshka dolls, encased with larger containers filled with smaller ones. The next cupboards held all of the normal trappings of a kitchen: pots and pans, cutlery and utensils, dishes, cups, and glasses. Moving to the last cabinet, it held canned food stacked in neat rows. Beneath that were bags of rice and beans, and beneath those were various types of pasta, including ramen noodles in their brick-shaped packets. On the last shelves were plastic containers filled with flour, cornmeal, steel-cut Irish oatmeal, powdered milk, and several plastic containers of a product labeled Tang. She moved on to a refrigerator that was ancient to her. It was bone white with a single door, GE in chrome cursive adorned the top right of the door. At the center of the door was a chrome horizontal latch. She pulled at it, and it swung open easily. A freezer compartment sat atop with paper-sealed packages. The only things in the refrigerator were containers of the usual condiments for sandwiches, salad dressing, a jar of pickles, a six-pack of Laughing Skull beer, and a box of baking soda opened at one end. An index card resting against the box had printed in bold block letters, "DON'T WASTE ANYTHING."

Lane and Robert stepped inside as she closed the refrigerator.

"What are we doing?" Beth asked Lane, putting her hands on her hips, clearly irritated.

"Robert, get a fire going, and I'll explain," Lane said as he strode to the window, looking out at the forest.

Minutes later, Lane sat in the armchair as Robert and Beth took spots on the futon. The warmth from the fire started to fill the interior, and Lane spoke.

"I knew the man with the wheelbarrow. The kid on the bike was his grandson. I used to come up here with the family quite a bit. My ex-wife and I had a fondness for the food at the Troll Tavern. We'd sit on the patio while the kids played in the stream. So I got to know a few of the locals. The old man, Benjamin, was the mayor. He said there are some Humvees that have been going through periodically. It's been a while since they've been here, though, but he expects they'll pass through any day. He said they haven't had any issues, but his almanac is calling for snow."

"Do you really think those books are accurate?" Beth asked with a hint of a smirk on her face.

"My grandparents swore by them," Robert offered in Lane's defense.

"They aren't the Weather Channel by any means, but people have been using them for over two hundred years. And the clouds rolling in validate the prediction," Lane said with a small grimace aimed at Beth.

"We're going to hold up here for three days or until Benjamin's grandson pops back and lets us know they've passed through. There's enough food here for us, so we won't have to unpack any supplies. So let's get settled in case it does snow. We need to bring in wood and survey what's here. And..."

"Wait, this guy Benjamin is doing this for us out of the kindness of his heart?" Beth interrupted.

Lane grimaced again. "That, and five ounces of silver."

Beth and Robert exchanged a quick glance at each other and wondered to themselves what else was in the box. Robert raised his eyebrows, and they both stood up. Lane went back to the truck and grabbed an AR; Beth grabbed the AR from the backseat and her pack. Robert soon joined them, removing his pack and the box of mags. Beth made a trip back to the truck and retrieved their new clothes. Robert came back and grabbed Lane's pack and the med kit.

When they returned, Lane had opened the electrical panel and was flipping on fuses. The silence was disturbed by a soft whirring. He opened the tap over the sink, a mechanical thumping grumbled from outside, and after a brief gurgling, water poured from the spout. He waited a minute for the line to clear, then shut it off. He opened the propane valve and lit the pilot on the water heater. He opened the water valve, and they could hear the water spilling inside. He then took three packets out of the freezer and set them on the hearth to thaw by the fire.

Beth was taking inventory of her pack when Robert stepped back inside carrying an armload of split wood. He set the wood down in a crate and took a seat on the futon. He removed his new boots and flexed his toes. As he rubbed his feet, Beth shrugged off her coat and bent over near the fire. He noticed her bottom and finally admitted to himself that it was getting more difficult to ignore his attraction to her. She turned to look out the window and saw him watching her from the corner of her eye. She then turned and looked straight at him, catching him in the act. His face suddenly turned beet red, realizing he'd been caught. He looked away in embarrassment, and Beth turned back to her pack and smiled.

Robert put his old cross trainers on and took his embarrassment outside. He walked around as Lane suggested, seeing what was adjacent to the ranger station. He pulled a flashlight from his pocket and ventured into the steel shelter. He found two cords of split wood at the rear; to the left was a small wooden enclosure with a door. It wasn't locked, so he flipped a simple wooden latch-up, and the door swung free. Inside on one wall was a bank of marine batteries stacked on shelves floor to ceiling. On the other wall was a black flat box nailed to a sheet of plywood fastened to the wall of the enclosure. The box appeared to be some kind of electrical transfer from the batteries, one yellow and two green lights blinking in unison from its exterior shell. Wires ran from the batteries to it and another box with a metal shell. From this box, wires disappeared through the wall. He figured this was to run to the station. He ventured outside, and a huge pole stood in a clearing. At the top were twelve solar panels that faced at a tilt to the eastern sky. At the bottom was a crank; he figured this lowered the panels for cleaning.

At the rear of the station were two small shacks. He opened the first, inside a pump worked; it was piped into the ground. This was the well. He opened the next shack. A small Honda generator sat on the floor; a fuel line was connected to it, and it had a line connected that disappeared through the wall. On another wall hung several pairs of snowshoes constructed of aluminum and nylon webbing. Beneath it were three trout baskets and three fly rods in tube-shaped cases. On a nearby eye-level shelf were three Altoids peppermint tins.

He opened each one, finding various tied trout flies. Fly-tying tools, spools of thread, small hooks, and a glass mason jar filled with an assortment of feathers and pieces of plastic ribbon in different colors were next to it on a separate bench. He took a spool of fishing line labeled Spider Wire from the shelf and stuck it in his coat pocket. He exited the shack, and after rounding the corner, a large propane tank painted forest green came into view. Robert guessed from its car-like size, it would supply fuel for many, many months, assuming the tank was full. Robert ventured further out and quickly discovered a game trail. After a hundred yards, he found deer and bear tracks, one stamping over another. He stood still and listened for any sign of life, and after five minutes, he followed the trail back to the station. Rounding the corner of the station, he saw Lane walking back inside.

As Robert walked to the front door, he looked up and noticed the sky was filling with clouds. Before he stepped onto the porch, puffy white flakes started to fall straight to the earth without wind to guide them. He grabbed another armful of wood and went inside.

Beth was sitting cross-legged on the floor by the fire reading a book when Robert opened the door. As he approached her, he looked over her shoulder and saw it was a *Farmer's Almanac*. He looked to his left and saw Lane in the kitchen stirring about. He sat down on the floor beside her. Beth's pulse increased slightly as she felt Robert's knee rest against hers. Lane entered the room and went to the fireplace, retrieving the paper packages. He went back to the kitchen and removed the wrappers of three venison steaks. He placed them in an iron skillet with olive oil, salt, and pepper. He rummaged through the cabinet over the stove and found garlic powder, which he sprinkled lightly over the steaks. He flipped the steaks over and repeated the seasoning. Beside the skillet, a pot of rice was boiling. When the rice was done, he drained a can of peas and carrots and blended it with the rice. The steaks were beginning to sizzle as he stepped back and popped another antibiotic capsule. He touched the wound and was surprised that it wasn't as tender. He stepped quietly to the doorway and watched Beth and Robert in silence. Two young lovers waiting to love each other, he wondered who would take the first step in revealing their emotions of longing. His thoughts moved to his ex-wife and children. He wondered if they were alive and well. He made a decision at that point to go see for himself. His last contact had been a letter from his daughter two months before D-Day. The letter wished him well and hoped he was okay. It was written like it had come from a business announcing changes in customer policy. His oldest was in Alaska, gold mining. His oldest daughter was working for a local veterinarian while she finished her biology degree. The youngest wrote the letter, announcing that she would start her first semester at Murray State University in the fall; she was going to be a CPA. Her mother and stepfather were opening a bed-and-breakfast on the edge of Mark Twain National Forest. She had ended the letter by again wishing him well and that they would be thinking of him. He hadn't written back; he had regretted it ever since D-Day. Now the phones were useless, and every satellite was floating space junk, or at least he thought they were.

Lane finished cooking, and they all ate by the fire on paper plates. The meal consisted of boiled rice, canned carrots and peas, and venison steaks, and they each drank one of the Laughing Skull beers. They all took turns showering using individual bar soaps that Lane had collected from hotels. Robert changed Lane's bandage and was pleased when he discovered the puckered wound was no longer puffy and an angry red. Beth found linens, blankets, and pillows sealed in trash bags for the beds. Lane retrieved a gun cleaning kit from the truck and instructed them all about gun cleaning. He handed Robert and Beth the ARs and guided them through disassembling them and putting them back in working order. He then guided them through the mechanics and cleaning of Robert's Beretta and Beth's .357. They finished off the evening by playing six games of Rummy with a deck of cards Lane had found in one of the kitchen drawers; Beth won every hand.

"We need to keep watch from now on. I don't know if there's any kind of *Deliverance* crap going on out there. There's smoke coming out of the chimney, and I have no clue how much of that is being shielded by the snow. We need to be careful." Lane said, picking up one of the ARs and slamming home a magazine.

"Deliverance?" Beth asked quizzically.

"It was an old movie, backwoods people... They, uh...never mind. We need to be on the lookout for bad people," Lane finished.

"I'll take first watch," Robert offered.

"No, that's okay. I won't be sleepy for a few more hours," Lane told them.

"Okay," Robert agreed, shrugging his shoulders.

Lane ushered them off to bed and took a seat in the armchair, holding the AR by the barrel with its stock resting on the floor. He rose perhaps an hour later and placed another log on the fire. He then looked out the window to find the ground completely covered in a thick blanket of snow. He guessed at least four inches had come down. He pulled the ham radio from his coat hanging on the rack and switched it on. He ran through frequencies for half an hour, hearing nothing but static, and then turned it off, replacing it in his coat pocket. When the log had burned down, he spread the coals and placed another log into the red embers.

He found Beth and Robert sharing the first room. He gently nudged Beth's shoulder until she freed herself from an old comforter, rubbing sleep from her eyes.

"Your turn, Beth," Lane told her in a whisper.

She nodded and stretched as she got out of bed. Lane returned to the fire and waited to make sure she got up. She soon padded up beside Lane and warmed her hands by the fire.

"I found some instant coffee if you want it. There's even sugar and creamer packets," he told her.

"Oh, that's awesome," she whispered, smiling.

"And don't forget, we've got hot water. Just let the tap run for a minute," he reminded her. He patted her on the shoulder and turned to leave.

"Lane, can I ask you a question?" Beth whispered. Lane nodded in return.

"Why are you doing this for us? You haven't known us but for a day and change," she asked, looking at him with innocent, imploring eyes.

Lane thought for a second and asked himself internally. He smiled at her the way a parent would their child, as if they had asked why the sky was blue. "I would want the same thing for my kids. I would hope that someone would help them if they were in the same situation."

He patted her on the shoulder again and turned for bed. He removed his boots and crawled under the covers. Before sleep took him, he wondered if his kids were in the same situation.

DECEMBER 20, 2024

LANE WOKE TO DAYLIGHT PEEKING AT THE corners of the curtains. He felt stiff and hadn't slept well. His dreams were troubled by visions of his children in peril. He swung his feet onto the floor and pulled the curtain back. The sky was overcast, and a thin layer of frost adorned the edges of the window.

He laced his boots up and soon found Beth and Robert sitting on the futon, sipping instant coffee. They were deep in conversation. He went into the kitchen and opened the tap to let the hot water run. He looked out the window and guessed the total snowfall was perhaps eight inches. He emptied two spoons of Folgers crystals into a mug with Charlie Brown on the side. Above his picture in faded letters read, "Good Grief." He took the armchair by the fire, and Beth and Robert greeted him in unison.

"Good morning," they spoke.

"Mornin'," Lane said, raising his cup to them. He noticed one of the freezer packs by the fire.

They sat silent for a few minutes, enjoying their coffee. Beth picked up the almanac and began reading again. Robert took his cup to the kitchen and began opening and closing cabinet doors. He returned moments later with a rounded lump covered in foil. He set it by the fire. "It's bread, found it in the freezer!" he said excitedly.

"What's on the agenda today?" he asked, facing Lane.

"It wouldn't hurt to scout around a bit, not too far though. I saw a shoeshine kit under the sink, you might want to put a coat of mink oil on those boots before you go out. Beth, there's also a can of Scotchgard, I'd spray those shoes you got a few times and let 'em dry by the fire," Lane advised them.

Lane rose from his chair, grabbed the freezer pack, and went into the kitchen. He grabbed a pot and filled it with water. He put it by the fire, completely forgetting the stove, and returned to the kitchen. He took the venison steak and cut it into bite-size chunks, running them through with a skewer. He returned to the fire and took the fire poker, wedging the loop of the skewer on its tip. The skewer was resting above the flames when he was finished. He sat in the chair watching the meat and water and started to coach Robert on the fine arts of polishing boots but remained silent when he saw that Robert was polishing them with practiced experience.

Lane occasionally turned the meat, then satisfied, he took the water and skewer to the kitchen and prepared three bowls of ramen, dividing the venison chunks evenly. He took a bowl for himself and returned to the armchair. "Breakfast is in the kitchen."

Like the night before, they ate in silence by the fire. They tore chunks off the loaf of grain bread and ate the ramen and venison. When they'd finished, they all washed their own plastic bowls and forks with a disposable packet of dishwashing fluid. Moments later, they followed Lane to the truck, where he dug out three of four Motorola radios and distributed them. Lane retrieved the ham radio and stuck it in his back pocket.

"You two stay in sight of each other, set your channels to 4. Try to keep silent. Turn your radios on now. If I key the mic, it will make a click as the channel opens. When you hear that click, click back once each if you're okay. Two clicks to standby. Three clicks mean trouble. After that, you switch to channel 2. Finally, if you have to respond, make it short. You got that?" Lane challenged them.

"Pretty straightforward. Beth?" Robert implied, looking at Beth.

Beth nodded and quoted Lane's instructions verbatim.

"We're going to try for a little fishing. I saw a terrain map in the shelter. There's a stream about three hundred yards from here. Gonna see if we can bag some trout," Robert explained to Lane, pointing through the trees to the east.

"Don't stray anywhere else. Take the ARs," Lane said and turned on his heel.

Beth started to say something smart but thought better of it. They retrieved the fishing gear and the guns and were soon plodding their way through the snow. Their progress was slow, and it took nearly thirty minutes before they found the stream. The stream wasn't deep, and the bottom was visible regardless of the current. Within minutes, Robert had rigged up flies to the rods. He spent the next ten minutes demonstrating how to cast the fly, gently flipping the tip of the rod between the ten and two positions. Beth caught on quickly, and after a dozen or so attempts, she was able to manage feeble but somewhat competent casts. Robert walked upstream until he was sure they wouldn't cross lines.

Twenty minutes passed before Beth made the first catch. Robert made his way back to her and helped her wrangle out the brook trout. Robert guessed that it was an adult by its size, probably fifteen inches and around three pounds. Robert deposited the fish in a shoulder basket. As Beth celebrated her trophy, their radios clicked. They fished their radios out of their pockets where they were clipped on. Robert nodded at Beth, and she clicked the mic; Robert followed suit.

An hour later, they had enough trout to feed them all for several days. With their basket full, they packed up their kits and started making their way back to the station. It was easy to retrace their steps, and they were making good time when they heard three quick clicks over their radios. They switched their channel to 2.

"Company behind you, move!" Lane said quickly.

Robert and Beth looked over their shoulders. In the distance, they could see three individuals coming from the stream, their figures black against the snow.

"Let's move," Robert urged her on.

They hastened their steps, and ten minutes later, they found Lane standing under the cover of their porch, holding the binocs to his eyes with one hand and his Mossberg in the other. Robert wondered how long Lane had been watching for them.

"Get inside. Beth, you stay hidden," Lane ordered her.

"I can hel—"

"No!" Lane growled, cutting her off. "Robert, crouch behind the woodpile. Hold your fire. If you hear me say 'Deliverance,' shoot starting at the left and work your way to the right."

Robert nodded and dropped out of sight.

Lane continued watching them. The trio of men took longer than expected. They were taking their time. What at first appeared like out-of-shape people turned out to be deliberate steps. They started close together; now they were spreading out, leaving twenty yards between themselves.

"Left guy coming in front of the truck," Lane warned through clenched teeth.

Lane lowered the binocs to his chest, gripped the shotgun in both hands, and racked a round. The shick-shack was loud, echoing in the still windless surroundings.

The three men were all wearing various designs of woodland camo coveralls that could be bought at any Walmart or Bass Pro, with ski masks covering their faces. Two were armed with scoped hunting rifles; the third on Robert's twelve o'clock held a scoped crossbow loaded with a broadhead tip on the bolt.

The guy in the middle shouldered his rifle and rolled up his ski mask, revealing an older man with a jet-black beard. The other two held their weapons at the ready.

"Howdy, how you folks doing?" the man asked cheerfully.

"Doing," Lane answered flatly.

"Well, that's good, that's really good. We saw your young folk down at the stream. Looks like they did real good. Got themselves a good haul!" the man announced as if he were a town crier.

Lane was even more alarmed now as he realized they'd been watching long enough to see them catch multiple fish. He didn't respond. He decided to wait. It was a trick he used often so that people would get to the point. Mr. Cheerful didn't disappoint.

"Anyhow, we've been hunting for days, and we ain't done so good. Was wondering if y'all minded sharing a little bit. We don't need much, just want to get out of the cold, chat a bit. My name is Billy, that's Carl on the left, and Chester to my right," Cheerful Billy called out.

"Sorry, Billy, can't share. I can let you take one of these fishing kits, you can catch all you want then," Lane offered him.

"I didn't get your name, Mr. uh…" Billy questioned.

"Didn't give it," Lane countered.

"I see. Well, normally I'd say that wasn't very neighborly at all. Thing is, we're hungry now," Billy told him.

"How old is your daughter? Is that your daughter?" the man on the left queried.

"One warning. Turn around, go back the way you came. If you don't, it's a bad day," Lane said without emotion.

"You don't seem to get it, do you, buddy?" Chester asked with a giggle.

"He's right, buddy. We're hungry, and that shotgun ain't much for three of us. And, seeing as how you got those young'uns of yours hid away, I don't see much of a chance for you or them. Or you could just let us in to warm up and share some of your food," Billy countered, unshouldering his rifle and holding it at the low ready.

"Tell ya what, Billy, I was a kid when I saw this movie about four businessmen on a trip in the mountains of Georgia. Some backwoods trash decided to have fun with those businessmen. I vowed then and there that I would never allow myself to fall into some shit as fucked up as that movie *Deliverance*." Lane finished by pulling the trigger.

The 12-gauge slug took Billy off his feet as Robert sent two rounds into Carl's chest. As Carl tipped over backward, he pulled the trigger on his crossbow, the bolt sprang free at 375 feet per second. The bolt slammed into Lane's left calf, distracting Lane and horrifying Robert. A fresh crack replaced the echoes. Robert and Lane both looked up just in time to see Beth emerge from the corner of the shack with her AR raised and a tendril of smoke curling into the air. Chester, aka the man on the right, staggered backward, still holding his rifle with one hand, its barrel head down in the snow. He did the stereotypical money shot by holding his blood-soaked hand in front of his eyes in disbelief. Unlike the others, he fell face-first into the snow.

Lane looked over at Beth as she inched toward the prostrate man. She was holding the weapon pointed at the face-first Chester. His leg twitched, startling Beth into firing two more rounds into Chester's back. She stepped back from the body as Lane walked toward her. She looked up at him and noticed the bolt protruding from his leg. She removed one hand from the AR and put her free hand to her mouth in a gasp. Lane followed her gaze to his calf.

"Don't worry about it," he told her, putting his hand on her shoulder.

Lane reached down and lifted his pants leg, raising it above his boot, revealing a prosthetic limb. Robert trotted up beside him as he exposed the false limb.

"Wow, that is really fucking cool! Glad you're not hurt!" Robert exclaimed.

"Language, please," Lane scolded him.

Lane brought the binocs back up and scanned the area. He did this for a couple of minutes, sweeping in every direction.

"We need to get rid of these bodies in case somebody comes looking. No way we can cover their tracks. Let's get rid of the bodies first, and I'll figure something out. Beth, keep a lookout," Lane ordered, removing the binocs from around his neck and handing them to her.

Lane removed a Leatherman multitool from a pouch on his belt and opened it. Using the wire snip, he bent over and cut through the aluminum bolt protruding from his rubber calf. After cutting through it, he raised his pant leg and cut it closer to the surface. He stuck the pieces in his back pocket and moved to Chester's feet. Robert moved to his shoulders and crossed his arms over his chest. He then raised his torso and stuck his hands through the crossed arms, grabbing his wrists. Robert straightened his legs as Lane grabbed the ankles and immediately cursed from the pain in his shoulder.

"There's a pile of gravel behind the shelter. Might be able to cover them with that," Robert suggested.

"Normally, I'd say that was a good idea, but with the snow, it'll be a dead giveaway, pun intended. Let's put 'em in one of the shacks," Lane offered.

The task was difficult but much more arduous for Lane. He needed longer to rest after each body was deposited. Finished with the relocation, Lane went to the shelter and found a four-foot sled constructed of sheet metal hanging from the wall. He found a shovel and handed it to Robert. Lane carried the sled sideways without dragging it. He approached the first patch of blood-soaked snow and dropped the sled, making a flop noise.

"We're gonna get as much of the bloodied snow on the sled as possible and drag it away. Then we're going to find a spot and dig out the clean snow and dump the dirty and cover it up. Then we're gonna dig up some more fresh snow and cover those bare spots as best as possible. Then all three of us are going to walk the area down and retrace their steps to the stream. That's the best we can do," he explained and watched Beth nod in understanding.

Close to two hours passed when Beth picked up their weapons and put them in the station under their beds. Robert and Lane returned, and they walked down the freshly scattered snow until no remnants of red remained. After they were done, it appeared like a well-trafficked area. Lane felt it looked suspicious but was indeed the best they could do in the snow. As an afterthought, he went to the shack and removed Chester's boots, told Beth to take hers off, and put his on. Satisfied, their boots were now all close matches. They retraced their steps until they hit the stream. Lane had Beth take turns scanning the area with the binocs.

"Y'all ain't gonna like this. Follow me and follow my footsteps," Lane ordered as he stepped into the stream.

Robert and Beth took sharp breaths as the freezing water stung their feet and ankles. Beth stumbled in the dead man's boots and immediately soaked herself from head to toe. Robert helped her up, but she brushed him off. Lane hurried his pace now, regretting having Beth wear the boots. He continued up the stream for what seemed like an eternity until he found a fallen tree with its top impacting into the stream. He found a small pine sapling and jerked it easily from the stream edge. Lane steadied himself with his hand and stepped onto the trunk. He used the sapling to sweep off the snow; it was easy as the pines were thick overhead, shielding it from heavy snow. After steadying himself, he slung his shotgun over his neck and began walking heel to toe with his arms outstretched to his sides for balance. The tree was old and large and made for easy walking. He repeated the sweeping, and step by step, he made it to the end and hopped off into the snow. Robert helped Beth up, and she clumsily traversed the tree. As she reached the end, she was shaking uncontrollably and fell into the snow.

"I can't feel my feet," Beth squeaked as she pulled one huge boot into her lap. She tugged at the laces, but her fingers wouldn't work.

Robert reached the end and grabbed Beth by the waist, hoisting her onto the tree, and she landed on her butt. He made quick work by unlacing her boots and taking them off. At least two cups of water poured out from each boot. He peeled off her socks, revealing blue feet from heel to toe. He then started undressing her. He pulled off her coat, and within seconds, he'd stripped her to her underwear. He took off his coat and put it on her. The coat swallowed her, making for a good layer. He began rubbing her feet vigorously and finally did the unthinkable.

"Don't be grossed out, okay?" Before Beth could answer, Robert stuck her foot in his mouth as far as it would go and started rubbing her other foot again.

The warmth of his mouth stung her skin at first, but the stinging soon passed. The stinging sensation was repeated with the other foot, and as the feeling began to creep back in, a surprising feeling crept into her, and her already blushed cheeks reddened further.

Lane wrung the water out of her clothes as best as he could and hung them over a tree limb sticking out from the fallen tree beside her. Beth's shivering wasn't lessening, and the color hadn't returned in the slightest. He stripped off his new fleece shirt and wrapped it around her feet and legs, leaving him bare-chested.

"You ready?" Robert barked at Lane.

"Yeah," Lane answered back in a defeated voice.

He picked her up in his arms and broke into a fast high step, leaving Lane to follow. Robert didn't feel the cold anymore; adrenaline took over, and he sped up his pace further, finding a stride. Lane grabbed Beth's AR and clothes, then followed with Chester's boots looped around his neck and Beth's socks tucked inside.

Robert pushed through the snow, high-stepping at reckless speed and coming close to falling face-first several times, but he regained his balance each time. He looked back once and saw that Lane was almost a football field behind him. What should have taken an hour to return took him half that time.

The fire had burned to embers when Robert burst through the door, his arms cramping and his heart pounding. He sat Beth down in the armchair and pulled it over in front of the fire. He put kindling on the embers and placed two split pieces opposite each other on the now smoking pile. Her feet were still blue and icy cold to the touch. He knelt by her, facing the fire, and started rubbing them again. Soon the fire grew, but her entire body was trembling, and her lips were blue.

"Robert, I'm g-g-good nuh-now," she said through chattering teeth.

"No, you're n—" Before he could finish, Beth spun his face into hers, hands still trembling, and she kissed him hard and long. Robert didn't resist. The kiss startled him, and he so wanted to enjoy her trembling lips and hands. He pushed his libido away as it dawned on him.

Robert pulled away from her. "I'll be right back."

He opened the small bathroom and threw open the shower curtain, heating the water until it was lukewarm. He returned and picked Beth up, carrying her to the shower. He carried her into the shower and let the water cascade over her body. After a few minutes, the shivering started to lessen, and he turned the heat up. After a few more minutes, the shivering turned to a small tremble, and he increased the heat a little more. Finally, after ten minutes, she stood erect without a hint of hypothermia. Only then did Robert become aware of the dark outlines that were visible through the light-colored underwear. Feeling embarrassed, he looked away, stepped out of the shower, and closed the shower curtain.

Robert stripped naked and grabbed a towel. "Don't look. I have to get out of these wet clothes."

Beth leaned against the wall of the shower and subconsciously used her pinky finger to pull the curtain back until one eye was clear; his back was to her when she peeked around the corner of the curtain. Steam billowed around him as he dried his back, and she caught a quick view of his muscled ass before he wrapped the towel around his waist. He turned, but she ducked back out of sight.

"I'll be back with some clothes," Robert called out as he shut the door behind him.

Robert went into their shared room and located her pack. He undid the straps and flipped it open. He rummaged through her clothing quickly and located her new hiking underwear. He took those and looked for something warmer. He spied a pink bundle at the bottom and smiled.

Robert knocked on the door. "Okay to come in?"

"Just a sec," Beth said as she finished wrapping a towel around her torso. She grabbed another towel and bent over, letting her hair fall. Then, with the skill only a woman possesses, she twirled the towel around her head into the wet-hair turban. "Okay."

Robert opened the door, and steam poured out. He stepped in, set the clothes on the sink, and turned to leave, but she grabbed him by the shoulder and pulled him into a tight embrace. She nuzzled into his neck and whispered, "I love you, Robert Fletcher."

He leaned back and looked her in the eyes, then he kissed her with ferocity. She leaned into the kiss, and Beth felt Robert's hands on her body. Robert felt himself stiffen and pulled back. Subconsciously, he put a hand over his groin and blushed heavily. "I love you too, Beth Holt." Then he backed away and closed the door. Beth bit her fist, giggling in response.

*****

Robert dressed in his hiking pants and a T-shirt and checked on the fire. The fire was catching the logs, so he placed another across them when Lane came through the door.

"Beth?" he asked with concern on his face.

"She's okay. I got her in the shower before hypothermia set in. Look, I know you had us doing what we did to protect us. She's fine, so you gotta let this one go, okay?" Robert said, trying to lift Lane's load of guilt.

Lane walked to the fire, then lowered himself to the floor and removed his boots. His right foot was blue as well. Since he wasn't sitting in a chair, his prosthetic stuck out at a weird angle. He rubbed his right foot vigorously for a few minutes, then rested it on the hearth by the fire. The bathroom door opened, and they both turned in unison to look. There stood Beth, covered in fuzzy pink pajamas from toes to chin. They all stood frozen for seconds, then Robert lost it and burst out laughing. Lane joined in, and after displaying a bewildered look on her face, she got the joke and started snickering. Beth sat in the chair by the fire again, and they talked. Beth said she was still a bit shaken from killing the man and was beginning to look distraught.

"Listen up, both of you. If I'd let those men in, they wouldn't have stopped at the food. Beth would have been next after they killed Robert and me. Unfortunately, there aren't many rules left that people would follow. And I'm pretty confident that won't be the last time you have to take a life. If it were up to me, everyone would live happily ever after. But I think you are both smart enough to know that something like that has to be earned. So, Beth, you actually saved my life today. I thank you for that. Don't you feel remorse for that man or any other life you have to take to protect yourself or anyone you care about."

Beth nodded at Lane solemnly, and Robert just looked at his lap.

"You probably saved her toes with that mouth trick. But if you ever try that on me, I'll break your jaw." Lane cracked a grin and turned to them.

Beth and Robert broke out in laughter, and it became contagious enough that Lane joined them. The laughter felt good to them and helped ease the tension. They spent perhaps an hour in front of the fire. Lane apologized to Beth for walking them through the stream but explained that he felt it was necessary to improve their chances of not being discovered. They then watched with fascination as he rolled up his pants past his knee. With practiced dexterity, he removed a rubberized calf prosthesis, revealing the metal tube that supported him. He removed his multitool once more and used pliers to remove the broadhead tip. If it had struck flesh, it would have caused serious or fatal injury. He handed the rubber calf to Robert and motioned for him to spread it open. Robert dug in his thumbs and spread open the rubber, revealing two .357 derringers seated in cutout depressions with a small Gerber tanto lock blade seated like-wise. Robert held it open for Beth to see, then handed it back to Lane. He fastened the rubber calf back in place and lowered his pant leg.

Lane rolled onto his belly and pushed himself up until he could get his knee into a crouch and push himself up to stand. It took maybe two seconds to get his balance. He grabbed the binocs and went to the window. The sun had passed over the station and was now spreading shadows into elongated dark gray silhouettes. He stood there for a long time before he turned and closed the drapes. Beth got up and disappeared into the kitchen. Lane went to his room and returned with a coil of paracord. He strung a line at eye level from a coat hook screwed into the wall, then to the curtain rod at the other wall by the front door. Lane picked up Beth's clothes that he'd carried and began hanging them over the line. Robert retrieved his clothes and the underwear Beth had left in the bathroom. After he hung the clothes and towels up, he set his boots and Lane's by the fire. Beth's new shoes sat dry next to the hearth.

"I'll take first watch tonight. I'll wake you up when I crash," Robert volunteered.

"Think you can handle dinner tonight too?" Lane whispered.

"Yep, not a problem. Any requests?"

"Whatever we have, preferably hot," Lane replied.

Beth came back holding three mugs of instant coffee. She handed the mugs out and sat cross-legged. She traded the almanac for a copy of *Popular Mechanics* and read leisurely. As Beth read, Lane studied her posture and appearance. She looked so young to him in her pajamas. The thought of someone trying to inflict any abuse on her made the coffee sour in his mouth. It surprised him that his parental instinct was impacting him the way it was. It wasn't that he didn't care about his own kids—he would do anything for them. In fact, he would have already left for them on D-Day, but his stump had been infected, and he had nearly died. He'd only been able to use his prosthetic within the last month.

Back on Falcon Crest Drive, the swelling went down, and he'd started walking to the end of the driveway and back. The pain was so fierce on his first attempt that he'd fainted on the steps of his front porch. He repeated this until the pain was reduced to a constant stinging. He stepped his game up again and started doing laps around the house. When he'd reached ten laps, he walked to the end of the street and back. When he was able to do that three times, he ventured out to see Myrtle. He hadn't wanted to advertise that he had a running vehicle. He broke away from his thoughts as Robert went outside and quickly returned, carrying the shoulder basket with the trout.

The sun had set when Robert announced dinner was ready. They ate a dinner of cooked trout with rice, canned green beans, and a handful of saltines. They were so hungry that they ate every piece of fish, leaving no leftovers. They tossed the remains of the bones and skin in the fire along with their paper plates.

"We leave at first light. I saw some tire chains that should fit the truck tires. As soon as we're packed and chains secured, we make tracks, literally," Lane told them.

He paused for a moment, staring into the fire. "We need to be on full alert. I'll drive. I want you two to be ready with the ARs. I want both of you to stow your pistols in your pack and start carrying the ones sealed in plastic—the Sig Sauer P250 .45s. They're great man stoppers. I'm guessing we still have 24 miles of unknown terrain, and adding the snow means it's going to be slow going. One or both of you may have to walk point and look for pitfalls," he explained.

Lane turned in early. He undressed and removed the prosthetic. The end of his stump was red and swollen, but it was no surprise to him due to the repeated impact. He gently massaged the stump, and all too familiar ghost pains came. When the nerves relaxed their relentless throbbing, he finally fell into a tense sleep. It was combat sleep. Though he'd never been in combat, it was a practiced skill every soldier developed in training. It was the ability to awake at the slightest noise, recognize it as nonhostile and drift back into sleep within seconds, or immediately recognize it as hostile and be ready for action. He believed that combat veterans' senses for this ability were ten times greater than his own. Unfortunately, combat sleep started up again for him two days after D-Day.

Robert routinely peeked through the curtains, as did Beth, gazing out the kitchen window. There was a full moon, and it illuminated the surroundings to a sunset quality. They took turns cleaning the ARs so there was one ready for trouble should it come. They talked about school memories and then finally grew quiet. They leaned into each other, embracing and kissing. Minutes passed before they let each other go at the sound of wood breaking.

Robert and Beth were both standing with their weapons at the ready when Lane appeared, hopping on one leg, stripped to his boxers and using the butt of the Mossberg as a cane. More breaking sounds came from the rear of the house. Robert dug a keychain flashlight from his pocket and sandwiched it between his fingers and the AR grip and moved to the door. Lane growled for Robert to stop, but he was already out the door.

The cold bit Robert's face as soon as he opened the door. He shut the door quietly behind him. The snow made an audible crunch as his boot touched down. He quietly cursed himself and repositioned his step to the packed snow. He moved across the front of the station and quickly found the trail they'd all used. He tiptoed until he was twenty feet from the pump shack. Noise reverberated from it; the sounds were alien to him. He took a wide berth of the shack until he was standing at an angle to the front. Even from there, he could see that the door was smashed inward. In the moonlight, all he could see was a black mass undulating back and forth. Suddenly, the movement and noise stopped. Robert let go of the grip and clicked on the flashlight. The next few moments happened in slow motion for Robert. Two eyes glowed as a very large black bear became visible.

It growled, then lunged forward, moving at incredible speed. Robert fired one-handed in a panic. He stepped backward hastily and fell. He fired repeatedly until he ran dry. The bear's jaws clamped down on his boot with feeble force, so feeble that Robert barely felt any pressure. One humongous paw dragged at his boot but stilled and moved no more.

Robert was still sitting in the snow when Lane appeared with his shotgun raised. He was still clothed in boxers and bare-chested, with his leg strapped on. He moved toward the bear and nudged its head with the barrel of the shotgun without response. He looked at Robert and spoke.

"I'm guessing about three hundred pounds. Should be twice that much for a bear that size. Must have been a bad year for it. Sometimes, if they don't put on enough fat, they'll break hibernation to keep from starving," Lane said with authority.

Robert picked up the flashlight and stood up. "I thought I was dinner. Guess the smell of blood or those burnt fish skins drew it in."

"You okay?" Lane asked.

"Yeah, I'm good," Robert answered.

Lane turned to go back, and Robert followed. Robert came to his side; as he did so, Lane clapped him on the back. "Please don't do that again."

"What, protect us?" Robert asked defiantly.

"No. Take on a threat without someone having your back," Lane said and put his hand on Robert's shoulder, gently squeezing.

Beth flung the door open, allowing them in. Lane immediately went to the fire to warm himself.

A few seconds later, Beth draped him in a blanket. He leaned his shotgun against the hearth and wrapped the blanket tightly around him. Beth then wrapped her arms around Robert, holding him tightly. Lane observed this from the corner of his eye, and a thin smile came to him and quickly vanished.

"We have to leave now. Those shots will've been heard for miles. Anybody looking for those men will definitely come looking. Get dressed, grab your gear. Go ahead and load the weapons they dropped in the trailer. We leave in thirty minutes," Lane told them and went to his room to change.

An hour later, they pulled out from beneath the shelter. The tire chains proved to be a good fit, but they'd been used in multiple winters, and their longevity was unsure. They drove without lights as the moon reflected off the snow sufficiently to see where the road was covered in unmolested snow. After they'd traveled five miles, Lane encouraged Robert and Beth to sleep. Beth was soon silently snoring; Robert took longer, closing his eyes for minutes at a time and waking in a start unsure, then drifting back off again. He was taking combat naps.

DECEMBER 21, 2024

THE RIDE OFF THE FORESTRY ROAD WAS uneventful. Three times, deep ruts in the road were encountered, but the large tires and chains traversed them with competence. The sun was rising when Lane stopped at the end of the forestry road. Robert and Beth woke when Lane got out of the truck. Lane walked ahead of the truck with Robert's AR shouldered. He was about fifty feet ahead, using the binocs to scan left to right.

The snow on the park road was neatly impacted by fat all-terrain tires, typically found on Humvees, two sets coming and two sets going out. He turned and returned to the truck.

"I don't see any way around it. Our paths are going to cross eventually with someone of authority. If things go south, try and get away, take the truck if you can. Regardless, we need to see what we're up against," Lane told them.

Lane pulled out a road atlas that was as big as a food tray and opened it to a blown-up scale of their area. After studying a route, Lane closed the atlas and wedged it between his seat and the console. Their breakfast consisted of peanut butter and dark chocolate Clif bars. They snacked on handfuls of raisins and water, making good time on an unobstructed road. It was cold enough that there was no melting, and the tires kicked clumps of powder as they rolled on. The truck clock read 10:20 when they met their first roadblock. They had crossed the state line into North Carolina after going east on Highway 64 for perhaps a dozen miles. Both sides of the highway were blocked with pairs of Humvees armed with .50 caliber machine guns. As they approached, four soldiers exited the vehicles with M4s at the ready.

Lane approached slowly until one soldier raised his hand for them to stop. Lane came to an immediate stop. Steam plumed from his nostrils as he came closer, wearing mirrored sunglasses that hid his eyes. As he got closer, he noticed the soldier wore a butter bar, a second lieutenant. He also wore jump wings, a CIB, and a Ranger tab above the Airborne tab and All American patch from the Eighty-Second. Lane rolled down his window as the soldier came up to his side.

"What's your business, sir?" the young man asked.

Lane studied the man for a minute. He saw him recognize the double A's sticker of the Eighty-Second Airborne displayed at the top right of his windshield. He decided on partial honesty.

"I'm taking my niece and nephew home to their parents. Was planning to jump back on 23 when we get to Franklin. Heading to Rogersville, Tennessee, Lieutenant," Lane told him.

The soldier looked at him, then ran his eyes down the length of the truck and the trailer. "Looks like a little more than an errand."

"I'm not coming back. Lane Stone," he said, extending his hand through the window.

The soldier slowly approached and tentatively extended his hand. They shook, and the lieutenant introduced himself as David Gold. He threw up a hand signal, and the soldiers got back into their vehicles. He and Lieutenant Gold briefly exchanged backgrounds and memories from jump school. He cautioned them to return home but would allow them to pass. He confirmed that all guard and reserve units were now under orders from the Army. He continued with a brief history of a gang called the Group and the terror it was inflicting on some of the northern states.

"Truth of the matter is, anybody that's above the Mason-Dixon that's done time or was doing time on D-Day is joining the Group like the French Underground joined the Allies on the original D-Day. I don't think there's a prison or county jail in those areas with a single occupant. Rape, murder, and slavery are the flavors of the day for the innocent. Be suspicious of everyone, they've taken over nearly all the military installations in their AO. There've been instances when they impersonated soldiers to get other soldiers to drop their guard.

They killed them, of course. So we started using verbal challenges. If you come across another soldier, they should know it. Start with E-4. They reply with 'Mafia,' you respond, 'Can't find them.' No deviations. Can you remember that?"

Lane nodded in response.

"If they don't respond friendly, I'd open fire," he advised.

"Why are you helping us?" Lane asked him.

The soldier pointed to a small tattoo on Lane's forearm in simple block letters; it read, "All the Way."

"What about it?"

"Well, any asshole could've heard about the military running things and memorized a few stories and, hell, could have just slapped a sticker on his windshield. But that neat maroon ink could have only come from Claydon's. And that particular piece of ink is only applied to those that wear a maroon beret. Safe travels, Airborne," the Army officer finished.

"Hooah, Lieutenant," Lane answered as he rolled up the window and put the truck in gear.

He shouldered his weapon and made a knife-hand gesture, and seconds later, one of the Humvees pulled forward to allow the truck to pass. After the truck passed, the Humvee backed into its original position. The lieutenant walked back and got in.

"Who was that?" a private asked.

The lieutenant sat silent for a second, then answered, "He wasn't a leg."

Beth immediately broke the silence. "I have a few questions. What is AO?"

"Area of operations," Lane answered.

"What was the code word stuff? E-4, Mafia, can't be found?" she asked again with her head cocked to the side.

"E-4 is a rank or pay grade, depending on who's asking. Anyway, they can either be a specialist or a corporal. What sucks for them is that sergeants weigh heavily on them to police the privates. That is a full-time job in itself that doesn't include their other duties. So NCOs—sorry, noncommissioned officers—abuse their rank quite often and micromanage the platoons. The other side of that is the specialists and corporals wouldn't be their rank without being the seedlings of future sergeants. They conspire with each other like the Mafia to avoid their abuse and inflict misery on NCOs and officers alike. Make sense?"

Beth giggled and nodded in response.

Five miles outside of Franklin, an old farm truck sat on the right side of the road with a sign hanging off the side painted in red with a brush. It read:

Diesel and Gas for Trade
Gold, Silver, & Dry Goods Accepted

Lane slowed the truck to a stop, and an old man stepped from behind the truck carrying a double-barrel shotgun. A younger man in his thirties followed close behind him, holding an AR. Robert lowered his window, and another younger man appeared from behind a nearby stack of hay bales carrying a scoped rifle. None of the guns were raised, but that could change in the blink of an eye.

They all wore the work clothes of a farmer. The old man wore a Carhartt coat that was faded and dirty from years of use. His pants looked like utility carpenter jeans, and his gloves had the index finger cut off on the right and left. Like the soldier, he paused and took everything in before he spoke.

"You folks need some gas?" he asked in an Appalachian twang, the "L" silent in "folks."

Lane turned to him with his left arm resting on top of the steering wheel. "We'd like to top off our tank, probably around ten to thirteen gallons if you can spare it."

"Depends on what you're trading," the man said confidently.

"You need anything besides what your sign says?" Lane pressed him.

"Got any guns you're looking to part with?" he asked in a whisper, looking to his left and right.

"Well, what I got to trade is worth more than the gas I need," Lane said.

The old man's eyebrows raised slightly in interest. "Why don't you hop out and show me what you got."

The old man turned to the younger man and told him to relax. Lane turned to Beth. "Hand me that camo rifle. Keep an eye out, be ready to go," he finished, addressing both of them.

Lane walked around the front of the truck, holding the rifle from a reverse grip, barrel down, making a point to let them see the way he was carrying it. He walked up to the old man and handed it to him. The old man leaned his shotgun against the truck and took the rifle from Lane. It was a Ruger Predator 6.5 Creedmoor with a Vortex 16×50mm scope. He checked the action and saw it was loaded. He then looked through the scope at a point in the distance.

"Mister, this rifle would probably get you way more gas than you need, even if I filled your tank six times. How do you feel about some silver or gold to make up the difference?" the man asked, still eyeing the rifle with admiration.

"I got another scoped .308 Savage," Lane confessed.

"Let's see it." The man smiled back.

Lane walked back to the truck, and Robert rolled the window down. He spoke for a second, then Robert handed the rifle butt first to him. Lane walked back, holding the rifle the same way, and handed it to the old man. The old man started to examine it but stopped.

"Can I trust you?" the old man asked innocently.

"Those rifles came from men we killed," Lane said bluntly. The moment he said it, he regretted it, but at the same time, it was cathartic.

"Were they bad men?" the old man asked, locking eyes with him.

"Yes, they were. They tried to take from us. When I refused, they tried to kill me and my nephew. I hate to think what would have happened if they had. My niece would have had zero chance against them," he said without blinking.

"Good enough for me. Tell your man to pull the truck behind that barn over there. That's where the gas is, plus I don't like advertising guns when I don't have to. He can just pull around it when you leave without having to back that trailer up. Tell 'em to get out if they want and stretch their legs. Hey, boys! Holster 'em," the old man finished, and the two men shouldered their rifles. One of the men flipped the sign on the truck over, revealing another message. It read in paint-brushed red letters:

Dead and Sick Inside
Enter at Your Own Peril

Lane returned to the truck and told Robert what to do. Each of the other men took a rifle and examined it as they walked to the barn. The barn, at first glance, looked like it was about to fall over, but on closer inspection, it was reinforced with pressure-treated timber painted the same distressed gray as the older wooden planks. There were similar improvements over the entire barn the closer he got. They stood outside the barn and waited for the truck to pull behind it. Robert and Beth got out with the ARs and handed Lane his Mossberg. They stood in a semicircle and exchanged quick introductions.

The old man was Phillip Talbert and owned the hayfield they were on. He explained that he lived at a farmhouse not too far from where they were. The two other men were his grandsons, Elijah and Matthew Phillips. After Phillip showed that he was at ease, the grandsons became friendly, and their postures weren't so severely erect. Phillip motioned everyone to the back and swung open one of two massive barn doors for them to enter. They stepped onto a dirt-covered floor illuminated by skylights on the back side of the roof. Sitting dead center were two identical Airstream trailers that looked like they had rolled off the showroom floor.

"Okay, on to business. How much do you say an ounce of silver is worth?" Phillip asked Lane with a shrewd look.

"It was around thirty dollars before D-Day. Where you at?" Lane asked, flipping the negotiation.

"Thirty sounds right. How about $2,000 for the guns?" Phillip sparred back.

"They aren't making any more guns. How about $2,300, and you throw in the gas?" Lane countered.

Robert, Beth, and the grandsons watched in amusement with impish grins on their faces.

"$2,100 and the gas?" Phillip hit back.

"$2,300 and the gas, and I'll throw in sixty rounds for each." Lane ducked and delivered a stiff negotiation jab.

Phillip rubbed a tight, weathered chin with gray stubble and thought. He took a minute doing his own version of country calculation. For theatrics, he paced several feet back and forth.

"Okay, you got a deal, under one condition." The shrewd look came back.

"What's that?" Lane asked suspiciously.

"Y'all stay and have a cup of coffee and exchange stories for a bit." The old man grinned a pearly denture smile.

"Deal!" Lane exclaimed and stuck his hand out.

They shook hands, and Phillip motioned for them to follow him and his grandsons.

The Airstream trailers must have been brand-new in 2023. They followed Phillip and his grandsons into the closest trailer. They were on their guard going into the trailer but soon relaxed when the grandsons and Phillip placed their weapons in a rack where pretty much anyone could get to them in seconds. Robert and Beth played it safe like Lane and leaned their weapons against the inside of their thighs. The grandsons sat on a table bench on the rear wall while Phillip made a fresh pot of coffee over a propane burner in the all-too-familiar camp percolator. Robert watched the old man warily as he disappeared into a bedroom at the front of the trailer. He relaxed when Phillip reappeared carrying a Crown Royal bag by its gold braided cinch strings. He set it on the table with a clink in front of Lane. Lane didn't open it; doing so would have been an insult under the circumstances after they had allowed them in on a secret they had no need to reveal.

"You folks hungry?" Phillip asked.

"We don't want to impose," Beth said in her sweet, tender lilt.

"Nonsense, we have plenty. Just do me a favor and keep that to yourself," he pleaded.

He opened an old Coleman cooler and returned with a stack of cloth-covered items. He handed them each two. They waited to see if they were going to join them, but after setting down cups and the coffeepot, they declined, saying they'd already eaten. Robert went first, unfolding the napkins to reveal ham and cheese sandwiches on homemade bread with homemade butter. He eyed the sandwich briefly and thought of Hansel and Gretel, wondering if he would end up being prepared as the next meal. The old man quickly picked up on his suspicion, took the sandwich, and used a spoon to cut the corner off, popping it into his mouth and chewing with delight.

"I'm sorry, Mr. Talbert," Robert said, blushing with embarrassment at the slight.

"Don't worry about it. Under the circumstances, I'd be wary too. And call me Phillip," the old man said with a genuine smile.

The three ate while Phillip talked. The COVID strain hit their area especially hard. The lack of medical providers and the rural isolation had protected the majority of the population, but after D-Day and the flood of refugees going both north and south through Franklin, the virus spread like wildfire. It had wiped out over 90 percent of the population in the city and the outlying communities. He went on, saying that all but one officer from the local police department died. That one officer left to go be with his family in Raleigh. Phillip lost his wife, three sons, a granddaughter, and two great-grandsons. He sniffed and wiped a single tear welling at the corner of his eye. He then told of a gang from Asheville that had been plaguing the area for a while. He explained that since Asheville had become a hotspot for government activity, the gang there became skittish of operating in that area and branched outward to satisfy their proclivity for criminal exploits. He and one of his grandsons went into town to scavenge for things they needed to keep the farm going and grab some dry goods. They'd already knocked holes through the rear wall of Lowe's and Ingles and covered the holes with plywood and dumpsters so they could regain access without advertising anyone had been there. They'd taken some wood and steel for repairs to the fence and barn and were making their way into Ingles for dry goods when they heard someone break through the front door of the store. They heard the glass shatter and decided to take a peek and see what was happening, though they already knew it was looting. They honestly thought somebody was hungry, and they'd let them be. But then they heard a woman scream and then another.

"The screams increased as we got closer. We got to the stock-room door leading into the store and saw it. Right between the bread and snack aisle, two young women were about to be raped. They'd ripped most of their clothes off, but we recognized them. We knew them, they were local girls still in high school. They went to our church just down the road. Five men were preparing to do the deed. We snuck up on them, they were having way too much fun to notice us. Just as two of them were about to drop their drawers, we shot them dead. They didn't have anything but bats and crowbars, but we weren't about to let this pass. The other three ran. Matthew dropped the other three in the parking lot with his AR. We took the girls back to the house and put them up in our kids' old rooms. That's the reason for these Airstreams. We took them from a local dealer in case we needed any more space for folks that need help. It's the Christian thing to do. We went back and loaded the bodies into Josiah's old Scout and took them to a nearby quarry and covered them with rocks. That was two months ago. Army fellas been by a few times, but they didn't cause no harm. They just asked for infor-mation about the area. Told them about some gang members that must have broken into the Ingles. Told them we boarded the doors back up and painted over their spray paint gang markings. He said he or somebody else in his unit would be by once a day, and if we needed anything to put up our mailbox flag. Nice fella, think his name was Gall, Gault...no, it was Gold," Phillip finished.

Lane smiled in recognition and gave a quick rundown of the last few days. Robert told his and Beth's journey up to meeting Lane, with Beth adding pieces that he had left out.

"Would you have any medicine to trade for something like a crossbow?" Lane asked Phillip.

The old man scratched his stubble again and thought for a min-ute. "What do you need?"

Lane pulled the same stunt as Phillip and scratched at his ever-growing beard. "Antivirals and antibiotics."

Phillip nodded at Josiah, and he disappeared back to the front room. Lane nodded at Robert, and he exited the trailer.

Josiah returned to the table with a black nylon duffel and set it in front of him. Robert returned and placed the crossbow on the table. Josiah picked it up and looked it over. It had double limbs; one limb was labeled Barnett, and the one beneath read Whitetail Hunter. It was covered in woodland camo and sported a stock scope that was probably good for fifty to one hundred yards. Underneath the limbs were two detachable quivers that held four bolts each; there were seven left.

Josiah pulled out a pocket-sized pharmacy guide and flipped it to the index. He flipped the pages back and forth for a few minutes, then fished into the bag and brought out two large pharmacy-style dispensary bottles. He then took out a pair of nitrile gloves and placed them on his hands. He took out a counting tray and sorting knife that pharmacists use and placed two typical brown transparent prescription bottles on the table. "Sixty ciprofloxacin and sixty baloxavir marboxil?" Josiah started, expecting Lane to counter.

"Add some antacids, and it's a deal," Lane countered cautiously, believing he'd already got the better of the deal.

The young man grinned, hopped up from the table, and disappeared again. He returned seconds later with a blister pack of Prilosec and a box of generic Tums and placed them on the table. Lane nodded and said, "Done."

"Let's get you fueled up," Phillip said, pushing himself up and away from his chair. They left Josiah to count and followed Phillip and Matthew outside. When they rounded the back of the barn, Matthew lifted a black tarp from a wide and tall bulge set against the barn. When the tarp was pulled further back, Lane could now recognize that it was an elevated carboy grounded into the earth. Matthew then pulled a hose with a fuel nozzle from a plastic tote and connected it. Robert opened the fuel lid, and Matthew stuck it in and opened a gate key on the carboy, allowing gravity to do the work.

"It's nonethanol gas. Don't worry about it being good. I threw in some octane booster when we filled it up, so that'll help a little." Phillip smiled with pride, sticking his chest out ever so slightly.

"I wouldn't have doubted, but thanks for telling me," Lane replied.

"One last thing." Phillip motioned for Lane to follow him so they could speak alone.

They walked to the edge of the woods that bordered the hayfield. They both stood shoulder to shoulder with their backs to the barn. Josiah exited the barn and stood with his brother, Beth, and Robert. "What's going on?" he asked them.

"No idea," Robert told him. He then looked at Beth and Matthew, and they both shrugged.

They stood there for the better part of an hour. It wasn't an animated conversation; for the most part, they stood with their arms crossed, nodding, and shaking their heads occasionally, and spoke in low tones so they couldn't be overheard. Finally, Lane dropped his hands to his hips, bowed his head in a defeated posture, then shook Phillip's hand.

Phillip walked over to Matthew and spoke to him quietly, then handed him a set of keys.

"I'll be back in an hour. Wait inside with the boys," Lane told them.

"What's happening, Lane?" Beth asked.

"Gimme an hour, and I'll explain," Lane pleaded.

Beth nodded in return and walked to the other side of the barn. Moments later, they heard an engine start. After a few more moments, a powder blue and white Scout drove down the path and turned left on the road. They watched until it was a speck, then saw it turn right and disappear behind a stand of trees. They followed Josiah and Matthew back into the barn. The boys didn't give them an explanation because they didn't have one. So they passed the time playing Uno and drinking coffee.

An hour turned into two, and just before three passed, they all heard the grumble of the Scout's engine.

They all emerged from the barn and waited. Lane emerged from the side of the barn first, Phillip soon followed with two teenage girls on his heels. Lane walked up to Robert and Beth and motioned for them to follow him. They rounded the corner back to the truck and got in, following Lane's lead.

"Lane, what's going on?" Beth asked.

Lane paused for a second, took a deep breath, and explained, "I'm going to abbreviate this as much as possible. Phillip has pancreatic cancer. He was in remission on D-Day, but he believes it's back. I won't go into the details of why he knows. His grandsons are heading to Florida when he passes. They both have girlfriends there. They would have already left, but Phillip's condition started getting worse. Matthew and Josiah aren't equipped to take care of teenage girls. The girls have no family here and want to leave. They've escaped rape countless times and are scared to stay. I've agreed to take them with us and care for them until they've come of age."

"It's going to be tight in here," Robert suggested.

"That's the other thing. He's giving me one of the Airstreams," Lane said, staring out the window.

"Can the truck haul one of those things?" Robert asked with doubt in his voice.

"It can. This truck has got a hauling capacity twice the weight of the trailer. We'll be heavy, but it'll be within limits. We'll leave the guns in the cab with some extra ammo, but we can unload everything else from the trailer inside it. They installed a fifty-gallon fuel tank below the water tank. It's already loaded with gas. He's going to load us up with some food and other stuff to make it easier for us. They're good girls, or at least that's what Phillip told me. He said they haven't caused any drama…other than being depressed over their family and friends being gone. He told me they've been good hands on the farm too. They know their way around hunting rifles and have been on their parents' farm all their life. They aren't lazy."

"I don't guess we have any say in this, right?" Beth asked.

"Sorry, but no," Lane said without hesitation.

"Well, I guess we'd better go meet our new travel companions," Robert said without malice.

They went into the barn and made introductions. Phillip introduced the brown-haired Shelby sisters first. The oldest, at eighteen,
was Crystal. She was pretty and shorter than her sister at somewhere
near five feet but had the curves of a woman that would entice boys
and men of any age. Blanche was sixteen with a tomboyish look but
still pretty and nearly half a foot taller than her sister with an athletic
frame. They both had green eyes that would burn right through you
if you let them. They shook hands like men but were gentle with
their grips. Lane introduced Robert and Beth, as he had already been
introduced by Phillip. Upon introducing Robert, both girls smiled a
little too much and held eye contact a little too long with him to not
be obvious. Beth noticed and stuck her hand in Robert's.

After introductions were made, the girls followed Phillip back
to the Scout and came back carrying Leokor backpacks, probably
the most expensive packs on the market. Sleeping bags, pads, and
assorted accessories were identically attached to both of them. Eyeing
the expensive gear, Phillip explained that he'd outfitted them well
from a local outfitter. The owner had, of course, died along with his
wife.

Phillip came a few minutes later with another cooler. They set
up a propane grill inside the barn and opened one of the skylights
with a cable crank. Phillip placed eight thick sirloins on the grill with
slices of onions. When they were done, they ate the sirloins on homemade rolls with a buttered horseradish sauce that added a little kick.

When they'd finished eating, Lane backed the truck into the
barn, unhooked the trailer in front of one Airstream, and then backed
up to the other. They finished unloading and loading easily in a short
time with all the extra hands. The Shelby girls proved their eagerness
to work, attempting to do more than the others. In addition to everything else, they added six 20-lb propane tanks for the Airstream oven
and burners, with another camp grill. They crammed in sixty rolls of
toilet paper and a sealed box of unmentionables for the ladies. The
last items were food that included 20 lbs of ground beef, 10 lbs of
pork chops, 10 lbs of sirloin, six dozen eggs, and three gallons of raw
milk. They continued to load milk crates of other foods until Lane
halted them, not wanting to overload going through the mountains.

Before they shut the trailer up, Josiah and Matthew loaded two milk crates of books. Lane frowned in protest but said nothing.

Phillip walked over and handed Lane another set of tire chains. "They were for the hay truck, but the transmission is roasted. Won't be using it anymore anyway."

Lane frowned slightly at the grim remark. Phillip walked away and reappeared holding a banker's heavy lock bag with both hands.

"I knew just about everyone in town, including the president of the bank. He was still alive when I took in the girls. Their parents banked there and had a bank box. I went in and got their birth certificates, and to my surprise, the Shelbys had fifty ounces of gold bullion bars. Reckon it belongs to them. So…Archie, the bank president, and I got to talking. He had COVID and knew he wouldn't survive it. His wife and daughter were already dead, lying in their beds, but he couldn't bury them. In fact, he'd moved into the bank and was leaving handwritten notes for the investors if any were still alive. He handed me a list of the box owners, red marks by most of the names. In exchange for handling his and his family's burials, he gave me the list and master keys for all the boxes for after. The dead didn't need what I took. The owner of the pawnshop was also dead, the guns and ammo had been cleaned out. But the safe was intact, so the boys and I…well, Matthew cracked his safe. It took him the better part of a week. Matthew actually did it like they do in the movies. He got a stethoscope from the clinic and a legal pad and spent about six hours a day until one day, he heard all the clicks hit the right combination, and it popped open. Needless to say, we were all surprised by what ole Delbert had accumulated. After the bank and the pawnshop, we'd pulled in quite a bit of silver, gold, and platinum. The boys have enough to keep them quite comfortable if trade picks up with survivors. Anyhow, minus the fifty ounces for the girls, the rest of this is for you to do as you please. I hope you'll use it to help you care for those young people," Phillip said, finally settling down the bag in fatigue.

"This is more than helpful, thank you. I'll put it to good use. It won't be wasted frivolously," Lane said stoically. He hoisted the bag up to the rear of the truck bed. He then turned to take on another task, but Phillip stopped him.

"Hold on, there's two more bags in the other trailer just like that one." Phillip grinned ear to ear.

The day was nearly done, and they decided to sleep in the other trailer and head out in the morning. The old man and the boys said their goodbyes and wished them all well. Tears were shed as Phillip and his boys hugged the Shelby girls. The old man blew his nose in an old bandana, and even Josiah and Matthew were sniffling. One final farewell wave and the men got in the Scout and left.

Having already eaten, they decided to turn in early. They went into the other trailer as the loaded one offered little room to move around. Crystal and Blanche unrolled their sleeping bags on the bed. The couch unfolded to allow two to sleep, so Beth and Robert unrolled their bags there. Lane unrolled his on the bench seat. Everyone was exhausted, and sleep took them quickly. The night was quiet inside the trailer, and their bags were more than warm. Lane's last thought before drifting off was wondering what he was going to do with two teenage girls indefinitely.

DECEMBER 22, 2024

THEY ALL ROSE EARLY WITHOUT COMPLAINT. IT was dark inside the trailer, with only hints of pink painting the skylights. Their breath was visible when they exited the trailer. Crystal took it upon herself to prepare some breakfast. Blanche walked around the trailer, checking the tire pressure. Two wheels were a few pounds light. Without being told, she extracted a foot pump and used her body weight to operate it and get them to spec.

Robert opened the barn doors as Lane started the truck to warm it up. Blanch checked the truck's tire pressure. The girl was smart; she bled five pounds off each tire so the chains would get more bite. Lane cursed himself for forgetting such an easy trick. His respect for Blanche went up a notch.

Twenty minutes later, with a hobo bag full of sandwiches, a thermos of coffee, and a cup for each of them, Crystal earned a respect notch herself.

They pulled into Franklin city limits ten minutes later. Robert rode shotgun with Beth sitting behind him. Crystal sat beside Beth, while Blanche sat behind Lane. There were gangland tags spray-painted here and there that were both Latino in style and reminiscent of Crips they'd seen around Atlanta. They pulled directly through the intersection and veered onto 23. Lane kicked himself again, realizing the reduced tire pressure was indeed helping. It was easy driving even with the trailer.

Crystal handed out fried ham and cheese sandwiches. They ate in silence, and after they all finished, she poured coffee for them all. They'd gotten about a dozen miles when they encountered a jack-knifed tractor-trailer covered in snow, blocking most of the lane.

Lane pulled into the oncoming lane at a turnoff for a sideroad. He grinned to himself at the freedom of being able to do so. He drove in this lane until they got to Dillsboro, then got back onto the proper side. They averaged 20 to 35 mph until they made Waynesville. Lane eased to a stop getting off 23 and pulled out the atlas.

They drove under I-40 when they made Canton. They encountered two men on ATVs, one of them dragging a doe strapped to a game sled. Lane drove wide of them as they passed. The men slowed to a stop, watching them until they were out of sight. Lane was pleased to see that both Robert and Beth were ready for trouble, clutching their ARs. It was 11:08 a.m. when they entered the city limits of Mars Hill.

They drove across 23 and made a right onto 19 East to go by Pisgah National Forest. After traveling for fourteen miles without issue, they encountered a pickup and a snow drift blocking the road just before the small town of Burnsville. Lane stopped the truck, and he and Robert went out to investigate. Beth stood by the truck, watching the area, but it was quiet except for the distant squawking of crows.

Lane rummaged in the bed of the truck and came back with a shovel. Robert handed him the AR, took the shovel, and got to work. He'd only cleared maybe a dozen scoops before he hit something hard. As he cleared away the outermost layer, a figure began to take shape, revealing a macabre scene. What at first appeared to be one figure turned into three. It was a skinny red calf with an older man and a teenage boy. It appeared they were trying to butcher the animal where it had fallen. The animal must have been frozen because their skinning knife hadn't even broken through the hide. The man and the boy were huddled together against the underbelly. The general assumption was they were so hungry they'd died in a last-ditch attempt to feed themselves or perhaps others as well. It was heartbreaking to see. The old man's last act was to shield the boy by opening his coat over the boy's shoulders, trying to protect him from the weather.

Lane left the scene and returned to a nearby fir tree and attached a come-along. He played out the cable, then secured it around the calf's rear hooves. He then ratcheted the slack until it became taut. Cranking down tighter, it didn't move. Robert took the shovel and started prying, first at the back of the calf, then its head, and finally under the buttocks of the man and boy. Nothing budged, so Robert repeated the process three more times. Lane cranked down again, and finally, the calf and the dead moved as one. They were somehow intertwined as one mass. Robert cleared snow from their path of travel, and slowly, inch by inch, they moved them so they could safely pass.

No one said anything when they got back in the truck. Crystal poured three coffees, which they graciously accepted. Before they entered Burnsville, Lane saw something that made him hope they could drive straight through this town without delay. An unbelievably large kettle of turkey vultures swarmed the skies in black masses. As they entered town, they could see them lining the rooftops, swollen and resting. An odor started to taint the air in the cab, and Lane closed the vent quickly, knowing what it was. The streets were empty except for one older woman pushing a shopping cart through the snow. As they passed her, she flipped them off and spat on the ground. Robert watched the woman in the rearview as she disappeared into a Dollar Store. They encountered no one else in Burnsville.

When they left the city limits, they'd gone perhaps five miles and were surprised to find that the snow had been well-traveled, but there were no vehicles in sight. After going a few more miles, they discovered why. Barbed wire ran from the forest edge along the road and disappeared into the forest ahead, in between sixty acres of pasture were nestled. In the pasture was an old John Deere tractor pulling a wagon filled with hay. A man drove the tractor through the snow while two figures tossed square bales to a herd of Red Angus that were lining up for their turn to eat. They didn't stop their work, but they clearly slowed to watch what had to be an alien sight to them as the truck and the shiny aluminum-skinned trailer drove by.

The last thirty miles took an hour and a half as they had to carefully navigate ever-increasing curvy inclines and abandoned vehicles. Many had been pushed to the side of the road, but some had been involved in accidents, and clearing these vehicles from the road would take the mechanical prowess of a wrecker / tow truck. At one point, Lane had to take the shoulder to get around a four-car pileup.

As he eased the truck onto the shoulder, he could see the trailer's rear slide closer to the trees. In a panic, he gunned the accelerator, and the chains found purchase. He pulled onto the road with pine needles barely kissing the roof of the trailer and missing the trunk of the closest tree by inches.

"We lost a chain," Blanche called out.

Lane straightened the truck and trailer out and stopped. Everyone got out and stretched their legs. Robert walked to the front of the truck, clutching his AR at the ready, while Beth stood beside him and scanned ahead with the binocs. Crystal sauntered up behind them, sniffing the air. Blanche picked up the broken chain and handed it to Lane. The link was broken in the cradle and couldn't be salvaged without a torch. Lane deposited the broken chain in the truck bed and retrieved one of the other sets that Phillip gave him. He laid the chain in front of the rear driver-side tire so that he could drive onto it. He spread out the center gap so that it was more rounded and hopefully wouldn't get bound up as he tried to fasten it.

"Can you drive?" he asked Blanche.

"Yes, sir."

"Hop in then, follow my hand signals."

She did as she was told, started the truck, and put it into gear. Lane held his hand in the air and pressed his index finger and thumb together back and forth slowly. She looked at Lane in the side mirror. Blanche let off the brake and slowly pressed the pedal until the truck started to creep forward. After about ten seconds, Lane closed his hand into a fist, and she hit the brake. Blanche put the truck in park but kept her foot on the brake. Lane deftly worked the chain around the tire. After some trial and error, he fastened the chain in place and stood up. *One more notch for Blanche*, he thought.

They all climbed back in and were soon covering the distance again. The mountains were all covered in snow. This is what the area was best known for, thick blankets of snow in the winter. He wondered if there were any surviving die-hard skiers who would attempt scaling the mountains to tackle the unmolested slopes.

A flood of memories tormented Lane as he drove by Sugar Mountain. He'd taken the family there skiing on multiple trips.

Squeals of laughter, bruised bottoms from falling on the bunny trail, snowballs, hot chocolate, and roaring fires. A tear threatened to well up, but he sucked it up and concentrated on the last few miles.

They pulled into the city limits of Banner Elk, greeted by dozens of people milling about here and there. With the exception of an old Toyota Land Cruiser, all other traffic was ATVs. And like the others, the truck and trailer made for a circus-like sideshow; everyone stopped to watch. Lane turned right on Main Street and found his way into a subdivision.

"Is this where your mother's cabin is?" Beth asked him.

"No, her cabin is higher up on the mountain. An old friend of hers lives here. He checked on it from time to time. Mom rented the cabin out when she wasn't staying here. I'm going to see if he's home," he explained.

They continued driving and turned off onto Shawnee Road, which was sheltered on both sides by fir trees drooping with snow. After another ten minutes, Lane stopped in front of a steep metal-roofed home that had been built to withstand winter snows. There was smoke coming from a stone chimney in a steady, even plume.

"Keep the truck running. Robert, take your Beretta out of the holster and give it to me. I haven't seen or talked to Earl in about six years. He was old and grouchy then. I don't even know if he's alive, but if he is, I doubt he's changed much," Lane told them and shoved the pistol into the back of his waistband.

The air was frigid as he got out. Simply exhaling sent large puffs of steam skyward. He'd taken no more than a dozen steps when the front door opened, and a giant of a man stepped out holding a coffee mug in one hand and a gleaming revolver in the other. Lane took his stocking cap off to reveal his mane of red curly hair.

"Earl! It's Lane Stone, Mirabelle's son," he announced.

"I know who you are! I'd recognize that bouquet of tiger lilies from a mile away!" the old man teased at Lane's hair. "Come on up!"

Lane trudged through knee-deep snow and went up the steps. The old man handed him a small broom, and he cleaned the snow from his jeans and boots. Earl opened the door for them, and they went inside. The home smelled of a mixture of coffee and wood-smoke. Earl placed the nickeled .357 Smith & Wesson on an end table, then picked up an open book from the seat of his chair and set it aside to sit down, gesturing to an opposite plaid high-backed chair for Lane.

"I know why you're here, Lane, and I wish I could have saved you a trip. Your momma's cabin is gone, son," the man said sympathetically.

"How?" Lane asked simply.

"Yankee hikers. I caught them up there about two weeks after the shit hit the fan. I went up there once a week like I always do. I guess they were planning it. They'd been there a few days, probably broke in as soon as I made my last visit. Anyway, I ran them off. There were four of them, two couples…said they were from Connecticut. I went back to the house, got some supplies, and stayed up there for a few days to make sure they didn't come back. So after a few days and no sight of them, I figured they were dust in the wind. They weren't."

Earl picked up his coffee and took a sip. As he exhaled, Lane caught a whiff of Scotch. Earl stood up and went into his kitchen and came back carrying a fresh mug and handed it to Lane. "Lees-McRae College" was painted on the side. Lane thanked him, and Earl took his seat again.

"Don't know what chain of events led up to it, but I was out in the garden, and I happened to see some smoke off in the distance toward Mirabelle's place. There was enough of it that I thought the worst. My fears were true enough. By the time I got there, it was a full blaze. Two fire engines couldn't have saved it. All I could do was wait for it to burn itself out. I came back the next day and started sifting through the ashes the best I could. I came across enough bones that at least two of them died, could've been all of them, all things considered. Anyways, it burned straight down to the foundation. I guess them old treated logs were pretty good fuel for that shingle roof. I'm sorry, son," the man offered again.

"Not your fault, Earl. You did what you could. Somebody wants in a place bad enough, they will," Lane told him, trying to ease any guilt the old man might harbor.

"What are you going to do, go back to Georgia?"

"No, I got some college kids I need to get to Kingsport. They were at Georgia Tech when it went down. By some twist of fate, they ended up on my doorstep. I'm taking them home, and I'll figure out what my next step is when I get 'em home."

Earl just nodded in understanding.

"How are you ladies doing back there?" Robert asked, turning in his seat to face the sisters.

Crystal was reading an old paperback, and Blanche was looking out her window, seemingly daydreaming. Crystal was preoccupied with her book and didn't respond. Blanche, however, was alert.

"Are we staying here or pressing on to Tennessee?" she asked, still looking out the window.

"Well, the plan was to stay the night and press on in the morning, but we're about to find out," Robert said as Lane stepped from the front door of the house. He and the old man shook hands, then Lane turned and descended the steps.

Moments later, Lane opened the door and climbed in. "Robert, can you signal for me? I need to back in to turn to the inside of the driveway mailbox."

Before he could answer, Blanche hopped out, volunteering. She high-stepped through the deep snow and took a position where Lane could see her. She knew what she was doing. She spun one hand in the air and used the other to signal forward, backward, and reverse. The young lady surprised him again. Once the trailer was straight to pull out, she hopped back in the truck.

"What are we doing?" Blanche asked, with a touch of excitement in her voice.

Crystal looked up from her book, and the rest listened.

"My mother's cabin burned down. We're pressing on. But not before we stop for lunch. Earl said there's some trading going on in town."

"Let me out. I'll go whip something up in the trailer," Crystal ordered.

"Not today. Lunch is on me," Lane told them without explanation.

He pulled the trailer back onto Main Street and soon turned left onto Shawneehaw Avenue. Seconds later, he pulled to the curb in front of a sign that read Avery County Farmer's Market. Several vintage Army tents were set up, and snow had been shoveled, clearing paths to and from each tent. A few tents had woodstove pipes coming from the sides. People were entering and exiting the tents with bags, and some were eating, but they couldn't tell what from the curb.

Lane turned in his seat. "This area has some good people that have kept things pretty well secure, so no long guns. If there's something in these tents that you think you want, or we need, just tell me, and I'll work it out. Beth, you, Blanche, and I will go first. Robert and Crystal, you stay with the truck and keep an eye on things just in case."

Beth made a small scowl on her face; Lane noticed but said nothing. He knew why—she didn't want to leave Robert alone with Crystal. She'd have to get over it.

They got out of the truck and made their way to the first tent. They pushed the flap aside, stepping inside, and let their eyes adjust to the gloom. People had folding tables set up for trading goods, and the people barely took notice as they moved inside. A man who was about Lane's size, height, and age approached them. He was wearing a state trooper campaign hat and an insulated vest with a star on it. He also wore the utility belt common with all law enforcement.

"Jeff Nelms, formerly of the North Carolina State Troopers," he said, extending his hand to Lane.

"Lane Stone," he said and shook the man's hand.

"What are you folks doing around here?" he asked politely.

"Well, I was planning to relocate here, but some assholes burned down my mother's cabin," he answered bluntly.

"Oh, I'm sorry, Mr. Stone. Didn't make the connection. I didn't know your mother personally, but my mother did. She used to make quilts with my mother. That's her back there." He motioned over his shoulder at a portly woman with silver hair standing behind a stack of quilts. "I'm sorry I never got the chance to know her. Come on, I'll introduce you." Jeff walked them over and made the introduction.

Mrs. Nelms just about burst out of her skin, maneuvering herself from behind the table. Attempts at a handshake were useless as she wrapped him in a hug and pulled his neck to her shoulder in a sickly sweet, perfumed embrace. He turned to Jeff Nelms for help, but he turned away, trying to hide his laughter.

"I loved your mama to death, Lane. She talked about you all the time. My goodness, we used to talk for hours with these silly old quilts draped over our laps. The stories she used to tell me about your family. What a bunch of characters. I heard about your mama's cabin, just a shame…just a shame. I reckon she's going to be fit to be tied. Where is that woman?" she asked, looking around Lane's shoulder.

Lane answered by just looking down at her and gently shaking his head.

Her hand flew to her mouth. "Oh no, sweet Jesus, no."

"I'm afraid so, ma'am," he said in a low tone.

"Did she die peacefully? Oh, I hope she did. She had such a sweet soul," she continued, not giving Lane a chance to respond. She carried on for another five minutes before she snapped her fingers and thumbed her way through a stack of quilts, then extracted one near the bottom. She unfolded the quilt, letting it fall to the floor. "Your momma left this one with me on consignment years ago."

It was an extravagant ten-point star in colors of green, dark blue, and magenta. At the tip of one of the star points, the letters M and S were stitched in cursive. "I reckon it belongs to you now," she said, wiping a lady's handkerchief under her nose. She took the quilt, folded it back up, and placed it in a reusable Tractor Supply shopping bag, then handed it to him. He thanked her for the quilt and said goodbye. He looked over at the tent entrance and saw Jeff Nelms watching them, unable to keep a straight face.

He and the girls made their way to a table selling honey. Lane felt his pocket jingle. He had fished a handful of pre-1965 quarters and dimes from one of the bags that Phillip had given him. The coins were 90 percent silver and should be good use for barter. Blanche explained that Crystal could use the honey for baking, so Lane gave the woman eight silver dimes for two quart jars, which she gladly took. He quickly discovered that most of the vendors here were trading for silver and gold, salt, sugar, and coffee.

Lane found one vendor in the corner who was trading cigarettes and chewing tobacco. Lane traded nine quarters for two cartons of American Spirit smokes and three homemade twists of chewing tobacco wrapped in cellophane.

Seeing nothing else of interest, they moved on to the next tent. Before his eyes could adjust, the girls made straight for the rear of the tent where a little chubby bald man with tufts of white hair sprouting around his ears was busy making pizza. His pizza oven was wood-fired and looked homemade. A shelf made of bricks had a steady fire burning from two dozen rows of split logs. Above that was another level of flat rocks pieced together like a jigsaw. The girls turned to Lane and swooned.

"I got pork sausage, ground beef, peppers and onions, mushrooms, jalapenos, but no olives. Mozzarella and provolone made in-house. By the slice or a whole pie, you pay...I make," the little man boasted.

Lane fished a small handful of change from his pocket, but not all of it, and told the girls to get what they wanted. It ended up costing a whopping three dimes for six slices of whatever they wanted. They stood in the corner of the tent, eating their pizza and watching people come and go. A couple of boys eyed Blanche and Beth, looking them up and down, smiling. Lane gave them the stink eye, and they moved on.

They finished walking around and decided it was time to let Robert and Crystal fill their bellies. They walked back, and Lane fished the rest of the change out of his pocket and handed it to Robert. He briefly explained the rate exchange of their transactions to give them an idea of what things cost. Crystal and Robert practically skipped to the pizza tent.

Lane opened the passenger door and fished around the glovebox, then he opened a pack of the American Spirits and lit one up.

"Ewww! Yuck!" the girls exclaimed as smoke filled the cold air.

Lane took in a drag and exhaled with satisfaction as a small nic-otine buzz grabbed him with a slight spin in his head. Beth took his keys, wrinkling her nose, and loaded their things in the trailer.

Fifteen minutes later, Robert and Crystal came back with their arms loaded. Crystal carried four five-pound cans of Sam's Choice coffee with two containers of Sam's Choice vanilla creamer. Robert was weighed down a bit more. He carried a huge duffel on his shoul-der, similar to the utility bag he carried his military-issue clothing in. He dropped the bag at his feet and stooped down to unzip it.

"Figured you might need this at some point after you drop us off," Robert said, grinning at him.

A huge lump formed in Lane's throat, and he had to walk away.

"Lane, what? I'm sorry. I didn't mean to waste the money! Hey, wait—" Beth stopped him from following. "It's not the money." She smiled at him, gently rubbing his arm. It suddenly dawned on him. He zipped the bag up and loaded it in the trailer.

Lane walked around the trailer to compose himself and suddenly felt silly. These kids had families that they needed to get back to. His feelings of loss were selfish, and he decided then that he needed to space himself a bit emotionally. As he approached the driver's side door, Jeff Nelms approached him.

"None of my business, but where you all heading?" he asked without any hint of subterfuge.

"Taking two of them to Kingsport. The other two, I'm their guardian. Parents died," Lane told him.

Jeff pulled out a business card and scribbled on the back with a pen, then handed it to Lane. "You'll need this."

It was a normal business card from the North Carolina Highway Patrol. Jeff's name and badge number were displayed in opposite cor-ners at the bottom. He flipped it over, and in a brief message, he'd written in cursive:

Allow passage, hardship journey.
Family in-state TN, VA, KY, NC.

Signed: Trooper Sgt. Jeff Nelms

96

"Thank you, Jeff. Would you add Missouri?" he asked, handing the card back.

He took the card, scribbled MO on it, and handed it back. He pulled a notepad out of his pocket and wrote down some directions, which he handed to Lane. "Follow this route. It'll save you some time and bring you out on 23 in Unicoi."

"I really appreciate your help. Hopefully, I can make it back here someday. Beer's on me." Lane shook his hand and got in the truck.

Everyone else piled in as Lane started the truck. Blanche asked how much farther, and Lane handed the atlas to her. Robert and Beth started talking about home, and then the girls started asking questions about where they were going and what it was like there. The time passed quickly after they left Banner Elk. He'd spent so much time with Robert and Beth that it'd slipped his mind of their actual ages. They were only separated by a few years and actually had more in common than Lane expected. They talked about music, movies, and other things that Generation X could care less about.

They soon pulled onto 23, and within an hour, they hit another roadblock after getting through the Johnson City limits. This time, the road was blocked by Tennessee State Troopers. They had Humvees with magnetic THP placards stuck on the sides. The troopers were in full uniform without deviation; their shoes looked like black mirrors. As one trooper approached, his body language read all business. He motioned with his finger for Lane to roll down the window. Another trooper joined the party and also motioned for Robert to roll his window down.

"Put your hands on the dash, Robert. Girls, put your hands on top of the back seat. They need to see your hands. Trooper, we've got loaded weapons." The trooper stopped short and held up a closed fist for the other trooper to do the same.

"Leave your left hand on the wheel and reach under your arm to open the exterior door handle. Then step out of the truck," he ordered.

Lane did as he asked with some difficulty. He stepped onto the snow-covered highway. The trooper approached him with his hand on his firearm. He motioned for the other trooper to approach the truck.

"Okay, thanks for showing us respect with the hands and weapon declaration. Now tell me what you're doing and where you're going. Judging from that Peach Pass sticker, I'm guessing you're from Georgia."

Lane went into the explanation, not leaving anything out except for the killings. He told him about Phillip and the girls, Robert and Beth being from Kingsport, them being students at Georgia Tech, and finally his stop in Banner Elk, producing his driver's license and the card Jeff Nelms gave him. They got everyone out of the truck and questioned them individually. They then peeked into the bed of the truck and looked inside the trailer. Satisfied, the lead trooper returned to him.

"I'm going to be honest with you. If this was pre–D-Day and I stopped somebody with a $30,000 trailer loaded with all the firepower you're carrying, ammo, and a truck full of young pretty girls, I'd hold you here indefinitely even if the ATF had to fly in from Alaska. But as it is, I'd say you're doing some pretty heroic shit." He pulled a card out and copied Jeff Nelms's message, then handed the card to him. "Safe travels. Take care of those kids."

The trooper turned on his heel and marched back to the Humvee, with the other trooper following.

The trooper turned back to Lane, walked up to him, and whispered, "Kingsport, Bristol, Johnson City…it's been bad. Eastman Chemical is completely shut down. There might be two hundred people left in Kingsport, not counting the gang. You might want to prepare those kids for the worst. And if you see anybody wearing green bandanas, that's the gang. They call themselves Shamrocks. Mostly white kids, but since the recruiting pool has been depleted, they aren't too picky now. Intel says they're holed up at MeadowView Marriott, so be prepared. My advice is to bypass them. Get off on Rock Springs Road. The kids probably know their way around." Then he turned and got back in the Humvee.

*****

98

They took the Rock Springs exit. The twenty-mile detour was slow going. Beth directed Lane where to go. The sun was setting when Lane pulled into a parking lot with a sign that read Laurel Run Park. Everyone got out and stretched their legs while Lane and Robert refueled. They emptied six of the jerry cans. It was dark when they finished; manually pouring gas from a jerry can just took longer.

"Beth, how much further? We're in Church Hill, right?"

"Yes, we are. About fifteen minutes," she murmured.

"Are you okay, Beth?" Robert approached her and took her by the hands.

"I'm scared. I'm afraid of what's there...or what's not there," she said, hanging her head.

"Whatever happens, I'll be there with you and for you." He lifted her chin and kissed her. She smiled at the display of affection.

"We'd better go." They turned and walked back to the truck hand in hand. Crystal watched the exchange and frowned.

The truck was running when they climbed in. Beth gave Lane directions, and they pulled out. There were a few places where the road was iced over, and they almost wrecked. The snow turned back to powder, and Beth told Lane to turn left on Mt. Zion Road. Beth's tension was so potent that everyone in the truck could feel it. "Up ahead on the right. The gray trailer with the ramp."

Her mother's Blazer was in the driveway, covered in a foot of snow, but the wheelchair-accessible van for Allie wasn't there. There were no lights on anywhere in the trailer park, not even the glow from a candle. Lane rolled down the window, parked the truck, and turned it off. They all sat and listened to the quiet, waiting for unexpected voices or worse, gunshots. Beth suddenly exhaled in a gush; she'd been holding her breath.

Lane handed her a flashlight. "I'm not going anywhere. I'll be right here."

Beth got out, and Robert followed in her footsteps. They walked up the ramp; the snow was undisturbed. No sounds came from inside the trailer, no footfalls, no voices. A rocking chair sat at the edge of the porch. Beth approached it and picked up the cushion that padded the seat. It was one of the zippered cushions where you could remove the covering for washing. She unzipped it and stuck her hand inside. A minute later, she pulled her hand out holding a key.

She stuck the key in the lock and turned it. She cracked the door open and called out, "Mom? Dad? Allie?"

No answers, only silence.

She opened the door wider and swept the room with light. It looked the same as she'd left it last Christmas minus the Christmas decorations. There were no decorations now, only a thin layer of dust. There'd been a tree last year, and lights were strung everywhere. Her family didn't have a lot of money, but they were proud. Her father had worked at least fifty hours a week for as long as she could remember. Her mother had worked too until Allie's car wreck had put her in the wheelchair. Even with all that, Christmas was always celebrated. She was hoping to come home to a tree lit up by a lantern hanging from the ceiling or something like that. Not even the smell of her mother's cinnamon stew. She would fill a pot with some water, cut tangerines in half, and put them in with cloves and cinnamon sticks and let it steep all day. It made their home smell like Christmas.

A very different odor hung in the air. Robert pushed past her. "Wait here." She objected, but he put his hand over her heart and pleaded with her in the darkness. She nodded her head.

Robert clicked on his flashlight and went to the kitchen first; nothing was out of the ordinary. He moved back and went into the first bedroom. This room was empty and must have been Allie's. A support hung over her bed from the ceiling on a chain; Robert figured she used it to get herself in and out of bed.

The next room was Beth's. There was a stuffed Pikachu on her bed along with a heart-shaped pillow. The walls were covered in academic awards and posters of tech giants that he'd heard of but knew nothing about. The odor was stronger now; there was one room left.

The door was shut. He knocked gently but knew there would be no answer.

The smell overtook him, and he pulled his shirt up over his nose. A large figure lay under a discolored sheet, stained from decay. Nausea grabbed him by the throat, but he fought it back. There was a wedding photo of Lenore and Greg on the nightstand. Lenore was blonde, and Greg was Native American. Robert pulled back the sheet until the top of the figure's head was visible. Jet-black hair stuck out from beneath.

He replaced the sheet and turned to leave, but something caught his eye. There was an envelope on the floor in front of the door that he hadn't noticed. He picked it up and looked at it. Beth's name was on the front in cursive. He started to open it but didn't. He walked into Beth's bedroom and grabbed her Pikachu, tucking it inside his coat. He decided that he would quickly skim over the letter to know what she faced. He quickly skimmed it and headed to the front door.

Beth waited anxiously by the door. She saw Robert's light dance on the floor as he approached. He came to her and took her arm, guiding her out the door and shutting it behind him. He walked her to the side of the trailer and handed her the envelope. He held his flashlight up so she could read it. She moved her fingers over her name; it was her mother's handwriting. She pulled the papers from the envelope and read.

10/8/24

My sweet daughter,

I hope this letter finds you well, and I am truly sorry to pass on this news in a letter. I wish I were there in person to hold you and tell you how proud I am of you.

Again, I am sorry to give you this news by letter. Your father passed away three weeks ago. The COVID took him from us like so many others around us. In his last words, he wanted you to know just how much he loved you and how proud he was of you. I would often find him standing in your room holding your stuffed animal. He missed you terribly. I've never lied to you, and I won't start now. His illness was difficult, and it was hard on myself and your sister. He hung on for so long.

Four days after your father passed, Allie went on to be with him. I cared for her as best I could, but like your father, she clung to life, but in the end, her body was too weak to fight off the sickness. She too was very proud of you and loved you. She wanted you to remember her the way she was before the wreck. She wanted you to remember the summers on the reservation when you ran in the forest and played in the stream.

Sweetheart, I wish I had some small piece of good news to give you, but I don't. As I write this, I am at Holy Spring Baptist Church. A couple of the congregation have been taking care of the dead and those that are close to dying. I have fought this damn virus as long as I could, and I'm afraid that I, too, will soon join your sister and father. I had the virus once, not long after D-Day. I laughed when I got it because I never had any symptoms. I just tested positive for it.

It wasn't long after that the neighbors started getting sick, and it went out of control like wildfire. Thank God for the church. Pastor Daniels had been preparing for quite a while for just such an emergency. Unbeknownst to the congregation, he'd been spending almost all of the offerings on food. Pastor Daniels and his wife were shopping geniuses. They had memberships at Sam's and Costco, clipped coupons, used apps, and were always looking for sales. They kept us from starving. Every single day they prepared meals for fifty people twice a day. I honestly don't know how they did it. Regardless, God bless them for what they did for all of us.

Sweetheart, if this letter finds you, please survive, please live.

I hope that you will never have to read anything remotely like this again for the rest of your life, ever.

I hope that you will find an honest man that loves you for all that you are, good or bad. I hope that you will love him for all his good and bad. I hope that this world will heal, and you are able to live some kind of normalcy. The last thing that we all want is for your grief to end the moment you read the last words of this letter. Remember the good times and shed no more tears, not for us. We all love you. Someday we'll see you on God's golden shores.

With love,
Mom

Beth, your mother passed away two days after writing this letter. We buried your mother and sister beside the tulip beds behind the church. We'll send someone to collect your father when warmer weather allows and place him with your family. We would have collected him sooner, but things have been busy with other members of the church. Please accept my warmest condolences. God bless you, child.

Sincerely,
Pastor Daniels

Beth folded the letter and stuck it back in the envelope. She stared at the envelope then looked up at the star-filled sky. The tears were cold as they streamed down her cheeks. She turned into Robert's chest and sobbed quietly. Robert stood there and held her close to him; he wouldn't move or encourage her to stop. He let her cry and whispered, "I love you, Beth Holt."

"Blanche, why don't you hop up front for a while?" Lane suggested as he watched Robert and Beth hold each other; he guessed the worst for Beth's family. Lane closed his eyes and said a prayer to himself and asked God to help ease Beth's grief; he then asked God for guidance and asked that he protect them on their journey. He finished his prayer asking God's forgiveness for the sins of his past, present, and future. He finished as Beth and Robert got in the back and shut the door. She clung to him, and he wrapped his arm around her. Crystal patted Beth on the leg, and Beth took her hand and gently squeezed in appreciation.

The tire chains spun in the deep snow, and the combined weight of the trailer made it impossible to move forward against the small incline that the truck faced. Balance hopped out and went to the driver side at the rear of the trailer. It was hard to make out Blanche's hand signals but after five minutes, he'd backed the trailer into the street and straightened out the truck to leave. Blanche resumed shotgun and picked up the AR. She checked the action of the semiautomatic rifle and verified that a round was chambered; she checked the safety and replaced it beside the console. The young lady continued to surprise Lane.

Robert guided Lane until he came out on Stone Drive. "Go straight for eight miles. We're going to hang a left on Bloomingdale Pike. Follow that for about five miles to Newland Avenue on the left."

All disabled vehicles had been cleared from Stone Drive. Not only was the road cleared, but disabled vehicles of any kind were absent. They had been hauled away by some unknown housekeeper. Lane stopped in the middle of the road and opened the fuse box. He removed the fuse for the headlights; it was the only way to keep the daytime run lights from being on. He then removed the fuse for the brake lights. He reached into the side pocket of his door and handed Blanche the monocular night vision device. She turned it on and held it to her eye with her eye shut.

"There's enough moonlight that I can drive by it. Just keep an eye out for me. You see something, say something," Lane told her. "Robert, give Crystal that atlas and your keychain light. Crystal, start scanning our area. Northeast Tennessee. I think it's page 11E. Look for airports, hospitals, schools, and any other points of interest." Lane really didn't need Crystal to do that, but he wanted her to feel like she was needed, and he'd realized that he had been showing favoritism to Blanche, and he felt guilty about it. Before he turned around, he saw that Beth was clutching an envelope. In the dim light, he could make out Beth's name printed in ink on the front. He grimaced at the sight and felt her grief. He put the truck in gear and pulled away.

As they entered Kingsport's city limits, Robert encouraged Beth to look out the window. Allandale Mansion was on the right. The large Georgian-style two-story mansion had been rumored that the home was built by a slave owner. But that wasn't true at all. It had been built by a wealthy cattleman named Brooks in the early 1900s. Before D-Day, the mansion was used mainly for weddings and social events. The mansion was still bone white, but the well-manicured lawn was now overgrown like everything else, but surprisingly, a male peacock strutted around in the snow. There was candlelight or perhaps a lantern glow coming from the window of an apartment complex that was next to the mansion. He thought he saw a shadow from the window, but they had passed on out of sight before he could get another look.

They drove over the bridge that crossed North Fork Holston River, Robert had waded this shallow river many times in his youth with his father and brothers fishing for bass and trout. They had always released the fish because of mercury releases from the mines in Virginia upstream. The water was black, but the occasional hint of white was visible as water fell over rocks into deeper depressions. The absence of cars that Lane had noticed was now explained as the Walmart was jammed full of cars in nearly every vacant patch of space. They passed under 23 and crossed another bridge before Robert spoke up. "It's on your left after that Putt-Putt course."

Lane slowed to a crawl and spotted the street sign that read Bloomingdale Pike. He took the left and discovered that this part of the road had seen some traffic. There were multiple sets of footprints beside multiple sets of tire tracks, yet there was no evidence of anyone nearby. "Robert, be ready for anything."

Beth momentarily freed herself from Robert's arm and freed her pistol from the thigh holster. She noticed that Crystal was staring out the window like she might've been sitting on a train watching the scenery roll by. Beth tapped her on the shoulder, and she turned to her. Beth tapped the atlas, and Crystal took the hint, clicking the little flashlight on, and resumed her search over the area.

There was little to be concerned about. The truck clock read 8:45, and it was bitterly cold according to the truck's external thermometer, which displayed 8 degrees Fahrenheit. They drove on and soon crossed over an intersection; the street sign read John B. Dennis Highway. Crystal made note of their location, enthusiastically moving her index finger and following the lines on the map.

"Movement!" Blanche called out, pointing to a stand of fir trees in the distance.

Lane took the monocular and held it to his eye as he slowed the truck. Indeed, he could see a single person duck behind the tree and keep poking his head out back and forth. He couldn't see a gun. Robert maneuvered his way around until he'd switched seats with Crystal and sat behind Blanche. He had the AR ready for action. Everyone was alert and tense. Robert sped up and tried to put distance between them. They were just about to round the corner when a shotgun boomed; they immediately heard and felt the impact of birdshot pinging off the truck and trailer.

"THAT SON OF A BITCH!" cursed Lane.

"Motherfu—" started Robert before Beth cut them off.

"Language, boys!" Beth admonished them.

Lane sped up, and the girls giggled at Beth's rebuke.

There were no other shots; Lane chose to assume that someone had ventured outside to answer nature's call and sent a warning shot or maybe a shot of jealousy at someone who was still mobile and warm in a controlled environment.

They were now in Bloomingdale now, the little area that Robert grew up in. He narrated like a tour guide as they went.

"Back down John B. Dennis used to have a dirt racetrack, you could hear 'em in the summer from the house. That place on the left used to be Kingsley Elementary School, I went there through sixth grade. They closed it in 2013 and turned it into senior citizen apartments." Robert pointed to the left. "That's Ketron, used to be a middle school, now it's, or was, the elementary school. Dad said there was a ghost story about a girl that was in the band that died during band practice. Said that folks told tales about seeing her walk around the ball field in her band uniform playing the flute."

Blanche and Crystal both rubbed at the gooseflesh that was covering their arms. They all looked below at the field half expecting to see a specter strolling atop the snow playing a tune.

"The turn is up here just past that little store. It's a steep turn by the way," said Robert, pointing over the backseat ahead.

Lane approached the turn and tried to turn wide of it as much as possible. He accelerated into the turn and the chains fought for traction. The tires spun into the powder but made no progress. Lane allowed gravity to aid him back into the original point of entry. "Is there another way in?"

"There's a carpet cleaning business up on the right, you can turn around there. We need to go back and cut up between the churches on the right. After that, we go right on Cardinal. That'll take us back to Newland," Robert explained.

Lane took the advice and soon turned into the small parking lot and circled back out onto the road. They drove past Ketron and turned right onto Katherine Lane. The incline was less severe, and the chains had no problem battling the snow. They quickly turned onto Cardinal, and after a couple hundred yards, they were turning left onto Newland Road. The incline increased, but with the momentum, the chains managed the weight and gained ground. Robert told Lane to turn left on Page Street. The street was level but quickly turned into a vicious incline. Luckily for them, Robert pointed to a house on the left two houses before the incline.

"That's home," Robert said quietly.

Lane backed the trailer into the driveway, then pulled out onto the street and parked.

They all got out of the truck; after being comfortably warm, the frigid air had an extra bite. Beth walked up to Robert as he moved to his front yard.

"Wait here. You too, Beth."

Lane wrapped his arm around Beth's shoulder, and the girls stood beside her. Robert walked around the rear of the house and stood in front of the sliding glass door. His intent was to look through the door, but the vertical blinds were drawn. He took an old leather wallet from his front pocket. He kept the wallet more out of nostalgia than anything else. Thirty-two dollars in worthless currency remained in his wallet along with a driver's license, student ID, and a portrait of himself and his family. Behind the portrait was the key to the sliding glass door. He unlocked the door and slid it aside slowly until it was wide enough to pass through. When he stepped inside, the smell of weed hung in the air. He slid the door closed and opened the blinds.

He turned around and let his eyes adjust to the gloom. There was a hint of a glow coming from the den fireplace. As he approached, he noticed a lump on the floor. On the hearth was a nickel-plated pipe lying next to a large bag almost full of weed. He noticed a mop of curly blonde hair sticking out the top of the lump that he now recognized as a sleeping bag. "Grant," he said aloud.

The lump didn't move. He called the name again, still nothing. "GRANT!" he yelled and kicked the lump.

A hand suddenly appeared holding a Colt 1911. "Who the fuck are you!"

"Grant! Put the fucking gun away before I clean the toilets with your head!" Robert warned.

"Robert? Is that really you?" asked the young man, staring through reddened eyes.

"Yes, you damn stoner! Now lower Papaw's pistol. And where is everybody?"

Grant's eyes softened and welled up with tears. Robert's younger brother put a few sticks in the fireplace. These had no doubt been dug out of the snow or broken off dead trees. The pile of embers was small, and it took some time before the sticks actually caught flame. "You better sit down."

Robert's heart skipped a beat. It was never good news when someone told you to sit down for news. There was a picnic-style table in the den. Robert pulled one of the benches out and sat next to Grant.

"I don't know where to begin," Grant said, staring into the fire.

"Why don't you start by telling me who's dead?" Robert's eyes betrayed the hurt he was feeling.

"Okay… Mom died July Fourth. Her heart gave out when the meds ran out. Dad died a month later when his insulin ran out. I haven't heard from William. The last time Mom and Dad spoke to him, he was a month out before he deployed to Bolivia. He told them the first and third battalions were doing a legit airdrop and supposed to be linking up with a revolution force. He left you a hat, said not to go around telling everyone you're a Ranger." He finished by wiping his eyes and nose.

Tears streamed down Robert's face. "How've you been surviving?"

"Scavenging. I think there's an older man living on Rainbow Circle. Aside from him, I haven't seen anyone in two months. So I started here on the street. I went house to house. I've been living on whatever I could find. I killed a doe about a month ago, the fresh meat was a nice change. I found this bag of weed a few days ago. I haven't been sleeping too well," Grant told him as he pulled the sleeping bag from his legs.

"None of the Shamrocks make it up here?" Robert asked, wiping his face.

"How'd you hear about them? But no. Like I said, I haven't seen anyone in two months."

"It's a long story. Where are Mom and Dad?"

"They're in the backyard, under the magnolia tree."

"I'm not alone. I've got people with me. Do you have more wood?"

"Enough for tonight," Grant said, pointing to a tall stack of broken branches.

"I'll be right back." He got up and pushed the bench back. He opened the door and turned back. "Oh, yeah, there's one big guy and…three hot girls, just in case you want to fix yourself up a bit. Just saying, the one with the long black hair is mine," Robert said, looking back over his shoulder.

Robert found them all pacing around, checking the area out. Beth saw him and ran up to him. She looked him in the eye, and he couldn't hide it from her. She just threw her arms around his neck and hugged him. Lane and the girls watched the two, then turned away out of respect.

"My brother is alive inside the house," Robert whispered in her ear.

"Really?" she asked, and he nodded in return.

Robert called out and gathered them all around him. He gave them an abbreviated version of his news and invited them inside.

Lane secured the truck and followed them around the house. The fire was blazing now, and the room was noticeably warmer. An oil lantern sat on the mantel, lighting the room sufficiently that you could read if you wanted. There was a large pot sitting in the flame with a lid on it. The bag of weed and pipe were gone.

"Hello." Grant walked into the room wearing clean Levi's and an orange University of Tennessee sweatshirt. Beth noticed how much Robert and his younger brother resembled each other. He invited everyone to warm up by the fire. He excused himself briefly and reappeared carrying a plastic jug of sweet tea and a stack of red Solo cups. He set the tea and cups on the table as a *pop* sounded, then another. Everybody turned at the sound, and it multiplied and multiplied again.

Twenty seconds later, popcorn lifted the lid off the pot. Grant took two potholders and removed the popcorn. He removed the lid and shook liberal amounts of buttered salt over it. He unfolded a newspaper on the table, then dumped the popcorn on the paper. He invited everyone to sit down and poured tea for them all.

They talked for hours; Beth laughed too hard at stories Grant told about Robert. She continued to giggle when she noticed Robert burning holes in Grant with his eyes. Of course, the girls were smitten with Grant's good looks and charm. If Beth wasn't with Robert, she would have been smitten too. Lane would chime in occasionally, but for the most part, he allowed the kids to chat away. Lane excused himself and asked Robert to join him.

They opened the trailer and gathered their packs. "I'm sorry, son," Lane said. Robert nodded and looked away. "If you want to talk, I'm not going anywhere."

Robert nodded again and turned to go back inside.

They dropped the packs off and returned to the truck for the weapons and the money bags.

Everyone rolled out their sleeping bags and settled in for sleep. Lane took an armchair that faced the door. Instead of crawling into his bag, he spread it over his legs and torso with his shotgun resting on his lap. Robert and Beth slept beside each other while the girls did the same and were within a hand's reach of Grant. Everyone but Lane was soon asleep. He sat there alone with his thoughts, his children, and his new children.

DECEMBER 23, 2024

When Lane woke, the sun was coming up over the Appalachian Mountains. The sunlight blinded him when he opened his eyes. He put his hand in front of his eyes to shield them. He pushed up from the chair and saw that, for the first time in a long time, he was the last to rise. Robert and Beth sat at the table across from each other, whispering and sipping coffee.

Lane rolled up his sleeping bag and joined them at the table. Robert went to the fire and poured a cup from the percolator for Lane.

"Where are the others?" Lane asked after taking his first sip.

"Crystal is making breakfast for us. Grant said he would accompany her. Blanche decided she would help when Grant offered to accompany her," Beth explained.

"Have you two talked about what you want to do next?" Lane asked between sips.

"A little," Beth replied.

"We were going to wait until everyone finished breakfast," Robert added.

Lane nodded in understanding and kept drinking his coffee. He was extremely anxious about what was going to happen in the next few hours. The girls came in carrying covered plates, with Grant bringing up the rear. He had a 30-30 lever action over his shoulder with iron sights. He was smiling ear to ear as if he'd won the lottery; maybe he had. Crystal also brought with her a campfire toaster. She carefully toasted a dozen thick slices of bread and set them on the table with a jar of homemade butter. They all sat together, and for the first time in many years, Lane said grace over their meal.

"Lord, thank you for the food that you have provided. Please bless the hands that prepared it. God, please grace the loved ones that have gone before us. Please help ease the grief of those that have lost their loved ones. Lord, thank you for guiding us here safely. Thank you for our lives and sparing us the sickness that has taken so many. Please protect our loved ones that continue to live. Please guide us to make good decisions and forgive us for the bad ones. In your name, we pray, Amen." They all answered "Amen" when he finished.

They ate scrambled eggs, pork chops, and buttered toast. Grant ran upstairs and reappeared with Minute Maid apple juice boxes. They ate in silence, but the glances Crystal and Blanche exchanged with Grant were easily noticed. Lane hoped their mutual infatuation wouldn't create division between them.

They finished their breakfast and cleaned the dishes in snowmelt. Robert excused himself and went outside. Grant had constructed two crosses from the neighbor's privacy fence. Their names were carved on each, with "Mom" and "Dad" carved into the top of each. He'd done a good job. Grant had managed to find pink plastic carnations somewhere and planted them at the base of their mother's cross. Tears spilled again. He promised himself that no more tears would be shed for his parents. They weren't grieving; they weren't in pain. Robert believed they were in heaven, and that comforted him. He finished a prayer as Lane and Beth joined him under the magnolia tree.

Lane put his arm around Robert's shoulder, and Beth took his hand. It occurred to Robert that Grant had gone through this alone without anyone to comfort him. He'd been alone when they died, and he'd buried them alone. He felt a measure of pain and pity for his little brother and decided he would start treating him with a respect he hadn't shown in the past. "Thank you both. I'll be okay."

He turned and pulled away from them, but Beth reached out and took him by the hand. "You don't get to do that. You don't get to shrug off people that care for and love you," Beth told him. He pulled her to him and kissed her. He looked up at Lane, who was staring at him with a questioning look. Robert understood and nodded to him. Lane returned a nod in acknowledgment and left them.

Lane was surprised to find Grant and the girls engaging in a form of judo he recognized from a YouTube instructor known as the Red Beetle. Lane had first seen this form of judo in the *John Wick* movies. Later on, he'd seen the young men who were actually in the third movie of the series demonstrate various moves with Japanese nomenclatures he couldn't pronounce. He had later learned that the Red Beetle was a man named Monty Collier, with a mop of red hair like himself, and after several Google searches, he'd found that he'd been training stuntmen and movie stars for over a decade. Of course, Grant wasn't throwing the girls around but was instead demonstrating how to fall or land when thrown. The girls were watching mostly as Grant had stripped down to gym shorts and a tank top. Lane had to admit he was a good-looking kid. His hair was a bit curly and a little more muscular, but he could pass for Robert.

"Did you learn your judo from Monty Collier?" Lane asked.

"How'd you know?" Grant asked in surprise.

Robert and Beth came in holding hands; Robert immediately put his hand over his face in embarrassment.

"What, you can do better?" Grant asked, smirking as he crouched into a fighting stance.

Robert let go of Beth's hand and approached Grant. Grant quickly grabbed hold of Robert's shoulders to gain control of his mobility. Robert did the same and stepped toward the outside of Grant's left shoulder. Once Grant became off balance, Robert stepped back with his right leg, pulling Grant forward with a sudden jolt. Robert quickly brought his right foot forward again and swept Grant's feet, sending him into a somersault landing with a controlled thud.

"Ladies and gentlemen, that's what is referred to as Okuri-Ashi-Barai. The part where Grant landed on the floor with a grunt is called Ukemi-Waza," Robert explained with a mock bow to his brother.

Lane was genuinely impressed, as Robert had never mentioned he had such a skill. What amazed him the most was the speed and ferocity with which he'd performed it. He had no doubt that if he'd been thrown like that, a number of his bones would have been broken. Robert helped Grant up, who needed no assistance but did so out of sportsmanship. All the girls were slack-jawed. Grant clapped Robert on the shoulder, grinning like nothing had happened. Lane clearly assumed that this was not the first time the two had sparred in such a fashion.

"Do you mind if we all have a conversation, please?" Lane asked, pointing to the table.

They all exchanged puzzled looks at Lane and each other but took seats at the table without protest.

Lane sat there and looked at all their faces. Their youth energized and haunted him at the same time. He had a singular mission that hovered in his mind, but he was sitting with young adults who were disguised as kids.

"I'm going to Missouri to find my kids. I am also responsible for keeping Crystal and Blanche alive. However, Crystal and Blanche, I don't feel like you've been given a choice as to what you would like to do. Robert and Beth, I have known you for less than a week, but I consider you family. Grant, that means you too. What I'm trying to relay here is I would like us to stay together. But you have a right to make your own decisions. I can't promise your safety. I have no idea what is out there. I just know that, dead or alive, I'm going to find my children," he finished.

Robert nudged Beth. "Lane, I can speak for Robert and me. We're going with you."

"Robert, can I talk to you a minute upstairs?"

Robert nodded and followed Grant upstairs.

Grant walked into the living room and stood by the window. Robert joined him, sitting on a loveseat.

"What about William?" Grant asked.

"I thought about him. Do you think he'd want either of us waiting here for him, not knowing if he's dead or alive? Do you think he'd want you or me staying here and running the risk of freezing to death?" Robert asked.

"I don't know. This is all I've ever known, Rob. I can get through the winter. I can keep collecting deadfall, and worst-case scenario, there's about a hundred privacy fences I can scavenge. There're probably another forty houses I haven't touched yet, and I can still hunt," Grant debated.

"And then what? What about next winter? And the winter after that? What if you hang around here and William doesn't come back?" Robert reasoned.

"Okay, fine. Fair point. What do you know about this Lane guy?" Grant shot back.

"I trust him. Beth trusts him. He saved our lives, we saved him. We all saved each other. A perfect stranger trusted him, after knowing him for less than an hour, to take two teenage girls with us, knowing he'd never see them again. That's what I know about him," he said defensively.

"Well, you did bring me two very hot single chicks," he said with a half-hearted attempt at a smile.

"About that," Robert said, crossing his arms.

When Robert and Grant rejoined, everyone was quiet. Robert started to ask why, but Beth anticipated his question. "We were waiting for you."

"I'm in," Grant announced.

Blanche and Crystal didn't hesitate. "We go wherever Lane goes."

"Okay, that settles it. We've got planning to do. There should be plenty of vehicles to siphon gas from. We need to refill the jerry cans today. Grant, you need to pack whatever you're taking. First, we need to do something. Robert, would you grab my fire safe out of the truck?" Robert got up and took the keys from Lane.

Robert returned and handed the fireproof box to Lane. Lane opened the box, took out a folder, and set it aside. "I'm showing you the contents of this box because I don't ever want any questions of what is in the box after this day. Anything else that goes in here, everyone should be in the know."

Lane started removing tall and short prescription bottles. They were full of silver bullion, junk silver, and gold bullion. Lastly, he placed ten 10-ounce bars with his hoard. "I have roughly 375 ounces of silver and 12 ounces of quarter-ounce gold Krugerrands. Oh yeah,

Crystal, Blanche, this was in your mom and dad's safety deposit box." Lane handed them a Crown Royal bag with the 50 ounces of gold.

They all continued to look at Lane. "And there's another reason I did this. I wanted you to see mine before what happens next. The girls' former guardian, Phillip, gifted us with three very heavy bank bags. They raided the deceased's bank boxes and the local pawnshop. Apparently, they had more than enough and, as I said, gifted these to help us get by. Robert, if you would be so kind."

Lane unzipped the first bag and started removing the contents. He placed plastic tube after tube of gold rounds on the table, then a canvas bag with ten pounds of junk silver consisting of dimes, quarters, half-dollars, dollars, and loose silver rounds and bars. They calculated that, based on D-Day prices, there was around $300,000 in the first bag. The other two bags had similar contents with gold and silver. They all figured that there was close to $750,000 worth of precious metals. The question that worried Lane the most was whether or not it would buy more than pizza and honey.

It only took Robert and Grant a few houses and a few hours to fill the empty jerry cans and top off the tank. Grant took Lane on a tour of the house and started selecting things to take. The garage held a pleasant surprise as Grant's late father, Greg, had a 2013 F-150 FX4, one year newer than his. With Grant's and Robert's permission, Lane spent the entire day cannibalizing every part he could, including the tires and spare. By Lane's reasoning, he couldn't exactly stop at a parts store anytime he wanted.

The plan was to leave the next morning, make the most of the daylight, and try to find someplace to hole up during the night. By the time they'd loaded up Grant's gear, guns and ammo, dry goods, and spare parts, Lane estimated that he'd added another 400 lbs, not counting Grant.

They made a meal of several cans of beans and saltines. True to common knowledge, everyone was soon excusing themselves outside to rid themselves of bean-induced flatulence. Robert and Grant sat at the table, taking turns writing on a legal pad. They busied themselves for an hour, then finally stopped and went upstairs.

Robert and Grant stayed busy. Per Lane's instruction, they repositioned some of the gear so that two people could occupy the trailer. Grant attached a scope to his Henry 30-30 and left it with the gun his father won in a raffle, an FN SCAR .308, in the rear of the trailer. Grant also borrowed one of the Berettas and now wore it on his hip.

CHRISTMAS EVE
DECEMBER 24, 2024

LANE BEAT EVERYONE TO RISE; SUNUP WAS still an hour away. Nobody stirred as he started a pot of water to boil. He eased himself outside and lit a smoke. His lungs protested and threatened to cough, but the muscle memory abated the reflex, and he savored the sensation as he exhaled. He took the moment to mentally prepare himself not just for the day but for the whole journey. When he crushed out the cigarette, a hint of pink emerged over the peaks of the Appalachian Mountains.

Lane stirred in portions of steel-cut oats for everyone and poured himself a cup of coffee. He went upstairs and found cinnamon, chopped walnuts, and maple syrup in the pantry. He returned and added all to the pot of oatmeal, save for the syrup, which he set on the table. When the oatmeal was done, he made a point of smacking the spoon against the side of the pot. Everyone but Grant stirred, so he made another series of spoon rattles, and Grant finally rolled over and yawned.

Lane spooned out equal portions into plastic bowls, and the grumpy youths shoved spoonfuls into their mouths, then took turns adding the syrup to sweeten their breakfast. Robert and Grant ate seconds, complementing Lane's preparation. There was little cleanup, and within minutes, they had repacked and walked out the door. They finished loading up, and Lane rechecked the cannibalized wheels he'd secured the day before. He fished the radios out and gave Grant one. Lane snapped a twig off a tree and broke it into two pieces. He held them out to Blanche and Crystal to draw. Crystal drew the short twig; he told her she'd be riding in the trailer with Grant. He gave her a spare set of binocs and told her to scan their rear and radio anything of interest. Grant and Robert visited their parents' grave one last time and returned with an arm draped over each other's shoulder.

Lane reviewed his atlas and decided to take Highway 11W, which went all the way into Knoxville. They loaded up and left the same way they came in.

At Beth's request, they stopped at her house and picked a few things up that were sentimental. From the moment she walked through the door to the moment she climbed back in the truck took less than five minutes. The day was warmer, and as they entered Rogersville, the snow had started turning to slush. Lane decided to remove the tire chains. The clock read 11:20 when he stopped in Blaine, twenty miles north of Knoxville. Robert walked about twenty yards ahead, with Beth a few paces behind him scanning the area with the binocs. Lane unhooked the chains and signaled for Blanche to drive forward. Lane picked up the chains and was stowing them in the bed of the truck when Beth alerted them.

"We need to get in the truck NOW!" she yelled the last word and started to run back to the truck.

Unlike the movies, no one stood around looking confused, and nobody had to be told twice. Blanche climbed over the console as Lane got in. Beth pointed her finger over Robert's shoulder. Fifty yards away, three female lions trotted toward them. Robert radioed Grant, telling them to stay in the trailer.

The lions came up to the truck and sniffed it. As Lane watched one out his window, one of them stood up on two legs and licked his window. Its claws dragged down the door and left deep gouges in the paint. Lane cringed at the sound.

"Can we go now, please?" Beth asked nervously.

As Lane pulled away, the male lion with its humongous mane came up to the roadside to watch them pass.

"Anybody wanna take a stab at explaining that?" Blanche asked.

"Knoxville Zoo. They must've escaped. Hunger," Robert explained.

Grant broke radio silence. "Uh, anybody else see lions out there?"

"Yep, just let us know if you see any of them following us," Robert answered.

They passed through Skaggston and pulled into the parking lot of a Dollar General. Lane opened the trailer door and asked if Crystal wouldn't mind making some lunch. To his surprise, she'd already made them sandwiches and a thermos of coffee. Lane took the sandwiches and turned to go when Robert spoke up.

"We really need to be ready for anything. Knoxville can be a nasty place. I barely escaped getting stabbed to death after the Tennessee-Florida game two years ago. Grant, I know you love that 30-30, but I believe, for the time being, Dad's SCAR is the better choice. Crystal, you should be moving from window to window instead of just looking out the rear window. We need to keep moving," Robert told them.

"You heard the man, let's roll," Lane said.

They pulled back on the road; 11W turned into Rutledge Pike, and minutes later, signs for Interstate 40 appeared. The temperature rose to forty-three degrees when they pulled onto I-40. The snow was melting quickly, and it sloshed in sprays on both sides of the truck. Lane was thankful he'd removed the chains. Despite the melting snow, there was still enough of it that if he went too fast, he felt the tires spin, even with the four-wheel drive.

They'd almost made it through the city without incident until they got to an overpass. Beth sounded the warning before it was too late. "There're two guys on the overpass. One of them has a cinder block."

Robert rolled down the window and stuck the AR out the window. Lane slowed as they got closer. Robert lined up his laser optical and fired two rounds at the barrier. Dust exploded from the concrete, and the figures ducked out of sight. They passed under, and Robert spun to face the other way. One man held the cinder block above his head, ready to drop it. Robert placed the dot on the man's midsection and pulled the trigger. The man staggered, and the block fell on his head. He pulled himself back in and rolled up the window. Lane looked at Robert out of the corner of his eye. Just from his body language, he knew he'd shot the man.

They made it to Farragut when they encountered the largest and most imposing roadblock yet. The entire interstate, including the median and the shoulders, was blockaded by armored vehicles. There were two Abrams tanks pointing in opposite directions on both sides. The median was filled with at least a dozen MRAPs, and the roads were blocked by four Bradleys on each side. Countless support trucks and Humvees were scattered on the exits.

All of the Bradley 25mm chain guns swung around, pointing in their direction. Robert radioed Grant and told him what they were looking at and told him to stand down. Lane slowed to a stop, and they all waited.

Lane got out of the truck unarmed. One of the soldiers yelled and told him to get back in the truck. He ignored him. He leaned against the hood of the truck and waited. He lit up a smoke and exhaled into the air. He was never afraid of fellow soldiers, but he was afraid that these soldiers might take Robert and Grant. He was halfway through his cigarette when a Humvee skirted around the other vehicles and came to a stop directly in front of Lane.

A private and sergeant got out first; they were followed by a captain and a full-bird colonel. A strange look caught Lane's attention as the captain started to approach as if he recognized him. He opened his mouth to speak, but the colonel pushed past him. The colonel removed his IHPS, the updated version of the old K-Pot helmet. His high-and-tight haircut was beginning to grow out, revealing a graying crown of dark hair. They all wore the tree with stars patch of the Tennessee National Guard. Lane took one last draw off his smoke and squeezed the end off, stuffing the filter in his pocket, not wanting to litter in front of the officer. The soldiers observed this and relaxed. The colonel's name patch was missing, as well as other badges like jump wings, pathfinder, airborne, or combat infantry badge. Now he noticed they were all missing badges except for their unit patch, rank, and name.

"E-4," Lane said aloud.

"Mafia," the colonel replied.

"Can't be found," Lane replied to the challenge.

"Where'd you learn the challenge?" the colonel asked with a sneer on his face. The captain waved an open hand in the air, and the tension of being on alert vanished.

"A fellow grunt," he answered.

"Why are you out of uniform?" He kept the sneer going.

"Well, I guess the VA figured I didn't need to wear one." The colonel started to reply in anger, but Lane lifted his pant leg to expose the ankle joint of his prosthetic. The colonel didn't flinch, but he noticed discomfort on the captain's face.

"I think that's a fair assumption, airborne," the colonel remarked, noticing the Eighty-Second decal on the windshield. "What brings you this way?"

"You know, this makes the fifth time I've been asked that in as many days. Being honest, it's getting old, Colonel. Seeing as you're probably the battalion CO, I'll humor you." Lane handed him the business cards from the state troopers and went into an abbreviated story, finishing by pointing to the lion scratches on the passenger door.

"That's quite a journey," the colonel said, handing the cards back.

"Quid pro quo, Colonel?"

"Oak Ridge National Laboratory, making sure nobody gets their hands on our atomic goodies. Pretty important. I'd thought they'd deployed regular Army for something as important as this." The colonel said with an air of arrogance that only officers can express.

Lane couldn't resist such a gift. "Well, Colonel, that's because they use the regular Army to kill the people that come after our goodies so you don't have to."

The aging soldier's brow furrowed, and his eyes pinched in anger. The captain stepped in to de-escalate the situation. "Mr. Stone, if you'd like, we have the chow hall set up at the next overpass. We'd be happy to feed your group before you get on the road. I'll radio ahead and let them know you're coming."

"Much obliged, Captain. Do you know of anything we should be concerned about between here and Nashville?" Lane asked the captain while ignoring the scathing look from the colonel.

"There's a small contingent of guards and state troopers in Nashville. I'd be more worried about getting over the Mississippi. The I-40 River Bridge was damaged again. There was a significant seismic event that damaged the road surface and lateral support structure. The Army Corps of Engineers have closed the bridges. I know there's at least one barge operating around the Memphis area. I'd think some bargain could be struck to get you across. Thing is, that damn Group gang has migrated activity to the river. You might find some pirate activity as well. As it is, I hear they're only taking gold and silver. If not that, ammo, guns, or other nonperishables might be bartered. Do you have anything like that?"

"Afraid not. What we have, we need. Guess we'll have to strike up some other kind of deal," Lane responded, not wanting to reveal what they had for fear of having anything confiscated.

"Captain, why don't you fix these folks up with some of that DHS 5.56? Not like those bastards will ever be on the front lines to use it," the colonel suggested, surprising Lane.

"I'll meet you at the mess tent, Mr. Stone," the captain told him, and they all spun on their heels and climbed back into the Humvee.

One of the Bradleys moved to the side, allowing them to pass. Lane climbed into the truck and quickly explained what they were doing.

One mile later, they pulled directly in front of the tent entrance. It was an ideal spot under the overpass, as it was mostly sheltered from any rain or snow. A master sergeant was waiting when they pulled up.

"Everybody keep your lips sealed, don't get chatty. I don't want anybody to find out what we have. As a matter of fact, Robert, stay with the truck. Grant, as soon as you're finished, relieve your brother. Leave long guns in the truck," Lane ordered them.

"Merry Christmas," the senior NCO said cheerfully.

They all looked at each other with puzzled looks. "What day is it?" Beth asked.

"Why, it's Christmas Eve, young lady," the master sergeant said, smiling.

It all dawned on them that they had not kept track of the date. They each felt some sense of embarrassment not knowing. The sergeant held a tent flap back, and they all went inside. The space was illuminated by electrical lights powered by a generator rumbling outside. He motioned to the chow line where two soldiers stood ready to serve food. They all took trays and cutlery and filed in behind one another. One by one, they were served meatloaf, mashed potatoes, steamed broccoli and carrots, and fresh rolls. At the end of the serving line stood stacks of coffee cups with insulated dispensers of coffee and tea. They all sat down and dispensed with manners, quickly devouring the hot meal. Grant finished first and excused himself to relieve Robert. Seconds later, Robert got in line, followed by the captain. They both got in line and filled their trays. The girls excused themselves as Robert and the genteel officer sat opposite Lane. Lane used his roll to scoop up the last remnants of potatoes and popped it in his mouth.

Robert wasted no time digging in. The captain was a little more reserved in approaching his meal but not by much. After all, soldiers were trained to eat as fast as possible so they could be at the ready and return to duty without delay.

Robert savored the last sip of his fresh coffee and stood up to leave. "Hold on, sir." Lane went to the line and refilled his cup and stole another roll. Before he finished his roll, Robert took his tray to a wash bin and went outside. Once he was gone, the captain set down his fork.

"Our armory was effectively fortified about a week after D-Day. We've got a surplus of a lot of everything. This allows me to be generous. I'm prepared to be generous under one condition," the captain said mysteriously.

"I'm listening."

"Follow me." The captain pointed to the exit as he stood.

They exited through another flap and walked toward another tent that might be a comms station at the edge of the overpass. The tent was dark, and the only light came from the open flap. From the

125

light, he could see that straw was spread on the floor, and an odor of shit and urine hung in the air, stinging his nostrils. The straw stirred in the corner and undulated before two noses and two tails appeared from beneath. Two pups almost identical in markings pranced toward them. The captain bent over and scooped one up in each hand. The ears stood erect, and their thick coats were marbled with brown and black. Lane took one of their paws in his hand and studied its size. At first glance, the pups appeared to be German shepherds, but maybe not.

"German shepherd sire, Belgian Malinois bitch," the captain said, anticipating his question.

"You want us to take them?" Lane asked.

"The parents were working dogs. The sire served in Afghanistan for IED detection, the bitch was used as an apprehension asset. The mother died. I think she was too old for a litter. The pups are fine, though. We found a pet store nearby and found puppy formula. They got to nurse from her for a few days before her body just gave up. I've had a private taking care of them ever since. The colonel's patience is growing thin. Nobody here is qualified to train them for anything, and I need the private to resume his duties. Take them both, and I'm going to sweeten the deal."

Lane studied the pups and felt his heart melt a little. The Grinch That Stole Christmas came to mind, and he pushed it away. "Captain, what did you have in mind?"

"The young man already loaded it from the truck." The captain walked outside and said something to a private in a low voice.

The captain carried the pups with Lane following close behind him. As they approached the truck, Beth and Blanche immediately noticed the pups and became completely unglued. They swept in and each took a pup, cooing and gushing at the cuteness and snuggling them into their faces with kisses. Lane rolled his eyes at the captain and mouthed curses at him. The captain snorted with laughter and told Robert to show him. Robert and Grant both laughed. Grant opened the trailer door and stuck his head in.

Stacked inside the front door were ten ammo cans of NATO 5.56mm, one thousand rounds each. To the left and right were six

M4s, three with optics, three with open sights. Beneath that were six new IHPS helmets and two pelican cases with night vision attachments, and a third case held battery packs.

"All this for two pups?" he asked in astonishment.

"You don't recognize me, do you, Sergeant?" the captain asked.

Lane thought for a moment and studied the man's face. Now that he looked harder, there was something in his eyes and voice that was familiar. It suddenly came to him; he had been on crutches waiting for knee surgery. He'd been given light duty, more of a first sergeant's role, and was charged with keeping a half dozen E-5s on task with new company arrivals after the body of the Eighty-Second had already deployed. A young second lieutenant was among the new arrivals. Lieutenant Wallace was fresh from West Point. More often than not, West Pointers were given immediate respect over ROTC simply because they'd been taught at the Army's war college. ROTC officers were usually quick to try and earn favor and respect. Because he was a West Pointer and there was an absence of senior officers, Wallace was made company XO in absentia. The younger sergeants were quick to take advantage of this. In turn, the lower ranks picked up on it too.

After a few too many displays of blatant disrespect, Lane called formation and smoked the entire company for an uninterrupted hour. Lieutenant Wallace was hidden by partially opened blinds as he observed and heard Stone's booming lecture to NCOs, specialists, and privates collectively. He preached about respecting rank as he hobbled back and forth on his crutches. He scolded NCOs that had demonstrated poor leadership skills by not setting proper examples for junior soldiers, and that doing so birthed a cancer that would get soldiers killed and lose battles. After countless mountain climbers, pushups, donkey kicks, sit-ups, squat thrusts, and flutter kicks, he'd gotten the message across. Not a single soldier disrespected Lieutenant Wallace after that day. He'd never said anything to Sergeant Stone, but he'd never forgotten it.

"You're that Lieutenant Wallace?" Lane asked cautiously.

"Sergeant Stone," he answered with a slight grin.

"I figured you'd be a colonel by now, sir," he said with a complimentary tone.

"Would've, should've been. I spent eighteen months in Walter Reed. It was my fifty-fifth jump, my canopy streamered right off the static line. We were below eight hundred feet, might've been six hundred. I cut away and threw the reserve. As luck would have it, I blew over another, and my air was stolen. I slid right over his canopy, and when I woke up, I was in Walter Reed with a broken back. They should recycle me when I die with all the metal I've got in my spine. Anyway, I got my silver bar because of you. You didn't get to see how your brief leadership affected my career. When you jerked a knot in the company's ass, that allowed me to gain control and groom those other NCOs into useful leaders. I was four months away from making captain and deploying, then that last jump. I ended up in the guard, stayed a first lieutenant for a time. I never learned how to play politics. So no, it's not just the pups. And train those pups, I've seen videos of both parents in action. Good luck, Sergeant." He stuck out his hand to shake and handed him a piece of folded paper with his left.

Lane unfolded the paper and read:

Tennessee National Guard: All Armed Forces, Federal, State, and Local Municipal Law Enforcement

DECEMBER 24, 2024

The bearer of this document, Lane Stone, is to be granted passage along with any and all passengers. He is a liaison for the United States Army and National Guard. He should be treated as an officer and provided with all acknowledgments and privileges therein. At no time should any property be confiscated without exception. All passengers herein are to be provided with similar liberties within. If this liaison needs assistance to further his travel your cooperation is expected. Please endorse the issuer below for command field review upon surrender. Any deviation from this order is subject to disciplinary action. Any person(s) causing harm or interrupting travel may be subject to the UCMJ for field execution.

Captain Thomas Wallace
Battalion Executive Officer

LANE READ THE DOCUMENT TWICE. "ARE YOU sure you want to give this to me? Aren't you afraid of catching hell for this?"

"Don't give one single fuck," he said without emotion.

He shook hands with him once more as three privates came up carrying a poly tote and bags of dog food. Wallace opened the tote to reveal everything that a dog would need for the first year of its life. There were puppy pads, meds including dewormer, vaccinations, and antibiotics. There were puppy and adult collars, leashes, and collapsible food and water bowls. The dog food was in four 50-lb bags labeled Taste of the Wild. Lane did his mental math again; he could not take on any more weight until he'd lightened the load by a few hundred pounds. He hid his frustration, realizing the only weight he could deplete at the moment was food, fuel, and water.

They loaded the trailer with the dog supplies, and Blanche relocated to the trailer to help take care of the dogs. They all said their goodbyes again and got back on the road.

*****

I-40 West was painfully slow. There were so many disabled vehicles on both sides of the interstate, shoulder, and median that a constant zigzag was performed for miles on end. There were brief intervals where the road opened only to be clogged again within a mile. They got as far as Buffalo Valley and the sun was setting. They got off on Highway 76; Lane located Edgar Evans State Park and decided to take a chance on parking there for the night. Six miles after taking the exit, they pulled into a turnaround at Coves Hollow Recreation Area.

There weren't any other vehicles except for a Ford Explorer with park ranger markings and an old Winnebago that looked like it belonged to Cousin Eddie from *Christmas Vacation*. They all got out and surveyed the surroundings. Blanche set the puppies down, and they immediately bounded into the snow face-first like windup toys. Blanche walked to a nearby trash can and deposited a wadded-up puppy pad.

Lane handed Robert a radio. "You and Grant scout around, see if there's anyone around. Get back here before you lose light."

The puppies chased after Robert and Grant as they made their way into a pine grove. Beth and Crystal quickly scooped them up and were immediately rewarded with rapid licks that couldn't be defended. The girls giggled, and it made Lane smile.

"They need names if we're going to keep them," Lane said.

"What do you mean if?" countered Blanche. "And I've already named them," she announced, grinning from ear to ear.

There was a long silence as the others stood waiting. Crystal finally broke the silence. "Well, doofus?"

"Kirk and Spock!" she exclaimed, still wearing the goofy smile. She pointed to one of the pups that was currently coloring a patch of snow yellow. "See his ears? They're a bit taller and pointier, he's Spock. And the other? See how he prances around with his chest stuck out? He has to be Kirk."

They all rolled their eyes in exaggeration.

Robert took one of the M4s from the trailer and returned to the truck for a magazine. He pushed the mag home and chambered a round. The action was well-oiled, and it moved like it was freshly cleaned. He walked back to Beth. "Keep an eye out. I'm going to check out that RV."

Lane approached the RV from behind. When he got closer, he noticed that it had North Dakota plates and a lot of bullet holes. He moved to the passenger side where the cabin door was located and discovered a single set of footprints. There were no tire tracks, so it had been here since the snow. Looking closer at the tracks, there were toe and heel depressions in the same tracks. That meant that whoever made the tracks took a great deal of effort to keep the snow unmolested for security purposes. The tracks went off in the opposite direction as the boys, but with the way the tracks had been used, he didn't know if the RV was occupied or empty. Something caught his eye at the bottom of the door. An inch of pine needle protruded from between the door and doorjamb. Whoever opened the door wouldn't see the pine needle, and when the pine needle was discovered on the ground, it would tell the owner they'd been trespassed on or burglarized. Then he noticed that the tires looked new. *The Group*, he thought.

An uneasy feeling crept over Lane. He didn't bother stepping into his tracks; he pulled out his radio and keyed the mic twice. He came up to Beth and whispered in her ear. He then went to Crystal and Blanche and whispered to them. A few minutes later, Robert and Grant came into view. As they got closer, he could see their hands raised above their heads. Lane walked into the center of the parking lot where he was easy to see. He could see someone behind them but couldn't see clearly. They marched within twenty feet of Lane, and a female voice rang out.

"Far enough, on your knees." As Robert and Grant lowered themselves to the ground, a woman wearing a black balaclava and Realtree camo coveralls carrying an SKS came into view. The boys' guns were slung over her head and shoulders, and their pistols were tucked into her pockets.

"Good evening," Lane said to her.

"Didn't think you fellas had made it this far south yet. Really Facebooking the whole D-Day thing, aren't you? Pretty soon you'll have your own Group Visa and Mastercard," she said without any hint of emotion.

"Ma'am, we aren't part of this Group you're talking about," Lane told her.

"Sure, you aren't. Now how about you drop that bang stick before I make canoes out of these pretty little heads," she said with the barrel of the SKS rising from Grant's head to Lane's midsection.

"Ma'am, you can lower the gun. We are not part of this Group as you suggested. We'll gladly be on our way. We just wanted to rest for the night. We'll find another pla—"

"I said drop the fucking gun! My patience is at zero right now, and I'm goi—"

"You are going to drop your gun, or I'm going to add another hole to your anatomy," Blanche told her in a cold voice and put the barrel of an M4 to her head.

"Okay, take it easy." The woman leaned the rifle out, which Robert took by the barrel and dropped behind him. He aimed the barrel of the M4 at the woman's midsection. Blanche backed off a couple of feet. Beth was behind her with the AR at the ready position. Crystal stood beside her with another M4 at the ready position. She stuck her hands in the air as Grant reclaimed Robert and Grant's rifles and pistols. Blanche frisked her and found a cheap camp knife sheathed on her leg and a .38 snub nose in her bib pocket. Lane picked up her rifle, ejected the rounds, and handed it back to the woman. He popped open the revolver and dumped the rounds on the ground. He took the knife from Blanche; he pulled it from its sheath to find a well-honed blade, then replaced it in its sheath and handed it back to her as well.

"Like I said, we're not part of this Group. Put your hands down," Lane told her. He motioned to the others to lower their weapons.

"Lane," he said, extending his hand.

The woman eyed him suspiciously, then tentatively extended her hand and shook it. "Ruth," she replied.

"Is there anyone around here, anyone at all?" Lane asked her.

"I've scouted around for at least ten miles. I found an older couple that shot at me with a shotgun. They would've hit me if I hadn't been on my bike." She pointed to a public restroom where a green Kawasaki 250 was leaning against the wall.

Lane cursed himself for not noticing the empty drop rig on the rear of the RV. A scratching sound caught everyone's attention. Blanche walked over to the trailer and opened the door. Kirk and Spock tumbled noses over tails onto the snow and bounded toward everyone, ignoring their liberator. When they were about ten feet away, they suddenly clawed to a stop, sniffing the air, and then realized a stranger was among them. They growled in a miniaturized version until Blanche scooped them up again and carried them into the darkening pine grove. She dropped them into the snow, and they immediately resumed puppy-fueled zoomies.

"Robert, would you and Grant get a fire started? Beth, would you and Crystal mind collecting wood? We need enough to get through the night," Lane asked. The young adults set off on their chores.

"So, you tell me your story, and I'll tell you mine," Lane offered.

Ruth lowered her balaclava and swept the hair away from her eyes. She was an attractive woman standing somewhere around five feet eight. Her hair was so blonde, it was almost transparent. Her eyes were so blue, they almost glowed. Her skin would've been fair under normal conditions, but this woman had spent time outside, and her cheeks were windburned from riding the motorcycle. If she wore makeup, she would have passed for a lady in her twenties, but there was no mistaking the natural beauty of this woman.

"I'm from Fort Yates on the Missouri River. I was a high school history teacher. I moved there four years ago from Twinsburg, Ohio. Everybody was working together at first after D-Day. Then the prisons in Langdon and Mohall poured convicts out. It wasn't long before Drake, Warren, and Larimore spilled theirs loose. From there, it was like dominoes. Every criminal joined their cause. I didn't have any more students, so I fired up my '74 Winnebago and hit the road. I got as far as Watertown, taking side road after side road when I got into South Dakota. That's when I met those fuckers, they started shooting at me. They set up a roadblock on I-29. They were mostly bikers, but they had a few police cars too. They had those damn Chargers, fast as hell. Anyhow, they were going to do a pit maneuver on me, so I stopped after I was far enough away from the others.

"Now let me give you a little backstory. Two weeks before I left, a family of seven was stopped at a roadblock: father, mother, grand-mother, teenage triplets—one boy, two girls—and a twelve-year-old boy. They killed the father and teenage boy when they tried to pro-tect the women. They killed the grandmother and mother after they raped them on the side of the road. They took the teenage girls with them, said they couldn't be touched, they were for the cadre. The only reason anyone found out about it was because the boy ran into a culvert. He was close enough to see and hear most of what happened.

"Back to my roadblock. I had my windows down, you know, still summer. They came up to my windows. I had a spray bottle and a roll of paper towels, pretending to clean my windshield. The mistake they made was both of them coming to the driver's side win-dow. They didn't even have their guns drawn; they were both wearing biker clothes. What I will never forget was what one of the bikers wore on a chain around his neck and on his wallet chain. There were dozens upon dozens of wedding rings, wedding bands, high school class rings from boys and girls...most of them had blood on them.

"So the day I heard about this, I went back to the high school and went to the chemistry lab. Mr. Powell had briefed all the teachers to warn us about this supply of sodium hydroxide pellets. He used them to make solutions. And so he showed us a little demonstration. He mixed a solution that dissolved a Coke can. I paid attention to the parts that were mixed. When I went back to the school, I made my own solution. I doubled the number of pellets. That's what I sprayed into their eyes. I left them screaming on the side of the road. I expect they died. At the very least, they are blinded for life.

"I got back on the side roads after that. I cut through Iowa, Illinois, and Kentucky. I expect I had some of the same troubles you've had. As you've discovered already, it's not easy hiding big hulks like this. I made my way from neighborhood to subdivision, etcetera, scavenging gas, food, and this rifle. It had just started snowing as I made my way around Nashville. I stopped at a truck stop about an hour from here. There were only a few trucks and cars. I thought I might get lucky and find a candy bar or maybe a bag of peanuts. I was wrong. There were three meth heads that had literally eaten everything that wasn't nailed down. They would've eaten me if I didn't have this rifle. So I found this park in my atlas. There's a boat dock near here; I found some fishing supplies, and I've been enjoying grass carp. It's the only thing that's been biting. I got tired of chewing bones, so I decided to go hunting, that's when your boys crossed my path." She looked exhausted as she finished her tale.

There were no fancy fire-starting tricks. Robert and Grant dug away snow to uncover dry pine needles and pinecones. Robert cleared snow from a spot in the parking lot where the fire would be concealed by the trailer, and Grant dug his lighter from his pocket. The needles caught quickly; the pine tar in the cones lit up just as fast. Beth and Crystal returned with armfuls of deadfall and gently placed wood around and on top of the flame. Robert and Grant grabbed their rifles and went to get more wood. Crystal disappeared into the trailer and returned with the percolator and set it next to the fire. Ruth saw this and was excited but gave no indication. Crystal made another trip and came back with a soup pot and a skillet. While the water heated to boil, she made yet another trip and returned with a mixing bowl and spoon. When the water started to boil, Crystal poured in rice. When the rice was nearly done, she added dehydrated vegetables and beef. While the rice mix steeped, she spooned cornmeal into the skillet and fried cornbread cakes.

Blanche corralled Kirk and Spock as the smell of cooked food drove them insane. She took them inside the trailer and gave them dry food and vitamins. Being puppies, they immediately gobbled their food as fast as they could get it in their mouths. They licked their bowls clean and sniffed around for more. She put a few ounces of water in two bowls, and they drank until the bowls were dry. She opened a trundle beneath the bed and placed a blanket inside. She stacked boxes around the trundle with a puppy pad and left them. The pups started crying before the door was closed.

The crying only lasted for a few minutes. Crystal was handing out food and coffee as the pups quieted. Lane told their story again, more abbreviated than previous tellings. Beth and Robert added to the story, and they finished it for Lane. Lane gave an abbreviated version of Ruth's story but left out the sodium hydroxide blinding part. Ruth merely listened to Lane's retelling of her journey and was satisfied with his accuracy. Everyone ate seconds and successfully executed any possibility of leftovers. Beth refilled coffee for everyone, save for Ruth, who politely declined as she was buzzing after not having any caffeine for the last two months. The fire was sufficiently warm sitting close to it.

Robert and Grant excused themselves to answer nature's call. The tire tracks that they'd made upon arrival had frozen as they walked over them into the pine grove. The girls took turns visiting the trailer's toilet. Ruth disappeared into her trailer and returned with a bottle of Eagle Rare. She poured a few fingers into her cup and Lane's. Crystal and Blanche looked dejected, holding their cups as if they were waiting on some magic elixir that would transform them into adulthood. Ruth looked at Lane, and he just shrugged his shoulders as if saying, *Hey, why not?* She poured the same amount into their cups; she offered it to Beth, but she declined, shaking her head and smiling politely. Blanche and Crystal sipped at their cups. Ruth and Lane waited for a reaction from them that might offer an opportunity for humor, but the girls sipped quietly and finally tipped their cups back in unison, emptying the last drops of the bourbon. Lane and Ruth looked at each other, clearly puzzled. They both got up to leave. Crystal noticed eyes on them, and she remarked, "Daddy used to make sour mash, we were his official tasters. We never got drunk or anything, but we developed a taste for good liquor." Lane and Ruth raised their eyebrows in response.

The boys came back to the fire and warmed themselves. "What's the plan tomorrow?" Grant asked no one in particular.

"We can leave after breakfast. The more miles we make during daylight, the better," Lane answered. Lane faced Ruth. "What about you, ma'am. What are your plans?"

Ruth stared up at the clear sky and the eternal abundance of stars that shined in the darkness with a luminescence that was never visible pre–D-Day, unless maybe you were far out to sea. She marveled at the sight and audibly sighed heavily. "I never really thought about it. My internal compass just told me to head south, maybe the Gulf Coast. Beyond that, I never really developed a plan to speak of. I thought about it a few times and figured I was taking part in my own personal exodus. My biggest hope is that I wouldn't spend forty years wandering about looking for the promised land."

Lane nodded at the Old Testament reference. "I'm going to find my children, they live in southeast Missouri. That's my mission. I don't really have any plans after that. I know there's plenty of farmland out there. I suspect there's quite a few abandoned farms now. There's also a lot of game, plenty of deer, turkey, and a huge stopover for migratory fowl. If there aren't any survivors, there's a private hunting lodge between Poplar Bluff and Doniphan. I saw it for sale about 10 years ago. It sits on 3,000 acres, 1,200 of those acres are fenced in by a 16-foot-high steel-crossed enclosure. Four streams run through it; one of the streams keeps a 23-acre lake filled year-round. The seller advertised that it was stocked with bass, crappie, rainbow trout, and catfish. Once I know the kids are okay, that's going to be my next stop."

"Would you mind if I followed along?" she asked sheepishly, still staring at the stars.

Lane hesitated, then answered, "Ruth, last I checked, that lodge had sixteen rooms. I have no reason to say no."

It wasn't the response she wanted, but she took comfort that he hadn't told her no. "What if my Winnebago doesn't make it? I don't think I can make it all that way on my bike."

"Let's cross that bridge when we have to." He patted her on the hand in a friendly and sympathetic gesture.

Moments later, they all gathered by the fire and decided who was taking first watch. It was decided that among Robert, Grant, Beth, and Lane, they would take two-hour shifts with Robert going first, then Grant, Beth, and finally Lane taking the last shift. Ruth offered to take a shift, but they all refused her offer. Trust had not yet been established, but they merely said it wasn't necessary. They all said goodnight to Ruth as she excused herself, still feeling very much like an outsider.

Blanche and Crystal shared the bed above the pup's cubby. Grant spread out his sleeping bag at the foot of their bed near the pups. Beth took the other bed and left space for Robert to join her. Lane stretched out in the back seat of the truck and was soon snoring. Robert disappeared into the shadows of the pine grove, purposely avoiding the campfire so as not to be a highlighted target and to allow his night vision to acclimate. There were no threats here; the only sounds were an owl occasionally calling out for a fellow nocturnal companion and the wind that made the bare hardwood branches click together like muted drumsticks. When the fire had burned down to embers, he eased out of the grove and made his way to the trailer. He let himself in and found Grant's foot and gave it a gentle kick. Grant woke immediately, unzipped his bag, and climbed out. Without a word, he grabbed the SCAR and went outside. Grant walked a perimeter around Ruth's RV and the truck and trailer. He then walked to where Ruth had parked her bike. It was a good vantage point, so he backed into the blackness of the shadows and watched.

Robert took his boots off and crawled under his sleeping bag like Beth had done. She felt the bed move as he crawled closer to her. When he was beside her, she took his wrist, wrapped his arm over her midsection, and spooned into him. Robert breathed in her scent and was asleep within seconds.

Grant watched and listened. There was nothing to be seen or heard. He walked the perimeter when he felt sleepy, which was often, and then went back to the shadows. Grant kept watch until it was Lane's turn, allowing his brother to get rack time with his girl. He hoped it would pay dividends later. He tapped on the truck window with one knuckle. Lane answered back with a knuckle tap of his own to announce that he was awake. A few minutes later, Lane exited the truck and staggered for maybe two paces until his stump remembered the prosthetic. He stretched, holding his shotgun above his head. "I thought it was Beth's turn?"

"I was awake. I let her sleep through. I'm going back to bed now," Grant told Lane.

"Okay, we're leaving at first light. Better rest while you can," he told him.

Grant left for the trailer, and Lane took in the quiet and also marveled at the stars. After a few minutes, he returned his gaze downward, and the percolator caught his attention; it was still sitting near the fire. He picked it up and removed the lid. He took out the ground cup and stuffed clean snow in until it was three-quarters full. He set the pot on the embers and waited. When it started percolating, he let it go twice as long. Surprisingly, the coffee wasn't bad the second time around with the used grounds. There was just enough melt to make one very large and strong cup. He walked and sipped his coffee, checking the tires on the truck and then the trailer. He approached the RV and did a loop; nothing looked out of the ordinary. He followed Grant's tracks back to the bathroom. Like Grant, he melted into the shadows and watched.

In the shadows, he saw a light flicker in Ruth's window. Lane assumed she had lit a candle. He watched her outline move back and forth from the front of the RV to the rear, bending over, then standing up again. Like a vaudeville show from a long time ago, she undressed, and he could see the outline of her body. Her body was hidden in her bibbed coveralls; now her voluptuous figure was betrayed by the candlelight and the drawn curtain. Lane let his eyes linger, but then finally, shame overtook him, and he looked away. He saw the light vanish, then heard the squeak of her door opening and closing.

He saw her round the rear of her RV; she looked around for the night watch in vain.

"By your bike," he called out to her as he stepped out of the shadows.

She startled and swung her weapon in his direction but lowered it with the voice and shape recognized. "Thought I'd get an early start and load my bike."

Lane turned back and took the bike by the handlebars, walking it forward. The tires crackled over frozen snow as he inched forward. She came up on the right side, shouldering her rifle, and helped push the bike. When they got to the rear, she took hold of a hand crank and lowered a steel cradle that the tires would rest on. Once the cradle was on the ground, Lane maneuvered the bike until it was in the cradle. Ruth unlatched a bar and hooked it in place, securing the bike to the cradle. The crank was the same he'd seen on boat trailers, and it made the same clicking noise as she raised the bike. A couple of minutes later, the bike tires were even with the bottom of the RV bumper.

Lane took out a cigarette and offered her one, which she accepted. He lit hers, then his own. They smoked in silence as the horizon started to glow with the first hints of pink. Ruth broke the silence. "Divorced?"

"Yep, twelve years now. She took the kids and moved to her mother's farm," he almost whispered. "What about you? Did you ever have a boyfriend or husband?"

"I dated and had a couple of boyfriends for a while, but I never found the right one. Do you mind if I ask how old you are?" she asked.

"Nope, I don't mind."

She looked at him and waited. "Well?"

"I don't mind you asking, didn't say I would answer." He grinned at her.

Ruth puffed at the cigarette and crossed her arms.

Lane didn't know if she was just trying to retain warmth or express frustration, but he assumed the latter. "I turned fifty-four on October 12."

"Hmm, mine is October 15. I turned thirty-three," Ruth said.

She and Lane stared at one another awkwardly until the sound of the trailer door opening broke the silence. An audible thud filled the quiet, followed by puppy yelps and the staccato of paws running at full speed. A thought occurred to him. The puppies needed to start training now. Making a mental note, he would have to see who was willing to take on the task. With that in mind, he took out a pocket notebook and started writing.

CHRISTMAS DAY

DECEMBER 25, 2024

CRYSTAL MADE DROP BISCUITS AND SCRAMBLED EGGS over the fire embers; they all ate quickly, enthusiastic to get on the road. Blanche gave the pups bites of egg, which led to Lane immediately scolding her. She looked perplexed at being chastised and pouted.

"If you get in the habit of feeding dogs human food, they'll never want anything else. If you want to give them a treat, put a small handful of their dry food in your pocket. Which is a point I was meaning to bring up. As the pups are right now, they are a liability. They will bark or run off on impulse, they're just being puppies, but that impulse could lead to catastrophic results for everyone here. They need to be trained, and I need someone here to take on this task with all seriousness. I don't mean roll over, beg, or give me your paw. They need to be trained like military dogs. They can be an asset or a liability. I prefer the former. If genuine effort goes into their training, I believe the trainer will be successful. It's in the pups' DNA. The two breeds that contributed to Kirk and Spock are two of the primary breeds that police and military have used for a century. So who will take on training the doggos?" Lane finished and looked at everyone in turn.

"I'll do it," Grant volunteered. "I worked with an organization that trained seeing-eye dogs."

"That is sooo sweet!" Crystal gushed.

"Easy there, Grant groupie. It was part of his court-ordered community service for fighting," Robert announced with a chuckle.

Grant grimaced at being outed but reaffirmed his offer. "In the four months I was involved, we trained six pups before they were sent on to their secondary trainers."

"Well, I would say that would make you more than eminently qualified. Here, take this." Lane took out his notepad, tore out a sheet, and handed it to Grant. He explained that it was a list of one-word commands with English translated to German pronounced words.

"Why German?" Blanche asked.

"So others can't use the dogs against us," Beth answered. Lane smiled at her immediate understanding.

"She's right. Once they've started to learn, everyone should practice the words and their pronunciations so they won't be confused," Lane told them.

Grant studied the list, then retrieved collars and leashes from the trailer. He corralled the pups and fitted each with a collar, then attached a leash. They immediately pulled against the leashes, which Grant immediately responded to with a firm tug and an audible, "Nein!" The pups responded by turning and looking at the leash, then at Grant. Their desire to explore took over again, and they strained at the leash. "NEIN!" Grant responded again and deftly picked them both up and returned to the trailer, the pups whining in protest.

"We need to get going," Lane said and headed to the truck.

Everyone took his suggestion and cleared the area of their belongings. Ruth started her RV and was pleasantly surprised that it started without delay. The truck, of course, responded in kind. Lane came up beside Ruth's driver window, which she lowered with its manual rotating handle. He handed her a radio and explained that after the first round of communication, she needed to change the frequency to the next odd channel.

Ten minutes later, they pulled out of the park and back on the road. Fifteen minutes further, they were back on the interstate. The obstacles were still present, and forty minutes later, Lane decided to take the 840 bypass, hoping that the disabled vehicles would be fewer in number. He'd used the bypass before. The route around Nashville added time to his trip but made up for its length with substantially lessened traffic. They were now cruising along at the breakneck speed of 30 mph. Considering the snail pace they'd been traveling, Lane expected somebody to tell him to slow down.

Thirty miles in, they found their first roadblock. A farm truck, much like the one Phillip Talbert had parked by the roadside, was overturned in the westbound lane. The truck itself wasn't the issue; the problem was close to a hundred heads of cows munching on the scattered hay. Once the Shelby sisters figured out what was going on, they wasted no time approaching the cows, yelling loud whoops and clapping their hands. The cows paid no attention at first, but Crystal found a windshield wiper on the road and used that to encourage their departure. The rump tapping had the desired effect, and the unhappy bovines communicated disgruntled mooing that was quickly picked up on by the others. As Blanche waved her extended arms up and down, Crystal continued her rump tapping until there was a break in the herd that allowed the vehicles to pass through. Once they'd gotten a safe distance away, both girls removed their boots and beat them against the pavement to remove departing gifts left by the herd. They finally gave up and tied the boots together, lacing them over the trailer hitch.

The girls were met in the trailer by two uncontrollable noses sniffing at their ankles; it was like someone had dropped a pound of cocaine on the floor at a drug rehab center. "NEIN!" Grant yelled from the rear of the trailer. The girls picked up on what Grant was doing and pushed the pups away, copying the command as they did. The pups cocked their heads, then sniffed the air, still trying to identify the alien scent. The girls stifled a snicker at their comical expressions.

In the last 47 miles on 840, they encountered one last obstacle that needed their attention. A Ferrari was one of many vehicles involved in a group collision that blocked both sides of the highway, including the median and shoulders. Since the Italian sports car was the lightest, it was decided to move it out of the way. A male corpse was reclined in the leather seat. A Rolex hung from its desiccated wrist, and expensive rings adorned the equally desiccated fingers. Robert and Grant lowered the body to the ground respectfully. When the body was laid down, the shirt fell away, revealing a holstered pistol inside the belt. Grant removed it and examined it; it was a Glock 19 with a spare mag. Robert explored the sports car further; there was nothing in the glovebox except for an owner's manual and registration. The front storage was a different story altogether.

"Wait," Lane called out; he approached donning a pair of nitrile gloves. He came up and looked inside. He took a nylon weave squared pouch and unzipped it on the ground. A Heckler and Koch MP 10mm was secured with Velcro straps, a 30-round magazine was loaded with another mag taped to it upside down, and two more identical taped magazines were strapped down above it. He rezipped the pouch and explored further. The space revealed a first aid kit, emergency road kit, spare tire, and beneath it what appeared to be thousands of tiny blue pills that Lane assumed were fentanyl. They left the pills and took everything else. Lane removed the watch and jewelry, thinking they could be used for trade. Robert put the Ferrari in neutral as he and Grant moved the car out of the way. Once they'd gotten back on the interstate, it was back to zigzagging in and out of stalled vehicles. The congestion decreased the further away they got from Nashville. Lane took the radio and called out, "We've got about a hundred miles before our next turnoff. The next time we hit a mass of vehicles, we need to find gas. Respond if understood." Lane clicked off and heard two audible clicks in response.

Twelve miles later, they stopped at an exit for a small town named Bucksnort. With the jerry cans, they topped off the truck with two jerry cans but needed the rest of them to top off Ruth's RV. Grant and Blanche set off to siphon gas from the stalled vehicles while Robert and Beth provided overwatch. Blanche and Grant worked quickly together; the lids that couldn't simply be opened, Blanche broke open with a crowbar. The plastic hand pump made the transfer easy and quick. An hour later, the jerry cans were reloaded, and they were back on the road.

As they approached Natchez Trace State Park, they were forced to stop at an Army roadblock. The road was separated by a median occupied by mature trees and overgrowth. The emergency access used by state troopers was occupied by Humvees and two MRAPs. Several tents were erected, and the blockade of Humvees were armed with .50-caliber machine guns. Lane slowed to a stop twenty yards from the roadblock.

"There's a lot of brass on the ground, must've been some nasty business going on here," Robert said aloud.

A soldier approached, wearing a black beret and the gold oak leaf of a major. Another soldier followed with his M4 at the ready. Lane lowered his window. As the man came closer, he noticed that the soldier didn't look well. His eyes were sunken, his face was unshaven, and his skin was pale, not the typical appearance of a soldier. The soldier behind him wore sunglasses and hadn't shaved for a couple of days either.

"Afternoon, sir. What brings you out this way?" the man asked in a generic Midwestern accent.

Lane was on edge and suspicious, deciding not to reveal their plans. "I'm on a military assignment. E-4." He waited for the challenge response, but nothing came.

"Care to explain, sir?" he asked.

"Not at all, Colonel," Lane responded, expecting to be corrected about the rank, but he wasn't. Now he was really on edge. Three clicks popped from the radio, and he and Robert looked into their rearview mirrors. Emerging from the edge of the forest and the wooded median, a dozen armed soldiers stepped onto the road behind the RV.

Lane looked away from the mirror to the soldier and the man in front of him, who were both now pointing their weapons at him. "Tell you what, red, why don't you and your folks get out of the truck, the trailer, and that old Winnebago. Don't be a hero, and you won't be a zero. Get my drift?"

Lane saw now that they were surrounded from the rear and the .50s were now aimed in their direction. He picked up the radio. "Everyone get out, don't do anything stupid."

"That's right, it'll all be over soon. Tie them to the saplings. Put the girls in the party tent," the man said with a gleam in his eye.

They escorted the girls to the party tent. A female they hadn't seen appeared and followed them inside the tent. They tied the boys' hands together with paracord behind poplar saplings. The sunken-eyed man guided Lane to another tent. It took a minute for his eyes to adjust, but the man, too, had some issue with it and opened a tent flap to allow light in.

"So I bet you're wishing you'd stayed where you were right about now?" The man grinned at his own attempt at humor.

"The Group?" Lane asked.

"Bingo! You win a prize, Mr. Ginger! Now you have a couple of things you need to consider real hard over the next few minutes. Normally, we just cut throats and pack up the women. And…"

They were cut off by a young man carrying Kirk and Spock by the scruffs of their necks. They were nipping at their abductor, clearly pissed off at their handling. "Lookee what I got here!" the young man exclaimed in excitement. "We can keep 'em, right?"

"Cadre will probably let us keep one. Tie them to a tree for now." The man turned on his heel with the new task.

"Sorry for the interruption. Where was I? Oh yes. Decisions. So option 1: you join and convince the boys to do the same, or we kill you. Option 2: you do everything I or those boys outside tell you, or we kill you. Option 3: do everything I ask you to do, or…"

"You kill us," Lane finished.

The man smiled a stained, toothy grin. "You catch on quick. You'll do fine. Oh, there is one other option I always forget. You try to take anything out of the truck, trailer, or RV and…well, I think you know, don'tcha? Anyhow, you folks are gonna get transferred to our little college in Indiana to make sure you get on board with the way the Group does things. That is, except for the ladies; they will be shipped elsewhere, probably the Dakotas. We might keep that little black-haired beauty for ourselves."

Lane seethed at this. All he wanted to do was get his hands around this man's throat and end him. The younger man motioned for him to move. With the muzzle centered in the small of his back, the man guided him to a stand of saplings where Robert and Grant were tied. Another fake soldier came over to tie Lane's hands while the gun was on him.

*****

Minutes turned into hours as they went from standing to sitting and leaning against the saplings. At one point, two of the Group's minions came and untied them one at a time to relieve themselves and drink water, then got tied up again when finished. It was dark before they heard the girls' voices yelling, then cursing.

"Grant, spin around until your hands are facing in my direction," Lane told him.

"What!"

"Just do it!" Robert told him.

Grant spun around until his hands were facing Lane's feet. Lane twisted until he was able to put his foot into the outstretched hands of Grant.

"Robert, tell him what to do," Lane directed.

Robert explained to Grant what he needed to do. Grant worked the pant leg up by twisting around the sapling. He found the snaps and started on the first one. It wasn't an easy task; the first snap took nearly five minutes to unfasten. The next six snaps were still difficult, but each one was easier than the last. Once he had hold of the calf, Lane had to pull his leg back to free it. Pulling the knife free also proved to be a difficult task as the knife was seated securely in the cutout. Finally, Grant was able to use his fingernail to pry it free. Once he had it in hand, the prosthesis fell to the ground. The girls' voices continued to rise and fall under duress. Grant got the blade open, but manipulating his hands in unison was necessary to cut at the bindings. After dropping the knife several times and reconfiguring his grasp, he was able to free himself. He cut Robert loose, then Lane. They all scrambled around on their hands and knees for what seemed like an eternity until they found Lane's prosthesis. He removed a derringer and gave one to Robert. He took the other while Grant kept the knife. They crept to the leader's tent. Lane peered through a crack. The leader was sitting at a desk, drinking Ruth's Eagle Rare and looking at a magazine with a scantily clad woman on the front. He set the whiskey down and started rubbing his crotch with his free hand. Lane backed away and motioned for the boys to follow. In the distance, they could see a group of fake soldiers gathered around a fire, passing around multiple bottles. From their voices, they were very drunk.

Lane peered into a tent window; the girls were all tied up with their hands bound to their ankles. Two other women had apparently removed their clothes down to their underwear. One of the women was holding a torch to what appeared to be a branding iron. None of them were holding guns, but their ARs and three M4s were stacked in a corner.

"We're going to do this quietly. You two go in fast and grab them, mouth and neck," Lane told them.

He counted off three on his fingers, and the boys rushed and subdued the women. The girls were clearly emotional at their rescuers and angry at the women. Lane held his finger to his lips for them to be quiet as he took the knife from Grant and cut their bonds. Beth was the first to be freed. As soon as she stood, she took the knife from Lane and stabbed the woman holding the branding iron. She spat in the woman's face when she pulled the knife from her heart. She wiped the blade on the woman's shirt, then looked at Crystal, who took the knife from Beth and cut the other woman's throat. Blood spurted out in a fountain with each beat of her heart. Robert and Grant lowered the women to the ground, their eyes wide at what the girls had done. Once Blanche and Ruth were free, they, too, spat on the women's remains. Lane took the knife and motioned for them to dress and take the guns. While the others armed themselves, Lane took the knife back and went to the ringleader's tent. Looking through the crack, he had graduated from rubbing his crotch to full-scale masturbation. He was so concentrated on pleasing himself that he didn't notice Lane was present until the knife was at his neck.

"Nice cock, my son had one just like it when he was three," Lane mocked. "Now you have a few things to decide on real quick. Option 1: you answer my questions as I ask them or…" Lane waited.

"You kill me," the Group man answered.

"Excellent, you catch on real quick. First question, when are you supposed to have your next contact?"

"Supposed to have a messenger in Bloomington in three days. If we're not there by then, they send someone to look for us."

"Second question, how far does this Group intend to go?"

"The entire country. See, I met our fearless leader and his cadre. They won't be happy until this entire country is speaking Russian."

"Third question, what's his name?"

"Kiril Viktor."

"Fourth question, two-part: Bratva? How old?"

"No, not Bratva. Did hear a rumor that he's former KGB. And he's probably early to midsixties."

"Last question, what were they going to do with us?"

The man hesitated, and Lane applied pressure to the blade. "You were going to be soldiers. The girls are pretty…they'd be whores."

"Put your cock away," Lane ordered him.

The man stuffed his penis back into his pants and zippered his pants.

"One more question, where are the soldiers that wore the uniforms you're wearing?"

"They're dead. They're just beyond the saplings you were tied to."

Lane cut through his carotid artery and watched the blood spurt onto the ground. He picked up the bottle of Eagle Rare and took a long pull from it. He set the bottle back on the table and walked out of the tent. As he stepped out, Robert put an M4 in front of him, which he took.

"We get within shooting distance. Robert, Beth, you take the left. Grant, Blanche, you take the right. I'll pick off the stragglers. Crystal, go get the pups, they'll start barking as soon as they see us. Ruth, watch our backs."

Crystal snuck over to the pups; they were lying with their heads on their paws. They smelled Crystal before they saw her, and they raised their heads and started to wag their tails. The pups licked ferociously at her face. She was quietly shushing them when gunfire erupted.

"There's no turning back from this," Lane whispered to them. "We have to kill them all. Even if they are wounded and begging for their lives. Anyone that doesn't want to be part of this doesn't have to. This isn't a dictatorship, you still have a choice. I should point out that if we don't kill these men, we may likely face them again." He finished and looked each of them in the eye. They all nodded up and down, but Lane asked them for a verbal acknowledgment. They each affirmed yes.

"Start firing when I say now," he whispered.

The men were drunkenly blathering, their discipline nonexistent. One of them shakily rose to his feet and started pissing on the fire. "I'm going to guhh...go gert me that pretty shorty."

Another man with a belly spilling out of his Army blouse spoke up. "I'm going witcha, I bet she can suck a golf ball through a garden hose." He stood up and pissed into the fire as well. Some of the others poked fun at the fat man's manhood.

"Now," Lane said with a grimace.

Robert was the first to open fire. The man that stood first made the perfect target; his head painted three of the men in a red mist. Crystal placed two shots in the fat man's chest. The other men didn't move for a couple of seconds, then self-preservation set in, and they stumbled and tripped to stand. It was like shooting fish in a barrel. Blanche and Grant joined in, and within seconds, all of them were dead or bleeding and waiting for death. Lane stepped forward and approached the fire. Three of the men groaned in pain and cursed their attackers. Lane put a round through each of their heads. When he turned around, they were all closer and staring at him. They were stone-faced, and all changed in their own way by what had happened or what could have happened.

"It'll be light soon, and I want you to do something. Right now, I want you all to find a cot in those tents and close your eyes. I'll wake you when the sun is up. Go," he gently told them.

They all turned and walked back. Instead of picking different tents, they all chose one large tent and huddled close together in one giant spoon. Almost as soon as they were lying down, they were all asleep, including Kirk and Spock.

Lane pushed one of the dead men away from a milk crate and sat down. The smell of copper and cordite was in the air and a minute hint of pine. Lane stared up into the sky and looked at the stars. He thought that the stars could be beautiful in almost any circumstance, but at this moment, all he could think of was that for the first time in his life he'd spent his Christmas killing someone and not saying Merry Christmas to a single person. The thought saddened him. A single tear fell from his eye and landed on a bare piece of asphalt that wasn't covered in blood. He wondered if there would be any more Christmases that he spent like this. He wondered how this Kiril Viktor had spent his Christmas. His thoughts turned to his children. Where were they? Were they alive and well? Would he show up to an empty house? How would his children receive him? Worse yet, how would his ex-wife and her husband receive him? He looked back up at the stars and felt very small. It had been God's grace and luck that had kept them alive up to now. How would he manage to keep them all alive? He decided that he would allow all the self-doubt, uncertainty, and negative imagination to plague him until they woke up. After that, he would do everything he could to keep those feelings at bay. He closed his eyes and said a prayer. Somewhere in his prayer, he slipped away, sleep taking him. He woke with a start and looked around in a panic for a few seconds before he realized where he was. Ghost pains in his absent foot jolted him further awake. He might have been asleep for five minutes at the most; it was still dark.

Lane was staring at the stars when Ruth joined him by the fire. She, too, nudged one of the dead away, planting herself on a down-turned five-gallon bucket. She turned her gaze skyward to take part in the astronomical theater.

"You know it's not your fault, right?"

"Hmm?" he responded quizzically.

"Everything that happened today. There wasn't any way to avoid it. If you're feeling guilt, you shouldn't," she told him and patted him on the arm.

"Oh, that. No, I've just spent the last few hours trying to conceive how I'm going to keep everyone alive." A shooting star crossed the horizon as the all-too-familiar pink brightened the sky.

"Quick, make a wish!" she told him.

"Merry Christmas," he said aloud.

"Wait, what?" she asked, puzzled.

"My wish is next year for everyone to have a good Christmas and that I don't forget to wish people a Merry Christmas," he said, bowing his head and looking at his lap.

She put her hand on his shoulder, and after a few seconds, he covered her hand with his. They stayed like that for minutes until they heard voices. They stood and approached the voices. One by one, they all emerged from the tent with Grant in tow, wrangling the pups and repeating "nein, nein" in a stern voice. The girls took turns using the dead women's tent to pee while the boys used some nearby trees.

Lane wondered to himself why the girls had so easily killed the women, but he guessed they had committed some heinous act. Thinking it best to let sleeping dogs lie, he kept it to himself.

DECEMBER 26, 2024

AFTER THEY'D ALL RELIEVED THEMSELVES, THEY MET in a circle, joining Lane and Ruth.

"We need to make it look like this group, pun unintended, broke camp and moved somewhere else. That starts by loading all of these bodies in one of the MRAPs and hiding it somewhere with the other vehicles. I looked at the atlas, there's an airport about seventeen miles from here. Where there's an airport, there's bound to be a hangar or two. We can hide the vehicles there. So unless anybody has any questions?"

Nobody did. Everyone pitched in, and once Lane figured out how to get an MRAP started, he backed it up to the firepit and lowered its access ramp. When that was done, Lane backed up to the other tents, and they loaded the last three bodies. Twenty minutes later, they set out on a convoy with the MRAP leading, Lane in his truck, Ruth, and three Humvees bringing up the rear. Thirty minutes later, they pulled in front of four identical hangars. The hangar doors all had padlocks hanging from them. They used bolt cutters and removed them all. The first hangar was filled rear to front with single-engine Cessnas and other planes that couldn't be identified. The second hangar was completely empty; they drove the MRAP inside and all but one of the Humvees.

Lane turned to Ruth before they climbed in. "How attached are you to the Winnebago?"

Precisely thirty minutes later, they got back to the camp. An older 2 1/2-ton cargo truck with a 250-gallon diesel trailer attached, 1 Humvee, and 2 more MRAPs remained. Lane walked Ruth to her RV and helped her lower her dirt bike. They walked her bike to an

MRAP with the ramp lowered and, with considerable effort, walked it in. They returned to her RV and came back with duffel bags in each hand. They took the tents down and kept the largest one the girls and the boys slept in. They also kept the wood stove that was in the largest tent along with the dozen collapsible cots and the military-issue sleeping bags. They collected twelve cases of MREs and the Vietnam-era PRC-77 pack radio from the leader's tent. They loaded all of the guns in the MRAP and would take two of the .50s off the Humvees for spare parts for the other .50s.

They all stopped at noon and handed out MREs. Each pack had the same spicy penne pasta and vegetables with crackers, sports drink mix, a bag of Skittles, and a packet of peanut butter. Grant and the girls ate the Skittles as if they were manna from heaven. The pups had already eaten their food and were sitting alert by Grant, who was quick on the draw with the "nein" correction when they whined for anyone to share.

"Let's make the last airport trip in thirty. I'll be right back." Lane stood and walked back to the area where they'd been tied the night before. He pushed through brush and nettles before he came to a depression and the bodies of the soldiers who had been murdered. He stumbled into the hole and made his way to the first man. He wore rubber rings around his dog tags that were used to silence their clacking against each other during movement. He removed one and stuck it in his pocket. He had to pry the man's mouth open with his knife; once it was opened far enough, he took the spare and placed it between the man's front teeth and shoved his lower jaw upward until it was lodged. Should the country ever recover and if these men had any relatives left, they could at least identify loved ones, that is unless animals carry off the skulls. By the time he'd finished, seventeen dog tags rattled in his pocket. Before he climbed out of the hole, he bent over and vomited up the MRE.

The others had finished and were now loading trash from their meals and what the thugs had thrown down. Robert wet down the coals of the fire, and Grant used a shovel to put them in another trash bag. They threw everything in the back of the Army truck. They unhooked the diesel trailer and hooked it back up to one of the

MRAPs. Ruth climbed into her Winnebago for the last time; Lane got in his truck and turned it around. Robert and Grant manned the other two MRAPs. The convoy headed back to the airport, but it felt different this time. They all felt a sense of accomplishment. The only regret they all felt was not being able to bury the soldiers. Aside from the dead soldiers, there were few traces of The Group's presence.

When they pulled onto the airport tarmac, someone waited on them. A grizzled-looking man with silver hair watched them, unmoving like a statue. He reminded Lane of the guards at Buckingham Palace. Lane stopped his truck within spitting distance of the man and opened his door, lowering himself to the ground, then approached him.

The old man wore coveralls and was holding a .45 Colt 1911 at his hip. "You looking to take my plane?"

"No, sir, we're here to hide some vehicles from the Group," Lane told him.

"Well, I was hoping somebody would get some of those bastards. They killed my buddy. He was flying down here from Indiana, and they shot him on the runway. He helped me rebuild Mabel. After I move her out, you'll have plenty of room to hide those things. Follow me, Mabel ain't too patient." The man turned and motioned with his hand for Lane to follow. The man stooped over and picked up a duffel bag and asked Lane to grab the other.

They walked to the last of the four hangars, and the man spread the doors open to reveal a beautiful machine. Standing before them was a Martin twin-prop B-26 Marauder. The belly was covered in highly polished aluminum, and the top was painted in olive drab green. On the side beneath the cockpit was a hand-painted blonde with her large breasts bursting through a barmaid's blouse, holding a large mug of beer in each hand. Above the buxom beauty in red cursive letters was "Mabel." The man ran his hand down the side like he was touching a woman. He returned, grabbed his bags, then opened a hatch underneath and loaded them.

"So what's your story?"

Lane resisted the urge to roll his eyes and relented by abbreviating their story into a concise CliffsNotes version. The old man nodded during the story and then whistled out loud when Lane told him about the lions. He spat on the ground in disgust when Lane told him about their Christmas day. It was at this point that the old man clapped Lane on the shoulder like he'd known him all his life.

"I was fixin' to leave in the next few days anyway. I heard you from my apartment when y'all came over the first time. Figured I'd go ahead and get while the getting was good. I did my preflight a couple of hours ago. I heard that Winnebago coming about five miles up the road, figured I'd see who the new tenants were. Now I know. If you'll excuse me, I have an appointment in Tyler, Texas." He opened the crew hatch and started to pull himself in but turned around and came back. He stuck his hand out. Lane took it, and he shook it. "Garland Stapelton." The man gave his name, and Lane gave him his. "Look, if you folks find that you've run out of options, I got a ranch in Tyler. It's off Old Omens Road, there's a shamrock-shaped mailbox by the entrance, you can't miss it. It's nothing like one of them ranches you see in the movies, but I got two nephews that's been keeping it going. We could use some folks that earn their keep. If y'all are those kinds of folks, we'd be happy to have you. If not, well, good luck and God bless."

The man disappeared inside the plane, closing the crew hatch behind him. A few minutes later, he heard the props whine as the engine fought to turn over. Then the engine coughed exhaust, and the props spun to life. Within minutes, the restored Marauder rolled out of the hangar and taxied to the end of the runway. After braking and revving its throttles, the antique plane shot off like a bullet, and then it was in the air. Garland tipped his wings back and forth, saying goodbye, and quicker than anticipated, it was in the clouds.

Ruth drove the RV into the hangar and was sniffling when she rounded the corner. She ran her hand over the vehicle like Garland Stapelton had his plane. Lane took her by the arm and guided her to the six-wheeled all-wheel drive. The ramp was down, and they walked up. The others had gone to retrieve the .50s, so the MRAP was unoccupied.

"Might as well jump behind the wheel," Lane told her.

Ruth sat in the driver's seat; it was constructed like it belonged in a sports car. Each seat was equipped with a three-point harness. In the center of the roof was a retractable saddle to operate the .50. There were front and rear mortar tubes for smoke, tear gas, or fragmentation grenades. Seated in cradles throughout the vehicle were NVGs plugged into charging stations. Behind each cargo seat were multiple racks for different types of weapons. There were also multiple storage containers bolted to the wall, undoubtedly filled with combat-ready necessities.

They watched Robert pull the Army truck inside behind the RV.

"Ya know your new ride was worth about 1.5 million before D-Day?" he offered, trying to lessen the sting of leaving her RV behind.

"There's no bathroom," she chided.

"Actually, there's a unisex cup for urination and bio bags for taking dumps," he told her with a grin.

"How quaint," she replied with a furrowed brow.

"Well, you have a 6.7-liter Cummins diesel that will get you up to 80 mph once I figure out how to remove the restrictor. For now, 65 mph will have to do. Plus, the armor plating will withstand anything up to rocket-propelled grenades. It also has climate control with the most advanced filters that can handle tear gas, nerve gas, and, within reason, radiation protection. Regardless, this is the top of the line for doomsday protection," he explained.

She put on a thin smile and gripped the steering wheel. They watched as the boys walked out of the hangar pushing a cart with the .50s on it, and the girls pushed another cart stacked with twenty ammo cans. It took both Grant and Robert to lift in the .50s one at a time. The same was true for the ammo cans due to their size. The guns and ammo were secured, and the girls returned after closing the hangar doors.

"Well, as they say in the infantry...follow me." Lane got out of the MRAP and walked to his truck.

The convoy headed out once more with Lane leading and Blanche riding shotgun and Grant in the backseat with the pups.

Ruth followed with Crystal riding shotgun, and Robert and Beth brought up the rear in another MRAP. None of them looked twice at the sanitized Group camp as they passed by.

An hour later and thirty miles west, Lane pulled off the interstate into a Bass Pro parking lot in Jackson. Lane got out and looked around, Blanche followed, and Grant set the pups on the ground. He put their collars and leashes on and walked them to a nearby tree, repeating the words "regen" and "kacke," which he was using as commands for *pee* and *poop*. While Kirk and Spock scrutinized the identities of foreign smells, Robert and Beth were scanning the area with newly acquired Army-issue binocs. Blanche busied herself with a scope-equipped M4, looking elsewhere. Ruth sat in her MRAP watching. Lane motioned for her to exit, and she reluctantly climbed down. Everyone gathered around Lane, curious as to what they were doing here.

"First off, we're not going through Memphis. We're going to cut up here in Jackson. It's a shortcut, but we still have to cross the Mississippi. Second, if you need clothes or shoes, you might be able to find something here. It may be a long time before we're able to get replacement clothing. These MRAPs can haul quite a bit, so take what you want if it's available. It looks like the police have kept the area. There's only one of the door panels broken, and somebody boarded it up. Robert, you and Blanche keep watch. The rest of us will clear the building." Lane finished by grabbing a crowbar from the truck.

To successfully remove the plywood, Lane had to sit on the ground and plant his feet against the door. The wood splintered and popped around the screws when it came free. Lane put his finger to his lips, pleading for quiet. He listened for a couple of minutes, but the noise went unanswered. Lane activated a flashlight on the M4 and crawled through the opening. He walked into the turnstiles, the mechanism clunking loudly in the skylight-illuminated space. He walked to the end of the store, to the aquarium, and put the flashlight on it. All of the fish were dead except for two very large catfish who had clearly stayed alive by eating the other fish after their demise. The catfish gulped oxygen-depleted water trying to stay alive. He turned his attention left and right, quickly realizing he'd let his guard down. Ten minutes later, he returned with headband flashlights and handed them out.

Ruth and Crystal made the most of their shopping trip and crawled out with multiple bags consisting of several outfits of varied seasonal wear, including shoes. Beth found enough to fill two bags and was suspiciously grinning ear to ear as she left. Grant brought his duffel in and replaced all of his clothes, leaving the old gear in a pile on the floor. He, too, found shoes and a black cold-weather coat. A few minutes later, Robert and Blanche crawled in. Like Ruth and Crystal, Blanche had a field day finding new clothes and shoes. Robert found another pair of shoes, some T-shirts, and more underwear before he went back outside. Lane did his best at doing some mental sizing and filled four bags of clothes and shoes in multiple sizes for his kids. The only things that remained of food were hard candy, chewing gum, and gourmet hot cocoa mix; all of it went into a smaller bag. He went to the shoe rack, found his size, replaced his boots with black Doc Martens, and shoved an extra two pairs in a bag with over two dozen pairs of socks.

The gun shelves and ammo had been cleared out, not that they needed anything, but he did find a Mathews Phase4 compound bow hanging from a rack behind the gun counter and a box full of graphite arrows and several displays of target and hunting tips. He found the knife display largely intact but had to smash the glass to access it. Into another bag, he shoved four Gerber multitools with belt holsters, three fillet knives, two more Kabars with sheaths, and four lensatic compasses. He started to leave, but something under the display case caught his eye. In six boxes were Gerber Downrange Tomahawks; these, too, went in the bag. He exited the store and sent Grant back in to retrieve the bow, arrows, and tips.

They packed back up and pulled out of the parking lot. Lane took another unexpected detour when he pulled into a jewelry store. After a quick inspection, all of the displays were empty. A large safe stood sentinel at the rear of the store; as expected, it was locked. He returned to the truck and stopped at two other jewelry stores with identical results. Finally, he found what he was looking for at a store called Glimmer's. The store had no windows, and a sign read, "All customers are seen by appointment." A phone number and a website were listed below the message. The steel door was not accessible by crowbar. He had Robert back his MRAP to the door and hooked a chain to the doorknob. As expected, the doorknob hardware pulled free without the door moving. He expected a series of deadbolts, and perhaps a bar was included in keeping it closed. Lane attached tow hooks to the chains and stuck them through the hole previously occupied by the doorknob. Lane motioned with his hand for Robert to creep forward. Once the chain was tight, he stood to the side and signaled for Robert to floor it.

A cloud of dust and concrete projectiles exploded outward as the door ripped free of the structure. Indeed, the door was equipped with three two-inch deadbolts that were embedded six inches into heavy steel receptacles. Lane traded the M4 for his shotgun and a headlamp. He waited for the dust to clear and swept the room with his headlamp. There were no safes; the whole store was a safe. If there was electricity, a highly advanced alarm would have already alerted the police. In the rear of the store, a desiccated corpse sat upright, leaning against the wall. He'd huddled under a blanket during the final moments of his life. In his hand, he clutched a gold crucifix.

Robert stepped inside with his shotgun at the ready. "What are you looking for?"

"That drug dealer gave me an idea. That Rolex we took is self-winding. Moving parts, but nothing digital. I want to see if there's any of them here," Lane told him.

All of the extensive selection of jewelry was displayed on velvet benches elevated at chest height for easy viewing. Dozens of framed photographs adorned the walls, showing the owner and his famous customers. There were many rappers showing off their jewelry for the camera. One picture had a rapper by himself, holding up a diamond-encrusted gold chain across his neck that had to have been valued at a million dollars back in the day.

"Bingo!" Lane exclaimed, holding up a box with the Rolex crown on top.

Lane searched the entire store until he'd found fourteen boxes, eight women's and six men's models. Lane picked out what he thought were the most subdued versions for the girls and the boys. He picked out two Sea-Dweller models for the boys and handed them to Robert. He then set aside four Yacht-Masters for the girls. Ruth walked in and started looking around. Lane handed her one of the watches. She took it from the box and put it on her wrist, marveling at the fact that she would never have been able to afford one.

Lane picked up a cloth bag and emptied the contents into his hand. It was an assortment of gems that consisted of diamonds, sapphires, rubies, and emeralds. The cut and size also varied; the smallest looked to be about 2 carats, and the largest as big as 10. He put the gems back in the bag and cinched it closed. He found an aluminum travel case and started loading everything. The cut stones, rings, earrings, chains, and watches combined would have been two million plus under different circumstances.

*****

An hour and a half later, they pulled off Highway 412 and onto the shoulder of I-155 in Dyersburg. Ruth and Crystal made dinner for everyone, consisting of sandwiches, single-serving chips, and milk that was dangerously close to spoiling. Grant finished before everyone else and took the pups for a quick walk. He allowed the pups to sniff their way alongside the shoulder; their noses brought them to a grisly discovery. Off the shoulder in a clearing were dozens upon dozens of charred corpses. Grant returned and told everyone about what the pups had found. They quickly mobilized and drove the two hundred yards back to the horrid site. By the time the count was finished, there were sixty-eight bodies. They had been burned in a hurry, likely accelerated by diesel or kerosene. Vague remnants of clothing discerned both men and women and, by size, children. Nearly all of the visible skulls had gunshots in them. The used brass found on the ground confirmed that the people had been executed.

"We need to get out of here, now!" Lane told them.

They all mobilized and left quickly. Lane examined his atlas as they drove. Thirty minutes later, they pulled off the interstate onto a state road. After a mile, they turned left onto Bungie Road. They followed the road until they were parked in front of a barge company that specialized in cotton and grain transport. Robert and Beth scouted the business but found it was a ghost town, except for a barge that was loaded front to back with rotting grain. Robert lifted back a tarp to reveal a world of well-fed rats. He quickly dropped the tarp when one of the rats scurried their way. They walked on until they found an adjacent barge business that appeared to have offered mechanical services. One of the barges had a crane parked in the center. A tugboat was anchored behind another barge that was empty.

Robert took the lead and guided them to the grain silos, which offered excellent concealment for the vehicles.

"Let's set that big tent up against the silo. I don't think we're going anywhere tonight," Lane instructed.

While the others erected the tent, Lane and Ruth toured the grounds looking for signs of life. They went to the main office; the door was unlocked. There was nothing in the office that offered any information about any existing operational function. After a thorough investigation, they left the office to find the sun was setting. To Lane's surprise, the tent was already up when they returned, and Robert had dug a Dakota firepit and was waiting for wood to get it started. It didn't take long for the wood to arrive. There was an abundance of dry driftwood along the shoreline, and there was soon a pile large enough to keep a fire going round the clock for two days. Lane shook a cigarette out and offered Ruth one, but she declined. He lit his and leaned against the silo, exhaling smoke. Soon, small fingers of flame danced just above the pit opening. Crystal placed a percolator with a few inches exposed to the flames over the pit.

"What's the plan?" Robert asked with Beth on his heel.

"Going to check out that tug tomorrow and see if it's operational. If not, then we look for another way," Lane finished by shrugging.

"No coffee for you, sleep now," Beth ordered, took Lane by the elbow, and guided him to the tent. His sleeping bag was already unrolled on a cot. He heard Grant and Robert discussing watch shifts, and he started to relax.

Sleep overtook him almost immediately once he was in his bag. He slept a dreamless sleep and didn't move an inch during the night. Robert and Grant made use of the NVGs; there was nothing to be seen. To Robert, it felt like they were the only humans left on earth. When Grant took his shift, he appreciated the brief respite of privacy. Being around so many people in such a brief amount of time had drained him, and he was slightly disturbed by this. When Blanche came to relieve him, he chose to stay with her and slept in his bag on the ground. He remained this way when Ruth, Beth, and Crystal took their respective shifts.

Crystal surprised herself by kissing Grant on the cheek before she woke him when the sun came up.

DECEMBER 27, 2024

CRYSTAL MADE A HUGE BREAKFAST OF EGGS, fried potato cakes from potato flakes, and drop biscuits. Lane felt rejuvenated and near-immortal after he got some coffee in him. Despite the chilly temperature, he felt loose and limber; even the gunshot no longer itched or ached.

Everyone ate standing up, and the convenience of paper plates would soon be a thing of the past. The soiled plates went into the firepit, smoking and then quickly catching flame. Kirk and Spock lifted their noses in the air, and both sneezed at the curling smoke. Blanche was gnawing on a biscuit when she noticed something floating on the river. She caught everyone's attention by pointing to the river and, with a mouth full of biscuit, said, "Look!"

They all walked to the water's edge and watched as it floated by. In its day, it had once been a premier party barge, usually moored to a lake dock and serving as a place for social gatherings rather than boating. It had two decks and was listing to starboard, with bullet holes explaining its list. The floating hulk spun slowly, exposing its stern, where a neon green-painted rooster with a marijuana leaf for its comb and the name "Cock of the Dock" to its right. A younger man hung suspended from a ladder; his throat had been cut. There was no way to board the vessel, so they all watched it until it drifted by and disappeared around a bend in the river.

"Beth, would you go with me to check out that tug?" Lane asked, turning to the raven-haired beauty who was tying her hair into a ponytail.

"Sure, gimme a sec." She disappeared into the tent and returned with her rifle and his shotgun.

The walk to the other barges and tug only took minutes, and then they were traversing the gangway until they stepped on the barge. The tug proved difficult to board. He boosted Beth aboard but had to stack several crates before he could climb up and safely swing his good leg over the bow. The tug appeared to be well-maintained. He and Beth both remarked that they'd expected one huge grease stain, but what they found was a vessel that had been left to withstand weather and the elements. The mooring lines were coiled into bundles and covered with plastic sheeting, and all of the handles, latches, and simple moving parts were either greased or covered with Vaseline.

The door to the bridge swung open easily. Lane found a box of rags and took one to wipe the lubricant from his hand. The bridge looked typical of what a tug vessel might have. The whole bridge was sterile; even the coffeepot had been thoroughly cleaned after its last use, along with the mugs that hung from little metal hooks screwed into the wall. Suspended from a wall-mounted rack were a mop, broom, and miniature squeegee. Beneath that was a shelf with glass cleaner, Brasso, and paper towels. There were several monitors that tilted downward from the ceiling. Two separate radio banks had hand mics attached to their sides with coiled wire connecting them, hanging free. The instrument array was spotless, and wherever brass was affixed, it had been polished to a high sheen.

Beth found a large manilla envelope in the captain's chair; she opened it and withdrew a single sheet of paper. Lane nodded to her to read it.

Greetings, travelers.

Nowadays, I don't just hang out waiting for work. I can assure you that after the earthquake, there have been more than a few who have wanted to cross the mighty Mississippi. Some have even gone so far as to try and commandeer my little rowboat, but she don't move unless I want her to. If you want to get across, I don't do anything for free. Eight miles south of here, turn left on Simpson Road, go three miles, and you'll find a little bar on the right called River Suds. I'll be there. Be ready to barter and likely be pissed off if we don't come to an agreement. I can assure you that if you are looking for trouble, you will find it. I look forward to sharing a beer with you while we figure things out. By the way, this letter was dropped off last night after you mentioned you were going to check the tug out. Cute puppies!

Billy

Lane studied the note and replaced it in the envelope. He was furious with himself for sleeping all night and wondered how the spy or spies had gotten so close to hear their conversations without being caught. He made a mental note to not underestimate this Billy.

"Well, I guess we better tell the others," he said, clutching the envelope.

They got back and passed the letter around while Lane downed another cup of coffee.

"This isn't a dictatorship, I want feedback," Lane told them.

"I don't think we have another choice, unless we drive south and look for another bridge. If I remember correctly, that's Memphis, and we're still in the same boat with the earthquake damage," Robert suggested.

"Well, it's not like we don't have any guns. I say we all go in armed and show strength in numbers," Crystal said, looking much taller in her bravado.

Blanche put her hands on her sister's shoulders and said simply, "Same here."

They all agreed and didn't waste time mobilizing. They started to tear down the tent, but Lane stopped them, saying that they might end up spending the night again. They backtracked and were soon back on the interstate. They followed 155 back to Simpson Road and were soon parked in front of River Suds. None of the girls or boys knew how to operate the .50s, but he asked Beth and Blanche to man them anyway. Lane wore his Desert Eagle now and felt a little silly carrying a pistol that could bring down a grizzly bear. Robert walked at his side and carried Lane's shotgun.

There were a few vehicles in the parking lot that hadn't moved since D-Day. One vehicle did surprise him—an F350 King Rancher. Coming off the lot, this truck went for $110,000. Not the kind of truck you'd see parked at a rundown dive bar. There were several solar panels on the roof and a substantial array on the ground. The bar was constructed of cinder blocks and had plywood attached in various places for advertisements. The glass door was blacked out and had rebar covering it for security.

The bar was illuminated with strings of LED lights sunken behind decorative copper flashing along the edges of the ceiling. Inside, the floor was covered with granite tile, and handmade Amish tables and chairs were scattered across it. The bar also appeared to be handmade, but it was lavishly carved in wildlife reliefs. Behind the bar, a simple red neon sign flashed Billy's River Suds.

"Back here," a voice called out from another room separated by a leather-embossed swinging door.

Lane pushed the door inward and walked through. A silver-haired man in his sixties sat in an overstuffed leather armchair watching a football game on an older television. The TV was large, and the model looked like it belonged on an episode of *Happy Days*. Attached to it was a prehistoric VHS player. Lane recognized the game. It was the Orange Bowl from two years ago; Tennessee beat Clemson 31–14. An audible crack surprised him, and he noticed that two younger men further back in the gloom had started a game of 8-ball.

"Have a seat," the man said, motioning to empty chairs with a coffee table between them.

Lane and Robert took their seats, and only after they were seated did he realize the young men and their host's eyes were on them. The host picked up an ancient remote and paused the game.

"So you want to get those two behemoths and your truck and trailer across the river?" the man asked with a grin.

"We do. What will it cost us?" Lane asked, getting to business.

"I like that—no chitchat. Straight to the point. So what do you have that I would want?" he countered.

"Sir, I have no idea what you would or wouldn't want. Just tell me and save us some time," Lane bit back.

"Time, I have plenty of that. You might not, but I do. Ammo, guns, fuel, and food. That's what I want. And I don't need diesel, I need gasoline. Guns and ammo, well...let's just say there's a lot of different guns out there. Food, well, that speaks for itself. So whatcha got for me?" the old man finished.

Lane thought for a second. He thought it would be better to lowball starting the negotiation. "One thousand rounds, three M4s, and two night-vision goggles. And ten ounces of gold."

"'Give 'til it hurts.' That's what Mother Teresa said. What else can you offer?" The old man grinned diabolically.

Lane held his hand up and removed his watch. "One Rolex Submariner."

The man got up and took the watch from Lane's outstretched hand. "Woooo! That's a Ric Flair watch if I ever saw one."

Lane cringed slightly as he'd gotten accustomed to wearing the high-end timepiece. The man stood near a window and pulled a panel aside, letting light shine on his new possession.

"Do we have a deal?" Lane asked.

"We can leave at first light, or should I say 7:00 a.m.," he said, giggling at his joke.

"Shake on it?" Lane asked while the man still admired his new watch.

The man hesitated at first but relented and shook his hand with a firm grip. "Billy Glass."

"Lane Stone," he replied.

The young men postponed their game of 8-ball and introduced themselves to Lane and Robert. The men were brothers, but Luke and Darrel weren't related to Billy. He'd taken them on for his crew four years ago when Billy caught them trying to break into his bar. They were strung out on pills and were homeless. Billy told Lane later that he'd kept them on the tug for two months before he let them out of his sight. By that time, he'd trained them into competent deckhands. Years later, they could pilot the tug as well as Billy could. Lane's opinion of the man had changed after hearing the story. He gave him one of the M4s as a measure of good faith. He looked the weapon over, and they shook hands again.

"What do you know about the Group? Have you had any dealings with them?" Lane asked, spur of the moment.

"Yeah, I know about 'em. I've only heard of them. I never took my tug past Kentucky once I heard about what they were up to," Billy told him.

"Avoid them at all costs. Maybe move further down the river. Their size has probably doubled in the last few months. We got hijacked near Natchez Trace. If we hadn't broken free and killed them, we'd probably be dead right now. We also saw one of those party barges all shot up and floating down the river. Had a dead body hanging off the ladder. I've heard worse stories. One of the people in our group barely escaped with her life when a bunch of bikers dressed in police clothes tried to take her on the road. It ended badly for them. It would be in your best interest to never mention you helped us," Lane told him.

"We'll see you in the morning. Make sure there's coffee ready." He looked at his watch and walked back into the bar.

During the drive back, Lane stopped the convoy and gathered everyone outside Ruth's MRAP. "I'm going to show you how to operate a Browning M2 .50 caliber machine gun. Pay close attention, what I'm about to teach you could save lives."

Lane had Robert drag one of the .50s out, and after he removed the barrel, he started demonstrating the mechanics. An hour later, he'd taught them all how to load, clear, and fire the .50. They all took a turn, each firing a 5-round burst. Surprisingly, it was Crystal who proved the most adept at function and accuracy, with Grant and Ruth tying for second. He then took empty MRE pouches and attached them to pine trees fifty yards away.

Over the next thirty minutes, they all used the M4s and went through about ninety rounds each, zeroing in until they were all competent. Robert and Grant proved to be spot-on sharpshooters.

They all broke down their own weapons and cleaned them. Lane demonstrated the disassembly of the .50, and they all pitched in to clean its components. They then policed the brass and headed back to camp.

Crystal went into cooking mode as soon as her feet hit the ground. It had been days since Lane had removed his prosthetic. He had Robert guard the tent, undressed, and removed his leg. He put his pants back on and tied his pant leg in a knot. He used his shotgun as a walking stick and hopped around until he'd mastered his balance. He hopped outside and found himself sitting on the bumper of the MRAP. Everyone except for Robert and Beth was stunned when they discovered Lane was missing his leg. Everyone was polite about his leg, and neither stared nor mentioned it.

The meal took longer than usual to prepare, but no one complained once Crystal was finished. She'd made spaghetti, and unbeknownst to anyone else, she'd made dough. After placing it in the MRAP and checking it frequently, the dough had been allowed to rise twice. The dough had been baked in a camp pot, and when it was done, it had grown large enough to raise the cast iron lid by two inches. The ground beef was nearly past its use-by date, but Crystal had been monitoring the cooler's contents. Once the bread was finished, she put it in a large towel and used the pot to prepare the spaghetti. She browned the beef and used two packets of mixed powder to make the sauce. Once the spaghetti was done, she drained the water and dumped the sauce on top of it. By the time everyone sat down, the temperature had dropped again, and with every bite eaten, large plumes of steam escaped their mouths like they were chain-smoking. Having tired of water, Robert rummaged through Lane's food supplies until he found Gatorade mix and dedicated enough packs to one of the twenty-liter containers. Lane was the only one who forewent the sports drink and sipped at his coffee.

After they'd eaten, Grant made the mistake of allowing Kirk and Spock off their leashes. Crystal went to the river's edge and rinsed the pot and pan. As she used clean water to finish the job, the pups got curious and decided a romp in the cold stiffening mud was irresistible. The pups were covered in a gelatinous goo, running from Grant like naked children avoiding a bath. It brought much-needed laughter. The same Dawn dishwashing soap used for the cooking cleanup was now being used to wash the pups. When Grant was finished, he, too, needed a bath, but with new snow that had started falling, he thought better of it and opted to change his clothes instead.

The fire was loaded with more driftwood, and soon everyone, including the pups, was gathered around it. Before sundown, there were three inches of snow on the ground and still falling. Lane asked Robert to grab him one of the Rolex spares and put it on. He took everyone's watches and spent several minutes synchronizing all of them to the second. Everyone except for Robert and Beth thought it was a needless effort, but Robert explained that if they needed to do something time-sensitive, it was a necessary effort. Beth and Robert thanked Lane as they replaced their watches. The others remained thoughtful and eventually thanked Lane as well. Lane briefly lectured them that the watches were wound by perpetual movement and that the watches should be worn at all times so that they would get used to wearing them and that the winding mechanism stayed active.

"Tell us about your children," Blanche said to Lane.

She caught Lane by surprise with the request, and he seemed to drift off into a daydream, but he gathered himself and spoke.

"Blake is my oldest, he's a year older than Robert. He's a kind and gentle soul. When he was a child, he used to take the hand of strangers and help them cross streets whether they needed it or not. He'd read a book when he was little about a blind little old lady who depended on the kindness of strangers to help her cross the streets until she was stranded at a crossing one day. Many people passed her by and ignored her. A child saw her across the street and crossed over to help her. After he'd helped her, the little old lady asked why he'd helped her. The little boy replied that she needed help, and it was the right thing to do. That's how he's been his entire life. He fell in love with a young lady whose uncle owned land in Alaska, and she was going up there to help him mine for gold. He really didn't have a choice but to follow his heart. I hope he's made it home and his temper hasn't gotten him in trouble.

"Dawn is the poet of the three. She's nineteen and finds beauty in almost everything. We all knew she was different when she was little. She was deeply saddened when her great-grandmother died. She was inconsolable for several days. In the end, she felt guilty for reacting the way she did. She'd told her mother that it had been selfish to behave the way she had. She knew that her grandmomma was no longer in pain and that she was in a place now that was so beautiful and wonderful and with all the people that she'd loved. We should be happy for her and not cry anymore. She also developed an aptitude for Brazilian jiujitsu, which frustrated her brother and sister immensely. She would rather spend her time gardening than interacting with others. She is one of those people that operates on a wavelength that she rarely finds like-minded individuals.

"Claire, my youngest, is seventeen. She's the glue that holds her siblings together. She's an old soul in a young body. She's quick to laugh, full of biting sarcasm, and quick to argue her point because she's usually right. If her school had remained open, her senior class picture would probably read 'most likely to do whatever she damn well pleases.' In all honesty, she's accomplished everything she's set her mind to. She doesn't set her mind, though, she gets distracted by helping others before she helps herself. But she took it upon herself to be competent in a very large catalog of skills and abilities so that she doesn't have to depend on anyone but herself."

Lane rubbed his stump and massaged it. "The whole truth is that I love them and worry about them every day. A father couldn't be prouder of his children. I would've never met any of you if I hadn't lost my leg. If that hadn't happened, I would have already been there. But I must say if I was your father, I would be very proud of all of you."

He finished by gesturing to all of them with a coffee cup. He used his shotgun to stand up and hopped away. He was dangerously close to weeping and didn't want them to see. He hopped in front of the MRAP and lit a cigarette. Ruth came up beside him and extended her middle and forefinger until Lane put a cigarette between them. He lit it for her and returned the lighter to his pocket.

Ruth exhaled a plume of smoke and stood on her tiptoes and kissed Lane on the cheek. The gesture surprised him.

"What was that for?"

"You looked like you needed it," she said with a smirk.

Then he did the unexpected. He grabbed Ruth by the back of the neck and pulled her to him. He kissed her hard and passionately, in the way a man kisses a woman so there was no mistake of his intent. She leaned into him until her breasts were flattened against his chest. He heard the others move around the fire and let her go. She leaned back and ran the back of her hand across her lips. She exhaled heavily, and her entire face flushed.

"What was that for?"

"You looked like you needed it." He grinned and hopped away into the tent.

Lane reemerged with his leg attached. The others were giggling, watching the pups twitch and jerk in their sleep. Ruth blushed again when she saw him emerge through the snow. He leaned against the silo and stole glances at Ruth. She quickly avoided eye contact each time she noticed him watching her. Beth witnessed this but said nothing, making a mental note. She watched Crystal continue to inch closer to Grant; she also noticed that Blanche was frowning. She was trying to figure out a way to help when Robert wrapped his arm around her and pulled her close to him.

"I'll take first watch," Lane said. "Volunteers, anyone?"

"I got second," Grant offered.

"Third," Crystal chimed in a little too quickly.

"Fifth," Ruth called out.

"Sixth," answered Robert.

"Last," Beth said.

"Alright then, go get some shut-eye," Lane told them and poured himself another cup of coffee.

Lane looked at his Rolex Sky-Dweller. It was midnight. He was about to question whether or not he needed to wake Grant when Grant appeared through the blowing snow. The snow had stopped, but the wind was sweeping it into the air, making visibility difficult.

He looked at his feet and guessed the snow was around eight inches deep.

"You think that guy has a vehicle that'll make it here?" Grant asked him.

"We'll give him thirty minutes' grace. After that, I may send you and Robert after him," he spoke.

"Alright, alright, alright," Grant said, doing his best Matthew McConaughey impression.

Lane chuckled and wondered if the famous Texan was somewhere in the Lone Star state with his shirt off making a pitcher of frozen margaritas. Once he was in his bag, he thought about kissing Ruth. The moment of passion kept him awake, but after half an hour, he finally drifted off into a restless sleep.

DECEMBER 28, 2024

"DO YOU THINK HIS CHILDREN ARE THERE?" Beth asked Robert.

"I don't know, I just hope they are. He would be destroyed if they weren't. You saw how he lit up talking about them," he said, gently squeezing her hand.

Lane crunched through the snow and joined Robert and Beth by a blazing fire. The coffeepot was steaming as he tipped it into his camp cup. He sniffed the brew and sipped at it until his eyes took on another identity. Slowly, the others emerged, shivering against the cold. Lane looked at his watch; it was 6:45. He walked to the side of the silo and looked to the eastern sky as he watched the color brighten. His attention was drawn to the road. He blinked several times to make sure his eyes weren't betraying him. An ancient truck made its way through the snow with ease. As it got closer, it became even more impressive. Lane lit a cigarette and approached the truck as Billy and his crew exited the cab.

"1946 Power Wagon. Took me nine years to restore it. Had to order parts for it all over the country. Only 5,450 were made between '46 and '48. She's a hot rod with a top speed of 50 mph," he finished, patting the fire-engine-red truck's fender with a gloved hand.

"I've only seen these in pictures," Lane said admiringly.

"Yeah, it's hard to tell how many of these ended up in the scrapyard. I'm not gonna tell you how much it cost me. But I'd guess you're more interested in the other side of the river."

"That we would. Robert, get the tent broke down and put away. Make sure you get the other items that will belong to Billy."

The next hour was a flurry of activity. One of Billy's boys brought a milk crate of what appeared to be engine parts. Billy car-

176

ried the M4. It was loaded, so he hadn't revealed that he had ammo. He fired up his tug, black smoke billowing from an exhaust stack. He directed Lane to where to park the vehicles. Then once the vehicles were rigged, he picked them up with the crane, and his boys maneuvered them into place on the barge. The trailer proved to be difficult. The wind sent the trailer into a dangerous spin, and it took nearly twenty minutes before they could get it under control and set it on the barge. It was 10:45 a.m. before everything was in place. They all walked the gangway, and with the aid of a ladder stealthily hidden on the barge, they boarded the tug. Lane was impressed by the operation of the tug and the steering of the barge. Billy and his crew worked well together and knew their roles. They did their best to stay out of the way, but it seemed that no matter where they congregated, they eventually needed to move to avoid halting progress.

Luke, the tallest of the crew, yelled something to Billy's other boy, Darrel, in some slang that no one was able to decipher. Darrel replied by hitting a large cable with a sledgehammer. The cable broke free and hung from the starboard bow. He repeated the task on the port bow. He backed away from the barge upstream, causing the water to churn behind them in a massive white froth. Once he cleared the mooring dock, he steered downstream and swung wide after he reached the end of the barge. He then played with the engines until the nose of the bow kissed the barge. Luke and Darrel both sprang into action and looped the thick cables through cutout sleeves on the barge. Darrel ran to Luke and held the cables in place while Luke secured them together with a shackle longer than his arm. They then ran to the port and repeated the process. Darrel removed a radio from his pocket and jumped onto the barge. Luke did the same but ran to the bow of the barge. Luke took another sledgehammer and knocked two pins loose, and the barge started to move backward.

From the turbulent water, Lane guessed the engines were pushing against the weight of the barge to control its movement. Lane watched with interest as the boys continued to dance back and forth between port and starboard, talking into their radios and waving their arms in signal. Ten minutes later, they were in the middle of the river. Darrel and Luke joined Billy in the wheelhouse. Lane joined them as Darrel handed Billy a cup of coffee. Darrel poured one for Lane and handed it to him; he nodded his head in appreciation.

"It's about thirty-five minutes to your stop. If you have chains, I'd get them on your truck before you get there. I'm pretty sure those big tires on the military vehicles will be fine. I got adjustable tracks on the end that will get you to the shore, but getting up the bank is another story. As a matter of fact, I'd hook up your trailer to one of the hulks to make sure you get it out. Where I'm dropping you off is just flood plain, and it's usually pretty soft, but with the snow, it might have hardened it up a bit." Billy took a sip of coffee and went quiet.

Lane went outside and joined the others. The pups stood and wagged their tails. Grant said, "Sitzen," and to Lane's surprise, the pups sat.

"Very nice," he said to Grant.

"Thanks, they catch on pretty quick," Grant said with a smile.

"Robert, do you think you and Blanche can get to the truck and put the tire chains on?"

"Sure!" Blanche said, clearly eager to do something.

"Grab a couple of life vests from the wheelhouse. And one more thing, get the rest of the trade stuff, and add fifty ounces of junk silver from the bank bag." Robert and Blanche took off with enthusiasm.

The trip upriver was right on time. Billy slowed the barge until it felt like they were standing still. Inch by inch, they crept forward until the barge hit mud and jolted the tug, making it gently rock forward before it fell back into position. Darrel and Luke both took sledgehammers and hit the sides of the wheel tracks, likely to make sure they broke free. Robert and Blanche carried the weapons and the ammo into the wheelhouse and set them down. They removed their life jackets and returned to Lane outside. Blanche dug into her coat pocket and handed Lane the gold and silver. Lane walked inside and placed the precious metals on the instrument panel.

"As promised, thank you for getting us here."

"Y'all be careful. You seem like good people. I wish we'd had more time to get to know one another. If you make it back this way, stop by and see us," Billy said with a smile.

They shook hands, but Lane turned to him. "You should really head south, find another place to set up shop. Don't give those fuckers an opportunity to take from you. One more thing, if you come across any military, use this challenge. Say 'E-4.' They reply, 'Mafia,' you reply back, 'Can't be found.' If they don't answer immediately, start shooting."

"I'll remember and tell the boys too." Billy grinned back at him and returned to the wheelhouse.

Lane took off first, and once the tires touched mud, he gunned it. The tires spun and threw mud but eventually caught enough traction that they rocketed up the slight incline. Lane got out and started to make his way back to the barge but thought better of it when he saw the depth of the mud. Robert and Grant attached the trailer to his MRAP and checked to make sure it was secured. The trailer wheels barely matched the tracks to follow the MRAP. Robert lined his wheels up with the path that Lane had taken. He looked at Beth briefly and floored the accelerator. The six wheels lurched forward in unison, and despite the mud, both the MRAP and trailer topped the little incline, throwing mud toward the barge.

Ruth didn't want to be outdone and copied Robert but accelerated so hard that Darrel and Luke were rewarded with globs of mud from head to toe. She, too, topped the hill, and they were all delivered from the river. Once a perfunctory inspection was completed on the vehicles, they all resumed their seating assignments and headed south. It took some exploring, but they eventually found 155 again and were all in an evenly spaced convoy.

Lane's heart dropped when they got off 155 and onto 412 as they entered Hayti. A National Guard unit was set up outside an urgent care center, but there were no soldiers to be seen. Beyond that, in an open field, were hundreds of graves. Further on were multiple spots that appeared to be mass graves. An excavator was parked nearby, which almost solidified the mass grave reality. This makeshift cemetery hit too close to home—his children's home.

Déjà vu took over as an old woman stepped outside the doorway of a convenience store. The lines on her face made her look ancient. Her back was arched in an unnatural hump. She eyed them suspiciously, looking over the handle of a snow shovel.

He brought the convoy to a halt. He got out and grabbed a dozen MREs and a twenty-liter container of water. He walked up her sidewalk and took the shovel out of her hand, setting the MREs and the water just inside the door. He shoveled the snow off the sidewalk and the entry. When he was done, he leaned the shovel against the wall and shook the frail little hand. He exchanged a few words with her and said goodbye.

He'd made this trip many times in his past, both married and divorced. The road was familiar to him as if he lived here himself. Once they pulled into Kennett, he hung a right at McDonald's and turned onto Highway 53. "Home of Sheryl Crow. She was born here in Kennett," he said aloud to no one.

"Who?" Grant asked.

Lane rolled his eyes, took a CD from his console, and put it in the player. Music filled the air, and he turned the volume up to an obnoxious level.

> I hitched a ride with a vending machine repair man
> He said he's been down this road more than twice
> He was high on intellectualism
> I've never been there, but the brochure looks nice
>
> Jump in, let's go
> Lay back, enjoy the show
> Everybody gets high, everybody gets low
> These are the days when anything goes
> Every day is a winding road
> I get a little bit closer
> Every day is a faded sign
> I get a little bit closer to feeling fine

"That's Sheryl Crow!" he snapped, turning the music off.
"Why'd you turn it off?" Blanche asked, pouting.
"Yeah!" Grant echoed in disappointment.

Lane grinned in disbelief, then turned the music back on. The two of them bounced their heads with the tempo. Lane copied them, tapping his thumb on the steering wheel. The song ended, and the duo looked at him expectantly. He changed the song to "All I Wanna Do." He couldn't remember the last time he'd listened to music, but as that song ended and they got off the main road and turned into the small town of Campbell, he ejected the CD and replaced it with one that a friend had burned for him decades ago.

Pearl Jam's "Jeremy" played as he passed the Sugar Shack. A wave of nostalgia overtook him again as he remembered stopping there with the kids to get ice cream. They were so young and innocent then, the soft serve ice cream dripping down their chins and their huge smiles. It warmed him briefly; the little place grew smaller in his mirror. Coldplay's "Clocks" came on as he crested a hill and fell away to what had once been a cotton field. Nostalgia returned yet again as his favorite landmark had been reduced to a pile of ashes.

He'd called it Struggle Tree. It had been a white oak and was struck by lightning multiple times to the point that its entire exterior was blackened, and its limbs were fractured and broken. But each summer, there was new greenery sprouting from the top. The sight had always given Lane hope; it was metaphorical to him. To him, it was a symbol that said no matter how broken you are, you can still survive. Now that it was a pile of ashes, it cast a shadow of gloom over him. Ironically, U2's "Beautiful Day" was the next song to play. He was so close now, his palms started sweating with nerves. The countryside flew by. Someone had taken the time to clear the road, and the way was unobstructed.

Snow hadn't fallen here, and it was easy to maintain 60 mph. It was easy to see that the crops had largely gone unharvested. He passed field after field, and then something caught his eye. Two people were riding mules in the distance; their tall ears were easy to see. A stand of trees that bordered a tributary was their destination. There were no other trees except more fields that likely had grown milo. The scene brightened his spirit again, that is until Linkin Park's "In the End" came on. It was a very dark song to him, and he advanced it to the next song. Gorillaz's "Clint Eastwood" came on, and the lyrics seemed to carry a prophetic tone.

> I ain't happy, I'm feeling glad
> I got sunshine in a bag
> I'm useless but not for long
> The future is coming on
> I ain't happy, I'm feeling glad
> I got sunshine in a bag
> I'm useless but not for long
> The future is coming on
> It's coming on, it's coming on
> It's coming on, it's coming on

Several more songs came and went, but Clint Eastwood kept playing on a loop in his mind. He wondered what the next few hours would hold and wished he had a crystal ball to tell him what to expect.

It was 3:30 p.m. when they entered Poplar Bluff city limits. Aside from the derelict cars and the absence of people, the small town looked remarkably untouched. Lane slowed when an Amish buggy came into sight. A man and woman occupied the front seat. The woman, of course, had her hair concealed in the traditional white bonnet and a very modest, unrevealing black dress. The man wore his neck beard, straw hat, white shirt, suspenders, and black pants. It looked as though their lives were unaffected, just as they had been prior to D-Day. They looked in their direction, and the man raised one hand in greeting before he dropped it back to the reins.

Lane turned onto Pine Avenue, and two miles later, he turned right onto Westwood Boulevard. He drove on until he crossed over the highway. He slowed and pulled into the parking lot of an insurance company. The others filed in behind him as he circled the building. Everyone got out of their vehicles and stretched their legs. Lane lit a cigarette to calm his nerves and watched the others. Grant led the pups to a decorative tree; he heard him give the command "Regen"—it was German for rain. He'd figured this word was as close to *pee* as he could get. The pups squatted and relieved themselves, but he thought the timely urination was due more to being in the vehicle for so long rather than having been trained over such a short time.

Lane raised his hand in the air, and everyone gathered around him. "I need to go in alone first. I haven't spoken to my kids or their mother in quite a while. They don't even know I lost my leg, as it is when I lost my leg, I nearly died. Robert and Beth can tell you about me learning to walk again. I have my radio. When it's okay, I'll radio you to come in. Pull out of here and hang a right onto Utah Circle. It's the last house."

He turned and climbed back in the truck. Foo Fighters' "Times Like These" came on. "You gotta be fucking kidding me," he said to himself. He pulled onto Utah, and his heartbeat quickened. The circle looked unchanged, but signs of neglect were apparent. Lawns had overgrown and died in the winter, giving each yard a yellow, tangled mass of weeds. Two coyotes ran in front of him, baring their teeth, warning him that this neighborhood belonged to them.

He pulled to the curb at the last house. The yard wasn't the same mess as the others, but it, too, suffered from D-Day-type neglect. The driveway was full; Claire's Highlander was parked at the top, along with Mary's work car. Paul's truck was parked beside Mary's car, and Dawn's VW Bug was parked at the bottom. They all looked relatively clean, but Dawn's car looked like it had been driven. What disturbed him, but wasn't a surprise, was the absence of Blake's Crown Victoria, which he'd won at a police auction four years ago for two hundred dollars.

He got out of the truck and shut the door; the sound echoed through the neighborhood. He stood at the front of the truck and waited, hoping his children would burst through the door, run to him, and embrace him all at once. He stood there for ten minutes, but no one came. He walked around the house, as was the custom. They always congregated together on the back porch. He, too, had spent time there. After many years of anger and hatred, he'd set aside those feelings and became friends with his ex-wife again and got to know her husband, Paul.

Lane walked to the door and peered through the blinds; no one was there. He tried the door, but it was locked. He tried knocking, then after several repeated door beatings, he surrendered and sat in front of the patio fireplace. He lit a cigarette and felt despair slowly take over. He turned to look in the backyard; a doe was leading two fawns. They made no noise; they turned to look at him but showed no fear. The fawns munched mouthfuls of corn from a bucket. Then it dawned on him: there was no way a bucket of corn would've lasted so long. Then a door opened from the cottage at the end of the property. Mary and Paul had built it for her late mother; the kids later used it as a clubhouse of sorts.

Lane stood and spooked the deer. As they darted off into the woods, Dawn came into view. She saw him and dropped a cardboard box to the ground. "DAD!"

Lane moved as fast as he could; his daughter broke into a run. She jumped into his arms, and he hugged her tightly to him. She smelled like peppermint, and he could feel her tears wet against his cheek. She sobbed against his shoulder, and he felt his own breath choke with the emotion of love and thankfulness that he'd made it here. Time melted away as this young woman once more became his child.

He pulled away from her and wiped his eyes. "Where is everybody?"

Dawn composed herself and wiped her face with the hem of her shirt. She stared at him blankly, then spoke. "Mom and Paul moved into the bed-and-breakfast a few days after D-Day. Claire and I moved over about a week later."

"Where's Blake?" he whispered.

"He called us from Fairbanks on May 20. He was there with Madison to pick up parts for one of her uncle's bulldozers. He said he was heading back to Noatak after he got off the phone. That's the last time any of us spoke to him. He asked about you. But we didn't hear from you. What happened, Dad?"

Lane looked at his daughter with her question hanging in the air. Reluctantly, he raised the cuff of his left pant leg until his prosthetic was exposed. Dawn's hands went to her mouth in shock, then emotion overtook her again, and the tears fell. He shushed her, telling her it was okay, but the continued sobbing made him feel there was more behind the tears than shock over the loss of his leg, but he let it go.

"Look, I've got friends that I've brought with me in some very scary vehicles. I told them to wait at the insurance place. I need to tell them to come on over," he told her, taking out the radio.

"Robert? Yeah, I'm here. Bring 'em over. Roger that, be there in a few." He put the radio away.

"Once you've met everyone, maybe you should go let your mom know I'm here with people. Tell her we're not looking for lodging. Planning on seeing if the old game lodge is vacant," he told her.

They made their way to the end of the driveway and waited for the others. The MRAPs pulled onto the street and stopped beside Lane's truck. Everyone got out, and Lane introduced them. Of course, Dawn smothered herself in Kirk and Spock to wind up the intros. Lane excused himself and returned quickly.

"Merry Christmas," he told her and handed her one of the Rolex Yachtsmans.

She put it on and said a polite thank you. Dawn was never a materialistic child and probably had no clue she was wearing a watch that cost more than her car. Lane retold what he wanted her to tell her mother. A few goodbyes later, the '68 Beetle rumbled to life, sounding like a pissed-off sewing machine. She waved from the window and drove off. Lane couldn't help feeling empty with her departure.

An hour later, Dawn walked through the front door of the former bed-and-breakfast and found her mother and stepfather sitting in front of the fireplace, reading and drinking wine. Dawn went to the fire to warm herself.

"Hey there, girl. Did you remember my books?" Mary asked her daughter.

"Did the house look okay?" Paul asked.

Claire walked in with a mug of hot chocolate in hand and a book in the other and curled into a chair by the fire.

"Mom, do you remember all those times last year that you kinda dogged on Dad for not writing or coming out here when you had a few glasses of wine?" Dawn asked.

Claire raised an eyebrow and put her book down.

"Yep, what about it?" Mary retorted, sipping her wine.

"About that."

Everyone was sitting on the curb and had just finished pork chop sandwiches. Lane went into more detail about the conversation between himself and Dawn. The pups growled and cocked their heads back and forth. Then they heard it: the staccato rumble of Dawn's VW. The headlights appeared seconds later and pulled into the driveway. Claire leaped from the car and wrapped her arms around her father's neck. Lane couldn't stop his tears at his daughter's greeting.

She sobbed into his chest. "I thought you were dead!"

"I'm okay, honey. I'm sorry I didn't get here sooner," he apologized.

Claire bent over and lifted his pant leg, exposing his prosthetic. She stared back up at him and could only mutter a one-word question. "How?"

Everyone's ears perked up. Robert and Beth squeezed each other's hands. They had all wondered how he lost his leg, but nobody wanted to ask. Robert and Beth had gone to bed many nights making up stories, imagining how he lost it. Before he could answer, Mary broke the silence.

"When did it happen?" Mary asked.

"My birthday," he answered.

"How?" Claire repeated.

"I was leaving Target. A little boy was playing with a soccer ball his mother had just bought him. I was loading some things into my truck. The boy dropped his ball, and it rolled into the traffic lane. A kid in a new Corvette, going too fast and texting, didn't see the ball or the four-year-old that went after it. I managed to get the kid out of the way, but my left leg didn't. Rescue and the doctors were great, but infection won, and I lost," he finished.

Mary swiped a single tear away quickly. "Why didn't you call?"

"Because you would've stressed out over not being here and bringing the kids, and Paul would've insisted you come. I was lying in a bed recovering, and you would have all spent your time in my hospital room watching TV with me and bringing me fast food. I would still be the same miserable man you divorced, except you would've been keeping me company. And after I got fitted with the prosthetic, my stump got infected again, and it got bad. So after I got the infection under control, they sent me home. While I was at home, the infection set in again, and it got really bad again. Luckily for me, they sent me home with a Costco-size bottle of antibiotics."

"So you had to learn to walk on that thing without training bars and help?" she asked him with wide eyes.

"The driveway was the worst part." He laughed.

Mary walked to him and hugged him for a five-count, then let go. Paul approached him, taking his hand to shake but gave him a quick bro hug, slapping him on the back. "Glad you made it, Lane."

Lane quickly introduced his companions, and they went inside. Claire built a fire while Robert and Beth told their story, editing a few parts about their abduction and the killings. Lane simply nodded in agreement. Grant started to add the part about gunning down the Group thugs, but Beth pinched him to shut him up. Ruth eyed Mary and surprised herself that she was feeling some kind of latent jealousy.

"Nobody lives on the street now. Poplar Bluff was forgotten with emergency relief. The new COVID-X4 strain pretty much wiped everybody except for the Amish and maybe ten or twelve farm families. We probably wouldn't have made it if it weren't for the B and B. We started putting up vegetables and raising chickens there two years ago. The pigs were the last addition, we've got twelve piglets we're trying to get through the winter. Anyhow, Claire and Dawn can come out in the morning, and you can all follow them over. So there's room for everyone here, stay the night. There's extra blankets and pillows in the closet at the end of the hall. Lane, there's wood in the cottage if you want to stay over there," Mary finished by unlocking the front door.

"Sounds good. I'm gonna follow you out and refill Dawn's Beetle," Lane said, standing up.

Lane had Dawn back her Beetle up to the diesel trailer. When the tank was full, he took her spare can from the trunk and filled that too. The girls hugged Lane fiercely and finally said goodnight. They pulled away, and Lane went inside. When he went inside, a pot of water was heating by the fire.

"Where'd the water come from?" he asked curiously.

"Rain barrel," Grant answered.

"I'm going to bed." Lane turned and left without a word and retreated to the cottage.

He went into the cottage and lit a fire. He stripped down to his underwear and pulled a pack of baby wipes from his pack. He set an ottoman by the fire and began cleaning himself, tossing the used wipes into the fire. He removed his leg and massaged his stump. He lit a candle and hopped into the bathroom; the flames made shadows dance across the walls as he hopped. He opened the medicine cabinet and found what he wanted: Burt's Bees dry hands ointment. He hopped back in front of the fire, setting the candle on the hearth. After he rubbed a generous portion into the skin of his stump, he went to the door to see if anyone was around. Satisfied there were no peeping Toms, he stepped out of his underwear and thoroughly wiped down his nether regions. He wadded up his dirty clothes, put them in a shopping bag, and stuffed them back in his pack. He pulled the covers back and got into bed. The cool sheets felt good to him, and the down comforter quickly warmed him. Sleep came easily, but the last thing he thought of before he drifted off was, *Where is Noatak, and is Blake still alive in an Alaskan winter?*

DECEMBER 29, 2024

LANE WOKE AND LOOKED AT HIS WATCH; it read 4:04. If the time change mattered, they were in the Central time zone. He turned his watch back an hour and got on his knees. He prayed, asking God to watch over his son. He thanked God for giving him the strength to make it here, for keeping his daughters alive, and for blessing him to hold his daughters again. He asked God to forgive him his sins.

Lane stretched out his hands and arched his body, perching himself on both hands and his one foot. Then did something he hadn't done in years: he started doing pushups. He made it to eight before he had to stop. Disappointed in himself, he started again. After completing six more, he stopped again, his heart pounding, and thought of the cigarettes. He sat on the floor in front of the fire and put a small log on the coals. He stretched out again and managed six more pushups. When the pounding in his chest stopped, he raised himself to stand. He placed his hand on the hearth to balance himself. Slowly, he squatted until he was in a sitting position, then tried to rise. His leg ached at the effort but complied. He repeated the squat until sweat poured from his face.

A pile of wipes smoked on the log as he dressed. The dark was giving way to day when he looked through the blinds and saw Grant outside with the pups. He heard him through the door; he was holding a stick while they bit at it and chewed. "BEISSEN! BEISSEN!" The word meant "bite."

He waited until Grant finished with the pups, then left the cottage and followed him inside the house. Lane found everyone standing around the fireplace making small talk. They all hushed when he stepped inside.

"Don't stop on my account. That is unless you were talking about me, in which case, I want you to start from the beginning," Lane said seriously.

"We're just wondering what happens next," Robert told him.

"We all were," Blanche agreed.

Lane studied them all. They were rested but looked apprehensive. He couldn't blame them; they were on his team and in the home of the woman who divorced him.

"I promise, by the end of the day, you will all have a better idea of what to expect or at least be better informed. I can't do any better than that at the moment," he told them and poured a cup of coffee. He held the cup up to Crystal in thanks.

Just then, Dawn came through the back door with Claire bringing up the rear, carrying a plateful of homemade doughnuts. She set the plate down and joined the hug between her father and sister. Lane let go of his daughters and grabbed the plate of doughnuts, putting his arm around them protectively, hovering over them. Dawn and Claire giggled. Lane had done this routinely in the past; he pretended it was the last food on earth and his daughters were the best bakers in history. Lane crammed one of the glazed rings in his mouth and chewed. His daughters crossed their arms and stared.

"Mom made them."

"Oh," he said, looking disappointed and embarrassed with his mouth full, handing the plate to Grant. The truth was his ex-wife could have made shoe leather taste good, but he'd eaten real shoe leather if his daughters made it.

It took mere seconds to empty the plate of two dozen doughnuts. Grant's face betrayed just how good they were. Grant looked at the empty plate in disbelief and frowned. "I only got four."

His daughters now giggled at Grant; he wasn't sure how he felt about this, but it wasn't great.

*****

The MRAPs followed Lane, who in turn followed his daughter's forest-green VW. At first, Lane had no idea where he was going, but with each turn, suspicion became reality. When they turned onto a state-maintained dirt road lined on one side with apple trees, he felt pissed off and betrayed. Twenty years earlier, he and Mary had toyed with the idea of investing in a B and B. They toured the lower portions of southeast Missouri and had narrowed their choices to two properties, one of which sat on a hundred acres with a road lined on one side with apple trees. As they rounded a curve, the familiar Craftsman-style home with a wraparound porch came into view. Lane seethed as almost every detail of their long-dormant plans had become reality. As he got out of the truck, the seething continued. The gardens were arranged upwind of two beehives to promote better pollination. Rain barrels were piped into a collection tank. Pallets were used to construct mulching bins. And last but not least, Mary had found some old bleachers and turned them into a chicken coop. His design was complete with collapsible wheels to move the coop around.

He almost felt steam escaping from his ears. He looked up quickly and saw blinds snap back into place. Paul stepped onto the front porch and waved. "Come on in, Mary set up a buffet in the sitting room."

Lane was greeted by Marco, the devil cat, when he walked through the front door. Marco was a rescue cat he and Mary had adopted for the girls when they were little. Marco had to be fifteen years old now. Marco's tail had been broken two inches from the tip when he'd been rescued, and whenever he swished his tail, it looked like he was repeatedly pointing at something.

Mary had channeled her inner Martha Stewart; the house was decorated in such a fashion that it looked like *Better Homes and Gardens* had been hired to outfit the home. Lane walked into the sitting room, and as Paul said, a full buffet had been prepared, complete with linen napkins, antique dishes and cups, and fancy cutlery. There was even a carafe of orange juice. He guessed somewhere deep in the cellar, a cold hole had been dug very deep in order for perishable foods to keep longer. He took a cup from the buffet and approached the fireplace. Ironworks had been constructed from his design. The pivoting ironworks allowed for any meal to be prepared over the fire.

He swung back an iron, used an oven mitt to remove the coffeepot, and poured himself a cup. He sat in one of the many folding chairs that had been set out for them. The others came in and, with no surprise to him, made a huge deal out of the meal that Mary had prepared. And in magical fashion, Grant was already sitting and digging into his breakfast before anyone else had grabbed a plate.

Lane stopped midswallow when the mellow sounds of Dave Matthews drifted in from another room. "Crash Into Me" had been one of the songs that was on a loop whenever there were fond memories of his ex-wife. She walked in carrying a brass steamer filled with homemade potpourri and set it near the fire. He hadn't noticed the last time he'd seen her, but her chestnut hair was graying at one temple. He noticed that Mary was showing her age. He felt a little embarrassed that he noticed; it was like discovering that a noble tree had flaws. He'd loved this woman once and perhaps in some way always would. A sadness crept over him; their season had come and gone, never to return. He suddenly felt eyes on him and saw that Ruth was staring at him out of the corner of his eye. He averted his eyes to his coffee and ignored the world until his cup was empty.

"Dawn said you want to check out that old lodge near the forest?" Mary asked, as Dave Matthews kept on crooning to the background of violin and saxophone.

"That's the plan. Do you know anything about it?"

"It went back up for sale last year around April. The original investors moved back to California," Paul answered for her.

"I'd say it's a good chance nobody's there. The last caretaker was put on hospice care around the same time the investors pulled out. There's just that big gate to get through," Mary added.

"Then that's where I'm taking the fellowship of the apocalypse," Lane said, laughing at his own joke. The others joined in the laughter without prompting.

"How are you outfitted?" Paul asked.

"That reminds me!" Lane said, snapping his fingers, and went outside.

He came back moments later with the Bass Pro bags. "Girls, go through those bags, and see if there's anything that fits. Bass Pro had a sale, it was on the way."

The girls went headfirst into the bags and were soon trying shoes on. Claire was taller than Dawn, and they wore different sizes. They disappeared and returned ten minutes later, grinning from ear to ear. They had both selected at least three pairs of shoes each, along with multiple pairs of pants, shirts, socks, and sports underwear. They set the bags on the floor near their father.

"Mary, I think there's a few sizes in there that might fit you as well," Lane told her.

Her eyes brightened. "Are you sure? What about the other girls?"

"Don't worry, they did their own shopping."

Mary took the bags and went through them. She soon had two pairs of shoes for herself along with three pairs of jeans and four flannel shirts that she favored. "Thank you."

"No worries, they were on sale," he told her, stretching out the joke.

"Merry Christmas," he said to Claire, handing her a Rolex box.

Claire opened the box and took out an identical watch to Dawn's.

"Those on sale too?" Mary asked sarcastically.

"Yep, practically stole them," Lane answered sarcastically.

"Too bad you didn't pick up another one," she said, pouting.

"Ahh geez!" Lane exclaimed and tossed her a Rolex box across the room.

Mary caught the box like a wide receiver catching the game-winning touchdown and squealed.

Paul smiled but wore a pout on his face. "You're as bad as she is!"

Another Rolex box flew through the air, which Paul deftly caught.

"How many of those things did you take?" Mary asked as everyone was showing their watches off.

"I've got one left for Blake." Mary suddenly looked up from her watch and looked him in the eyes.

"Once I get everyone settled in at the lodge, I'm going to find our son."

Mary seldom cried; twenty years of hospice nursing had withered her crying into extinction. She wept now, tears falling from both of her eyes. "I know."

Claire and Dawn both looked at their father in shock.

"Dad, you know Noatak is north of the Bering Sea, right?" Claire asked.

"I do now. I haven't looked at my atlas yet. Regardless, it's winter, and I don't think he's going anywhere. The sooner I get started, the better chance I have of getting there before he decides to make a run for it. Regardless, I'm leaving in two days," he said sternly.

Lane got up and refilled his cup, then took a biscuit and folded a strip of bacon inside. Everyone was staring at Lane except for Robert and Beth; they knew he wouldn't back down from finding all of his children. Lane ate his biscuit over a napkin and ignored their eyes on him.

"What do you need from us?" Mary asked, leaning forward from her chair.

"Thanks for asking, but aside from refilling a few water containers, I've got everything I need. I was actually going to leave some weapons with you. Now, what I need to know—and don't leave anything out—is what do you know about the Group?" he asked.

Paul and Mary both stared at each other with faces that betrayed fear.

"You probably didn't notice, but we have a pair of mules out in the barn. Thing is, after D-Day did a plague purge on Poplar Bluff, I started going on scavenging runs. It started by finding pump mechanisms to raid gas stations. Then I actually started raiding the gas stations for fuel. Then one day, I was driving by the frontier museum, and I thought there might be something in there we could use. There was. There were several wagons that had been reproduced from historical specs. Now the problem with that is I didn't have anything to pull them. We didn't have any mules, but I knew who did. We didn't need six wagons," Paul explained.

"Amish or Mennonite?" Lane asked.

Paul smiled. "Mennonite. That's how I got the mules and the information about the Group. The son doesn't practice the culture, and he'd been picking up stories here and there. It might be hearsay, but what I heard, I passed on to Mary and the girls."

"Hearsay is all we have now," Lane told him.

Mary looked at Paul and nodded. He nodded back to her with a shrug.

"Point is, you need to make a bugout for your bugout. I'll help if you let me. There's a place in Tyler, Texas, we've been given an informal invitation to. I'll give you all the necessary information for you to gain entry," Lane told them.

"We aren't getting there in a wagon and Dawn's VW." Mary chuckled.

"No, you're not. You're getting there in my truck," Lane told her.

"What?" Mary asked in surprise.

"There's plenty of gas in the bed right now. It would make me feel a lot better if you all left now," Lane admitted.

"We aren't going anywhere right now. You said you were leaving in two days... We'll give you a decision by then," Paul finished.

"Are you deciding for the girls too?" Lane asked.

Mary bristled at the question but said nothing.

"Let's go check out the lodge," Lane said, standing up.

Everybody went, including Mary and Paul. Mary, Paul, and the girls all rode with him in the truck. The girls made the trip bearable, providing backgrounds to their activities since he'd last spoken to them. It was a much-needed distraction from Mary and Paul's conflicted demeanor. The sixteen miles into the forest was long but scenic. Claire's smartass commentary of "Look, there's another tree" made Lane smirk each time she said it. They passed the gate the first time and had to backtrack to find it. The driveway into the lodge was carefully camouflaged. The entrance was unmanicured dirt with dead weeds overtaking it, returning to nature. If it was springtime, they would never have seen it. Tree limbs and branches hung over the dirt road, blocking not only a clear path but also providing a natural screen from the leaf-strewn paved road beyond. A heavy alloy chain was stretched across the road, blocking access to the gate. Robert came back with bolt cutters but was unable to bite through the link. Robert took over and tried as well, but he, too, couldn't break the barrier. Paul took a turn but met the same result. After they'd given up, Lane took the cutter and walked behind the tree that held the chain. Two seconds later, Lane walked around with a severed padlock and the end of the chain in his hand. With a flick of his wrist, the chain fell to the ground.

"You have to go after the weakest link," Lane said with a smirk.

They all walked the twenty yards to the twelve-foot-high electronic gate. The numbered keypad was enclosed in a protective box. The gate was topped with wrought iron spikes, as was the fence. It was reminiscent of a wealthy Victorian landowner. Beth was front and center this time. "Lane, I need your truck jack."

They all looked at her with puzzled expressions. Lane simply smiled, nodding, and walked away. Lane returned with an eight-ton bottle jack. Lane assumed Beth's intention as she wedged the jack in between the bars and started pumping the jack. Half a minute later, Lane released the jack and removed it from the gap in the bent bars. Beth stuck her body through the gap, starting with her arm, then head, and torso. Once inside, she disappeared out of sight behind a brick column.

"I need a crowbar!" Beth yelled.

Beth was waiting at the gate when Robert returned with the same crowbar he'd protected her with on I-85. He handed it to her through the bars, and she disappeared again. Grinding and *twangs* were audible with Beth's grunts and squeaks, then a *thwack*. And then a click from somewhere inside the brick. Beth appeared and took hold of the gate. With a little effort, the gate started to slide away. They all looked at her expectantly.

"My cousin had her car towed once. It was impounded, and there was a pound of weed in it." She blushed.

They all snickered and returned to the vehicles. The paved driveway was longer than two football fields and circled around a pond that reflected a tall, hand-hewn lodge constructed from local timber. It was impressive. The builder had hired a father and son team from Norway to build the structure from the native hardwoods. They had used pumpkin ash exclusively due to its height and girth. The ironic part was that they'd harvested none of the wood on the property. The roof was covered in jointed metal panels that had been painted green, and six stone chimneys could be seen from its perimeter. Robert stood with his arms crossed and a funny look on his face.

"Uh, Lane?" Robert called out.

"Yeah."

"Isn't this the place on the magazine that was in your house?"

"Huh? Oh yeah! I guess it is. Wait, everyone get in the MRAPs, NOW!" Lane yelled.

Everyone piled in, protesting and asking questions. Lane went to his truck and put on his Desert Eagle. He returned to Ruth's MRAP and climbed the troop ladder; his leg didn't cooperate the way he wanted it to, but he made it to the roof.

"What the fuck, dude?" Grant asked from the .50 saddle. He cocked the charging handle and let it slam home for effect.

Grant disappeared, and Ruth took the saddle. "What's going on?"

"This is an exotic game lodge. A bunch of rich guys had trophy game shipped in from all over the world for other rich guys to shoot. So they brought over impala, nyala, kudu, gemsbok, and predators like jaguars, lions, black bears, and grizzlies." He finished by swiveling and looking around.

"And you were going to tell us when?" Ruth growled.

"If I told you about the critters, would you have come?" he asked her.

Ruth pursed her lips but remained quiet as she dropped down inside.

Lane drove through the open gate and pulled to the side to allow the others to pass. He grabbed the radio and asked Robert to get out.

"We're going hunting. Tell Beth and the girls to go back with Grant." Lane handed Robert his bow case.

Lane dug around in the bed of the truck and pulled out his baby, then took two boxes of ammo and stuck them in his pockets. Lane approached his truck and handed Paul the keys. "I'll see you girls tomorrow. I love you." Mary stepped from the truck and approached Lane as he backed away.

She crossed her arms for warmth and looked at him. "What are you doing? You just got here…the girls just got you back, and now you're going lion and bear hunting?"

"I can't leave these kids here if they aren't safe, and knowing it's something I can control, I'm going to do it." He pulled the magazine from the .30-06 semi-automatic, checking the magazine, then slamming it home again.

"What if—" she started, but Lane interrupted.

"What if one of these animals got loose and attacked Claire while she was feeding the deer yesterday?" Lane quizzed her.

"Lane, this is one of the reasons I couldn't stay married to you. You always have to fix everything. And you always tried to fix everything…everything except us. You didn't try to fix us," she growled in a hushed tone.

"Neither did you," he whispered.

"What?" she growled.

"I said I'm putting my best foot forward. I still have one." He looked her briefly in the eye, then walked away.

Robert hugged Beth; he then whispered something to Grant. Crystal and Blanche waved goodbye, while Ruth looked at him questioningly and raised her hand with a feeble wave. They left an MRAP, and the others all drove back to the B and B. Robert picked up the crowbar and shoved it through the belt of his pants.

"Cover me," Lane said as he ascended the front steps, then turned around and came back.

Robert leveled the AR and scanned the area, looking for anything that might be a threat. Lane looked through the shrubbery on one side, then he looked through the other side. He went back up the steps and started looking for anything that stood out.

He thought he'd found what he was looking for in a basket full of unread newspapers. He picked the basket up and dumped the contents on the porch but found nothing. There was nothing inside or underneath it. Lane scratched his head but continued looking.

Robert saw some movement in the brush, and he put the laser dot of the optic on the brush. At the corner of the porch stood a croquet set, and Lane was immediately drawn to it. He looked through the set carefully and found nothing. He kicked the set, nearly knocking it over, and as it rocked back and forth, a rattle could be heard. Lane picked up a mallet and shook it, nothing, then another and another. Then he picked one, and a rattle sounded from inside. He took the white plastic hammer piece and twisted it until it came free. He tipped it over, and a key fell into his hand. "Bingo!"

"Why are we going inside anyway?" Robert asked.

"We need to know what and how many critters we're hunting," Lane said.

Lane unlocked the door and stepped inside. The entryway wall was decorated with the heads of dozens of animals. At the end stood a grizzly bear that was at least eight feet tall from its three-foot pedestal, making it look monstrous. Lane was startled when Robert shut the door behind him. They walked into a library that was neatly stocked with hundreds of books. Each wall was covered in full bookcases from floor to ceiling with a wheeled ladder to access the higher shelves. Carved mahogany chairs covered in crimson leather sat around a mahogany table where undoubtedly titans of industry drank expensive whiskey, playing poker with stakes high enough to pay off the average person's mortgage.

The next room was a dining room that rivaled anything he'd ever seen in person. There was a masculine motif that screamed power and money, but he ignored it and moved to the kitchen. The kitchen would have made Gordon Ramsay blush with every conceivable pot, pan, and cooking device either hanging from a suspended rack over a prep table or sitting on a separate station or counter. He gave it a second look, then moved on. He found what he was looking for in an office that was equally furnished in money.

A picture board hung from the wall that was covered in pictures of game animals. Some of them had red X's struck through them, which he assumed meant a hunter had already sent them to taxidermy. He frowned when he found four pictures that did not have

X's struck through them. Two were male leopards, one was a male black bear, and last but not least was one female grizzly.

Robert stepped behind him, looking over his shoulder. Lane pointed with his index finger at each picture. He then directed his attention to an aerial map of the property. The property was divided into sections notated by number zones, with a circle around the lodge and "1" in the middle. There were eight zones, and three of the zones were shaded with red. Lane assumed these were the predator zones. He was happy to see that lines were drawn around the three predator zones; the legend notated it was a fence.

"We're going to hit these one at a time. All of them, because I don't believe for a second that predators are going to stay in their enclosures when food runs out. To be honest, I'm just hoping there were enough graze animals to keep them fed. Maybe some deer are out there as well. Let's get started. Get that bow put together," Lane said as he turned to Robert and put his rifle over his shoulder.

Lane and Robert stepped into enclosure three. The area covered 125 acres that was supposed to be a habitat for nothing but impala. Snow was coming in flurries but not enough to accumulate. Robert carried his bow with an arrow knocked in one hand and his pistol in the other. Lane held his rifle at the ready and pushed carefully between two cedar trees. As he emerged, two impala pawed in the turf, looking for anything that wasn't dead grass. Lane backed into the trees and moved to the east, motioning for Robert to follow. The wind kept their scent downwind, and the impala didn't take notice. They moved east until they found the fence. Robert put his bow down and holstered his pistol. He planted his foot into a square of the fence and started climbing. He got to the top and fished binocs out of his coat pocket. He stayed up there for nearly fifteen minutes, then finally climbed down.

"There's a pond about three hundred yards northeast. There's a dead impala hanging off a hardwood limb. Sitting above that limb are two large cats," Robert said proudly.

"Eagle Scout," Lane mumbled.

The impala now took notice, scampering away as Lane and Robert stalked their way toward the area that Robert had spotted.

The slow-growing cedar trees sparsely dotted the landscape as they continued toward their goal. Lane pointed at a pile of sun-bleached bones. "They've been here a while."

The white oak stood alone in the center of a two-acre field. Robert handed him the binocs. Starski and Hutch rested on limbs hanging over the dead impala. Each of the predators was given names for who knows what reason. Neither leopard could be distinguished as unique from their vantage point at what Lane's quick math discerned as maybe sixty yards. The wind was in their favor, and neither Starski nor Hutch seemed concerned about the flurries or aware of them.

"Can you make that shot and possibly get another off before the other gets wise?" Lane asked Robert in a whisper.

"I can get one, but there's no guarantee that I can get them both."

"Okay, start with the top, go for the shoulder," Lane told him.

Robert removed an arrow from the attached quiver and stuck one of them lightly in the dirt. He eyed the top leopard. He drew the arrow back until his knuckles rested against his cheek. He lined up the arrow tip with his eye until the shaft disappeared from his line of sight. He aimed the tip a few inches above the leopard's spine. It'd been over a year since he'd touched a bow, and that was just sending a few arrows into one of his father's buck targets. He'd done okay from forty yards, but one of his arrows sailed over the target into the neighbor's storage shed. He remembered that arrow now and steeled his nerves. He inhaled and exhaled slowly, then let his fingertips peel off the string. The rubber silencer quivered violently as the string returned to vertical, then went still.

The four-bladed hunting tip struck the leopard behind his shoulder. The fight-or-flight instinct played some part in the leopard falling from the tree, but the impact caused the hunting tip to inflict fatal damage with the impact to the ground. The other leopard stared at his kinsman lying on the ground, writhing in death throes. He leaped to the limb beneath him, sniffed his next meal, then agilely landed next to his hunting companion as he took his last breath. That's when Robert's second arrow struck him in the neck. The leop-

ard ran fifty yards away before he, too, fell to the ground and suc-
cumbed to his wound.

Twenty minutes later, both leopards were hanging by their
feet from the limb where the impala was still wedged between thick
branches.

"What now?" Robert asked.

"Now we see if we can find the black bear. Let's go kill Putin,"
Lane said.

"You're kidding me, right? They named the bear Putin?" he
asked incredulously.

"The notes on the animal board said he was a cunning predator
and killed the other black bear in his enclosure. So I guess it fits. The
next habitat is his," Lane said, walking to the north.

Lane took a ring of keys, fished through them until he found
the right one, and let them both in. This enclosure was subtly different. Pine trees were in abundance here, and in the spring, apple
trees and blackberry thickets would bloom. A stream cut through
the habitat, which was nothing more than a trickle at the moment.
The stream ran into a small pool that was little more than a mud
puddle but would be noticeably bigger when the stream grew. The
puddle had all the signs of being wallowed by a large animal. The
card said that Putin's enclosure was ninety-five acres. It took over
an hour before they found Putin's den. Three oak trees stood within
twenty feet of each other. At the center, the largest tree towered over
the other two by at least thirty feet. At its base, a den had been dug.
There was nothing significant about it. The hole was large enough
that if Lane had hugged Robert, they could have dropped through
the hole without touching the sides. Robert put his flashlight into the
hole and illuminated nothing but the walls and the darkness beyond.

"Start a fire but keep an eye on the hole," Lane said as he walked
over to a pine grove.

He took out his multitool and found plenty of trees that had
Putin's claw marks gouged deep in their trunks. The hardened pine
sap broke off in chunks and flakes, all of which he deposited in his
coat pocket. A few minutes later, he was sitting by the fire and breaking open an MRE. He opened the foil drink powder pouch that dou-

bled as a cup. Fruit punch with electrolytes was labeled on the side. He dropped the pine sap into the pouch and set it by the fire. Lane squatted on the ground and started plucking brown grass in handfuls until he had a loose pile the size of a football. He returned to the fire, picked up the foil pouch with the pliers of his multitool, and used a twig to stir the contents until it was a gooey red. He set the pouch on the ground and slowly started stuffing the dried grass inside. The sap sports drink oozed over the side as the grass became impacted.

"I don't know if this is going to work. Hell, I don't even know if the bear is in there. Hopefully, this will put out enough smoke to coax him out, but we need to find something to block the hole." They scoured the area until they finally settled on rocks. The first few attempts ended in the rocks falling into the hole and beyond retrieval. The next attempt, they used deadfall to build a support and stacked the rocks on them. They scooped dirt with their hands to fill in the cracks and left a hole big enough to get the smoke bomb through.

Lane cut the pouch down the side and held his lighter to it. The sap served as an accelerant, and the grass wick caught, and soon the foil was a small blaze in his hand. After several attempts, he blew out the blaze, and a small pillar of smoke curled into the air. He tossed the bomb as far into the hole as he could, then they placed another rock over the hole and scooped more dirt into the cracks.

They backed away from the hole and readied themselves. Lane handed Robert his baby and unslung his M4. Five minutes turned into ten, and nothing happened. Lane lit a cigarette in frustration and exhaled into the sky.

"Do you think the bear is down there or not?" Robert asked, fanning cigarette smoke away from his face.

"I'm starting to think no. We better pack it in and make use of the daylight," Lane confessed, standing up.

They turned and started making their way to the next enclosure when a garbled moan emanated from beneath the pile of stone and dirt. Lane and Robert stood transfixed as the ursine phoenix rose from the proverbial ashes. Putin's paws made brief appearances, swatting through the branches and stones. Putin clawed his way through the den's barrier and emerged, sneezing and shaking his head. Lane took his baby from Robert and leveled it at Putin. One shot into his ear collapsed the large animal.

Lane felt remorse in the killing but squashed his own guilt, thinking Robert was probably feeling the same. They both stared at the bear as blood pooled and soaked the earth around his head. Lane nudged the animal with his boot but got no response.

"We're losing daylight," Robert said.

"Let's go find BB," Lane replied.

"BB?" Robert asked.

"Yeah, BB. Short for Big Bear."

The next two enclosures they passed through contained ibex, elk, and one very cantankerous moose with a rack that was as wide as Dawn's Beetle. After dodging through trees to avoid the moose, they found themselves at enclosure eight. BB's habitat was 175 acres, and all signs pointed to BB being very much awake and not in hibernation. Bleached bones and fresh deer kills were in abundance. The fresh kills gave evidence that BB didn't leave anything left on the plate. Nearly every carcass's cavity was emptied of organs, and the legs were cleaned to the bone. In many cases, those bones were crunched to splinters to eat the marrow as well. The terrain changed from flat to a small collection of hills where the same stream they'd seen earlier flowed through. They followed the stream and found a set of footprints that swallowed his boot print when he stepped in one. The hill grew steeper until they came upon a clearing. At the end of the clearing, a cliff had been carved by erosion into the hillside, exposing an overhang with a hollow beneath it. The hollow had been expanded by BB; it had packed dirt surrounding it where the excavated soil had been thrown. The natural berm shielded the hollow and what was inside. Lane pointed to an oak and ash tree that stood close to each other. Robert hoisted Lane onto an ash limb and pushed him until he was straddling it. Once Lane had ascended two more limbs, he once again straddled the limb with his back resting against the trunk. Robert took a leap, swung himself into the oak, and climbed upward until he was almost even with Lane. They both sat there quietly for thirty minutes before Lane removed his open MRE and took out a pack of crackers and a pouch of peanut butter. He squirted a liberal amount of peanut butter on a cracker, smashed another cracker on top, then popped it in his mouth. Robert took Lane's example and pulled his MRE from his pack and rummaged through it until another familiar pack of Skittles made an appearance. Lane continued with crackers, only this time, he threw a large unbroken four-piece cracker with peanut butter on it toward the hollow.

Lane looked at his watch. It was 4:44, and the sun was well on its way to setting. The flurries picked up again but still didn't contain enough strength or volume to cover the ground. Robert copied Lane and threw another square of peanut butter cracker near the other. Lane and Robert looked at each other and read each other's minds. They slit open the remaining packets and threw them frisbee style in the same direction as the crackers. Lane tore open his Skittle pack and threw three handfuls across the clearing, much to Robert's dismay. He frowned at Lane, and Lane mouthed, "Sorry."

BB didn't crawl out of the hollow as expected but walked in following the same path that Lane and Robert had, nose to the ground, head swiveling right to left. The foreign smells led BB to the snacks that had been littered about. BB sucked the Skittles off the ground and found the other morsels. When BB ate the peanut butter cracker, her nose went to the air, sniffing with curiosity. While the nose was still in the air, Robert shifted on the limb, and BB noticed.

BB was in the 900-lb range and was around seven feet tall standing up. Robert's oak tree wasn't mature and began to sway. He clung to the tree tightly, and the swaying became more violent as BB started slamming paws against the trunk over and over. The bear roared angrily at Robert being out of reach. The tree's roots began to weaken and, in turn, weakened the stability of other roots; it was a domino effect.

The concussion of the Desert Eagle was deafening. The first round sailed past BB's snout; the second and third round hit BB behind the shoulder and infuriated the angry bear further. The wounds caused her to stagger, but she remained upright. BB now leaned against the tree with her weight because slamming against the trunk was no longer needed. The tree had reached the decisive moment that staying upright was no longer possible. Robert still clung tightly, literally hanging on for dear life.

The fourth and fifth rounds hit BB in the neck, causing the monstrous beast to fall on its front paws. A labored growl escaped her gigantic, gaping maw. The sixth and seventh rounds struck BB behind the shoulder, and the front legs collapsed. Heavy breaths sent puffs of dust into curling plumes that almost immediately fell to the ground. The oak tree groaned, and the root ball seemed to pop like a cork when it came loose from the earth. The tree fell in slow motion, allowing Robert to ride it to the ground, hopping off and sending three .45 rounds from his Sig Sauer into BB's head, causing the rear legs to splay out.

Lane fell to the ground from the lowest limb in a heap, causing his prosthetic to rip free and making Lane yell in agony. Despite his pain, he removed the empty magazine and slammed home a fresh one. Robert walked to BB and nudged the bloodied head with his barrel, and nothing happened.

Satisfied he wouldn't be eaten like a gingerbread man, Lane removed his pants. His prosthetic wasn't broken, but the impact and the strap's elasticity simply allowed his stump to slip free. His stump throbbed, but the skin wasn't broken and would be sore and swollen for several days. He reattached the leg and put his pants back on.

"You okay?" Robert asked.

"Yep, I'll be fine. Are you okay?"

"Other than riding a tree to the ground, I'm good," Robert replied.

"Let's pack up and get out of here. I'm hungry and need some rest."

Robert held out his hand to Lane and helped him to his feet. Lane stood and worked his stump into a comfortable position. He shrugged off his pack and dug out his headlamp, switching it on. Robert fished his out of his coat pocket and did the same. They secured their packs and made to leave, their lights sweeping back and forth with the subtlest of head movements.

Before they could take their first steps, an alien sound could be heard. Lane and Robert looked at each other. Both of their ears were still ringing from the gunfire. Comically, they both stuck their fingers in their ears and wriggled them back and forth. The sound came again; it was reminiscent of whimpering. They spun in circles, trying to zero in on where the sound was originating from. Robert walked up to the soil berm and gazed down. A ball moved in the darkness, then gradually broke apart into three individual balls of dark fur. BB was a mother.

The cubs were no bigger than footballs, and they were crying for their mother.

"What do we do now?" Robert asked, with his hands on his hips.

Lane looked at Robert with a dark look that he interpreted as euthanasia.

"I'm not killing babies, no matter the species," Robert said, huffing.

"Turn around," Lane ordered. Robert looked at Lane with anger in his eyes, and he stared back at him. Finally, Lane spun Robert around by the shoulder and started stuffing the contents of his pack into his own. Once he emptied his pack, Lane limped down the hollow and started placing the cubs in his pack with a very gentle hand.

Once they'd made it back to the lodge, they went inside and went to the rear of the interior. After a brief search, they found the mudroom that the hunters used. Lane went upstairs and found what he was looking for. He returned and placed two polar bear rugs on the floor. Robert went outside and returned with a bowl of water, placing it inside the mudroom, then shutting the door behind him.

Lane pulled in front of the B and B and shut off the engine. It only took seconds before everyone was outside. Claire and Dawn beat Beth and the other girls to give hugs. Beth immediately wrapped her arms around Robert's neck once he was free. All three girls pulled away in unison, complaining about their smell. Lane noticed that Ruth was leaning against the baluster with her hands in her pockets, smiling at him warmly. He winked at her, and she winked back.

Lane and Robert gave them the play-by-play and explained that there were three new mouths that needed to be fed and that they should all leave and head back to the lodge. They all got in the vehicles, Dawn and Claire included, as they insisted on having to see the bear cubs and spend time with their father. The girls said goodbye to their mother and stepfather and climbed in Lane's truck. Mary and Paul said they would drop by the next day, as their curiosity had gotten the better of them with the lodge.

When they all pulled in front of the lodge, they were still on edge, but Robert and Lane reassured them that the predators were dead. What lanterns they possessed were lit, and they all went inside and started selecting rooms. The lodge was vast, and each person was able to have a room to themselves. The lodge was chilly, but it was well-insulated and kept the inside somewhere in the fifty-degree range by Lane's figuring. He rummaged through the closet and found two thick quilts. He placed the quilts on top of a down comforter and undressed. He took out his baby wipes pack and set to cleaning himself again. It was only after he'd accumulated a pile of used wipes that he noticed an odor wafting up to his nose. He scooped up the wipes and balled them into a waste basket in the bathroom. Lane removed his leg and crawled under the covers; he was asleep within seconds.

DECEMBER 30, 2024

WHEN LANE WOKE, THE LUMINESCENT DIAL ON his watch read 5:08. Being under all the blankets kept him warm all night, and when he pulled them back, his naked skin erupted with gooseflesh. He sat up and massaged his stump; as predicted, it was slightly swollen. Several minutes passed before his massage therapy ended, and he replaced his leg.

He dressed, went outside, and removed a few supplies from the trailer. He went to the kitchen and removed a large cake pan from a cabinet. Tipping the twenty-liter container, he spooned in powdered milk and whisked the mixture until it was viscous. He went into the dining room, removed a candle from the table, and returned to the kitchen. He lit the candle, wedged it in the sink drain, and then positioned the cake pan over the flame. He went back to the dining room and lit a fire in the oversized fireplace. Moments later, the percolator was sitting by the fire warming as Lane exhaled cigarette smoke into the chimney flue.

When he'd finished the cigarette, he returned to the kitchen again. The concoction of powdered milk was warm to the touch. He stirred the contents and took the pan to the mudroom. The cubs were in a deep sleep and didn't stir when he opened the door. He placed the pan on the floor and dipped his finger in the thick milk, touching it to the cub's lips. The nose quivered, then the tongue shot out and licked its lips. He repeated the action until each cub had tasted the milk, and they woke to seek out the source. As Lane stepped out of the mudroom, each cub had its muzzle buried in the pan, lapping away with ferocity.

Lane pulled a chair away from the dining room table, sat down with his road atlas, and sipped his coffee. Noatak was a spot on the map that didn't offer a lot of background information beyond being very remote. It sat next to a chain of tributaries that fed Noatak River, bordering Noatak National Preserve, which was well over six hundred square miles. Dawn had mentioned that Blake and Madison were camped between low-lying mountains, thirty-five miles from the little village that consisted of an airport, a church, a tribal store, and one bar. He was eyeballing the general area when Grant walked in.

"Are you leaving tomorrow?" Grant asked him.

"Yes, I am," he answered simply.

"I want to go."

"No, I need you here. Somebody has to watch over the girls. I would prefer it if you didn't get either of them pregnant," he said seriously.

Grant stared back at him, dumbfounded. He started to speak but decided against it when he heard scratching coming from the mudroom.

"That's the other thing. I can't swear to it, but those cubs are black bear–grizzly hybrids, and bears are unpredictable at the best of times. I can't take them with me, and I'm not enough of a monster to kill them. Raise them and train them as best you can. Keep them safe and train them until you can't," he said, closing the atlas and standing up.

Crystal and Blanche came downstairs, and Blanche poured herself a cup of coffee and sat by the fire on the hearth. Dawn and Claire could be heard from the mudroom making baby sounds and were most likely on the floor of the mudroom playing with the cubs. Beth appeared, tying her hair in a ponytail, and Robert was close behind her, tucking his shirt in. Grant noticed and smirked at his brother.

A little while later, Crystal and Beth came in carrying plates of pork chops, eggs, drop biscuits, and powdered milk mixed with chocolate. The chocolate puzzled Lane; he didn't remember where they'd gotten it.

"Dad, can't you wait until warmer weather to go after Blake?" Claire asked him.

"Blake's smart. I don't see him starting a transcontinental journey in the middle of winter. The sooner I leave, the better chance I have of finding him in place. And I need to find him in place before he decides to go through Canada," he explained.

"Dad, can't you wait until Blake just comes home?" Dawn asked, her brow furrowed in worry.

"What if he meets the Group between now and then?" he asked her. Dawn stared at her lap in response.

Breakfast was finished, and slowly everyone emptied the table.

Lane stood by his truck and stared at the empty bed. Everything that had been loaded in Flowery Branch was now lying on the pavement, except for the spare tires and the gas cans. Lane set about divvying up supplies that would keep two to three people alive for two months. He then set aside three M4s and his Desert Eagle and cleaned them. Two hours later, he'd loaded the truck and sat on the tailgate contemplating the trip. Kirk and Spock ran beneath a row of box hedges and spooked a squirrel into flight. Grant strolled behind them and allowed the pups an opportunity to expel their morning zoomies.

Claire and Dawn walked backward into view from the side of the lodge. "Come on, Moe, Larry, Curly!"

The three cubs tumbled over each other following the girls. The small animals were a dramatic contrast in size to the super-predators they would someday become. The pups came running up to the three newly named cubs and slid to a stop, growling and barking. The stooges squirmed their way until they were hidden behind the girls' legs. Grant picked up the pups, one under each arm. As Lane studied the comedy, Mary and Paul pulled up in Claire's beetle. Mary joined the girls while Paul walked up to him with a picnic basket. He set the basket on the tailgate and sat beside Lane.

"You're really going, aren't you?" Paul asked.

"Yes, Paul. I'm going. Blake's out there. And I will be damned if I let him fall prey to this Group. My son will not be target practice for a bunch of lowlife fucktards," he said flatly.

Mary walked up to them, took something out of her coat pocket, and handed it to Lane. Lane took it and spread the items out like playing cards. They were wallet photos of Blake.

"Thought they might come in handy," she said, crossing her arms.

Lane looked at the picture. Blake was leaning against a barn door. His hair was parted to the side, the style reminding him of the type '20s and '30s silent movie actors used to wear. His smile was very devil-may-care, and he looked as though he had a secret that no one else knew. The picture reminded him of his mother's father. He tucked the pictures into his coat pocket and looked off into the distance as tears threatened the corners of his eyes.

"Lane, did you know that Noatak is above the Artic Circle?" Mary asked him.

"Yes, and our son is there," he answered bluntly.

Paul hopped off the tailgate and walked to the lodge. "I'm going to check out the inside."

"God bless you, you have the best intentions of anyone I've ever known. You're fifty-four years old with one leg, and it's been a long time since you jumped out of planes for a living. Do you really think you can make it up there? You're looking at over three thousand miles without the benefit of gas stations, Jiffy Lubes, hotels, or McDonald's. What if your truck breaks down?" she asked.

"Then I'll fix it, or I'll find another truck. If I can't find a truck, I'll walk. Whatever I have to do, I'm going to find Blake and bring him home," he said, looking her in the eye.

"It's too much for one man, Lane. You can't do this on your own," she told him.

"He's not doing it alone."

Robert and Beth stood on the porch with their packs slung over their shoulders. Beth held an M4, and Robert was holding his bow case and the SCAR Grant had been carrying. Beth walked down the steps, wrapped her arms around Lane, and hugged him. "Where you go, we go."

Lane looked at Robert, who just shrugged. "What she said." Robert smiled and walked down the steps to join them.

"Will you drop in on Grant and the girls and keep an eye on them?" he asked, turning to Mary.

"You're sure about this?" Mary asked.

"Yes, I'm positive. Although I'd prefer these two stay behind. I'm pretty sure they'd just follow me if I left without them." Robert and Beth nodded their heads in unison like little toy bobbleheads.

"I'm going too," Ruth said with an impish smile, standing in the doorway.

"I'm guessing it wouldn't do any good to say no?" Everyone looked at Ruth when Lane asked.

"Nope," she answered and walked back inside.

"Okay, change of plans. We're taking Ruth's MRAP. I'll leave the truck for you and Paul," he said, tossing the keys to Mary.

"You're shitting me, right?" Mary asked.

"No, I'm not. We'll be better off with the armor and firepower. I just need to remove the governor. Look, if you all head for Texas, you can take the trailer and hook up a horse trailer to the MRAP. Grant can rig a piggyback for the diesel trailer. One other thing, you'll need to take these with you." Lane went to the back of the truck and let down the tailgate.

He showed Mary the bank bags and told her how they'd obtained the gold and silver. He took out three hundred dollars in face value quarters and dimes, two hundred ounces of silver rounds, and thirty ounces of gold. He placed it all in the bottom of a field triage bag and put it in the MRAP. He tasked Robert with repacking their supplies in the MRAP while he busied himself removing the governor. He soon found that removing a physical governor was a fictional task. He located the field manual locked in a compartment beneath the driver's seat and discovered the governor was a programming task that he was ill-equipped for. He handed the manual to Beth and asked her to see what she could find. He helped Robert finish loading, and Beth hopped inside the MRAP and shut the hatch behind her.

"The kids are all going to stay at the house. We'll figure out what to do with the bears. I can't just leave three teenagers to fend for themselves," she told him.

213

"I'll be right back," Lane said, suddenly trotting to the passenger door and grabbing a package from the glovebox, then went inside.

Lane found Grant and tapped him on the shoulder. "Follow me."

He and Grant exited the lodge through the mudroom and found themselves on a patio furnished with Adirondack chairs and low-constructed side tables. "Give me the weed," he said, turning to him.

"Come on, man, I haven't smoked since I was home," he pleaded with a pout on his face.

"You and the girls are going back to my ex's house," he explained.

"In that case…" Grant eagerly fished out a fake Coca-Cola can. It was a clever device made just like a traditional soda can with a twist-off top. He handed the can to Lane enthusiastically and turned to leave.

"Wait. I need you to do something else. There are two leopards hanging from a tree and a dead grizzly all out in the enclosures. They need to be buried. Please take care of that after we leave. I don't want this place getting overrun by coyotes. Their enclosures are notated on a map in the office. Look, we're coming back. I'll do my best to keep your brother alive. You do me a favor and protect my daughters and everyone else." He withdrew a package and handed it to Grant.

Grant opened the package and emptied the contents on a table. "It's two ham radios. The instruction manual should be read as soon as possible. There are five frequencies I wrote on the back of each radio. Cycle through them until you're familiar with the range. They're fully charged, there's a car charger adapter, and that black bundle is a solar blanket charger. If I can manage the MRAP radios, my call sign is Peter Pan. The call signs for those radios are Wendy and Tinker Bell. There's a list of authenticator codes I wrote in the instruction manual. Cross the codes off as we use them, use them in sequence. There should be enough codes there for three months. Don't use the numbers after the hyphens in authenticating. If we run out of the codes, that's when the hyphen numbers come in. The hyphenated numbers end in a random sequence. Just start wherever 1, 2, 3, et cetera is at the end, and that will give another three months of authenticators. I'll call you at midnight each night and give you an update. After authenticators, I'll provide a number. That number will be how far away we are. TA means 'To Alaska,' as in we're still making our way there. FA means 'From Alaska,' which means we're leaving and headed back, and you'll get a number again to let you know how close we are. HB means 'Have Blake.' Of course, that means we have him, a mission success. It's all in the manual along with other codes. If you guys bug out and leave, the only thing you need to do is keep repeating on each frequency, 'Valkyrie.' It means I'll turn on the radio for five minutes every day just to listen at noon and then at six. If there are any problems and you need a response, use the codes." He finished by packing everything away again and handing the package to Grant.

"When are you leaving?" Grant asked.

"Tomorrow morning, first light," he said, extending his hand to Grant for a handshake.

Grant took his hand and shook it properly, three slow pumps, then let it go, letting his hand fall back into his pocket. Kirk and Spock trotted up beside his ankle and stared up at him, then at Lane, cocking their heads to the side in unison. Spock issued a bark, and Kirk barked back. If it had been translated into English, it probably would have been something like, "Kirk, do you know what the fuck is going on?"

"Nah, bruh, but it seems tense. Let's go over there where those furry things were that looked like us, but they aren't like us…I want to smell where they were."

They both watched the pups run to where the cubs had answered nature's call and skid to a stop to do what all dogs do, smell with unbridled ferocity.

"Keep up the work on the pups. You're doing a good job," Lane told him and turned to walk back inside.

Lane spent the majority of his time in the library with Dawn and Claire. They were making small talk and catching their father up on lost time. They found a Monopoly game, and the three played by themselves. It was the cheating edition, and soon they were all either cheating or getting caught cheating. When that wasn't available, they were accusing each other of cheating. The game wound down, and while a late dinner was being prepared, Lane snuggled up with his daughters on the floor in front of the fire. He reveled in the contact with two of the three people in the world who loved him unconditionally.

Mary and Paul were sitting at the table, looking through Lane's atlas, pointing at spots on the map, and conversing with each other about trips they'd taken over the years when Grant helped Crystal put food on the table. They all crowded around the table and helped themselves to chili made with the last of the ground beef and a huge pan of cornbread. It was a last-minute discovery made from a huge tin of cornmeal found in the pantry. The mood was made jovial by Dawn and Claire cracking jokes; they were soon joined by Blanche and Crystal with a similar sense of humor that only sisters share. Robert decided that Grant was laughing entirely too hard and told everyone about the time he'd mooned the student body at a pep rally, then fell flat on his face at half-court when he ran away. Robert burst out laughing when Grant screwed up his face in embarrassment. Grant, in turn, told the story of when Robert had gotten drunk and fallen down the side of Bays Mountain. The fall was over two hundred feet down a steep grade. He'd bounced off rocks and trees and had free-fallen close to forty feet into a shallow stream before he stood up and walked away drenched and dripping without a scratch or a bruise.

Ruth stared at Lane and read a coldness behind his laughter; it was as if he was steeling himself for the task at hand. No one else read it in him except for maybe Mary. She'd been married to the man and lived with the soldier. There are no soldiers without darkness inside them; maybe that's why they were no longer together. All she knew was the strength he possessed outweighed the darkness in Mary's eyes.

The laughter was the medicine they all needed. All of the girls cleared the table, save for Mary. Mary excused herself and returned shortly carrying a bottle of Glenfiddich twenty-six-year-old Grande Couronne single malt scotch. In her other hand, she carried four whiskey tumblers. She set the glasses on the table and poured a generous portion in each.

Lane picked his glass up and sniffed the pungent, smoky aroma.

"To Blake, may you bring him and yourselves home safe and fast," Paul said, sipping the expensive liquor.

"Bring our son home," Mary added.

Lane lifted his glass and started to speak, but Ruth cut him off. "He will," she said, then took the liquor in her glass in one gulp. Lane looked at her and replied by swallowing his own scotch and setting the glass on the table with deliberation.

NEW YEAR'S EVE
DECEMBER 31, 2024

EVERYONE TOOK ADVANTAGE OF THE NUMEROUS ROOMS the night before and discovered the next morning that motion sensors had activated a bank of batteries charged by solar panels on the roof of the lodge. Somewhere in the lodge, an automated system turned on the hot water heaters. The tank had to refill several times, but everyone was able to get a hot shower.

They all stood on the front porch of the lodge and exchanged goodbyes that were long enough to summon tears. Dawn and Claire clung to Lane as if they would never see him again, and in this new world, it was a harsh possibility. Lane kissed and hugged them both and promised to bring their brother home.

Mary stepped up to Lane and stood on her tiptoes to hug him around the neck. She kissed him on the cheek and whispered to him, "Bring Squishy home." She released him and wiped tears from her face. Paul handed Mary a bag, and she gave it to Lane. He opened the bag and smiled; it was his old travel coffee maker with his Eighty-Second Airborne insulated mug.

Claire and Blanche hugged Robert a little longer than Beth liked, but she said nothing. Robert gave cursory hugs to Dawn and Claire, then hugged Mary briefly. He asked her to keep an eye on Grant, and she assured him that she and Paul both would. Robert pulled his brother aside and walked him back inside.

He handed his younger brother a small paper bag. "Stay out of trouble, and *only* use these if you find yourself without a choice. I'm not endorsing or encouraging you to do anything."

"Geez, why all the big words?" he asked, then looked in the bag. Inside the bag were close to three dozen condoms.

"I'm being serious. This new world isn't ready for babies," Robert told him, then embraced him in a tight hug. "Keep it in your pants," he whispered in his ear, then surprised him by suplexing him over his shoulder and onto the floor. "Be ready for anything."

FEBRUARY 19, 2024

BETH TUGGED AT ROBERT'S SLEEVE TO FOLLOW her. Hours earlier, they had entered the city limits of Hugo, Colorado. It had been a struggle getting out of Missouri and through Kansas. Robert winced at the jostling; the previous day, he'd been grazed by a bullet on the shoulder. After they dispatched the gang that called themselves the Plains Kings, he'd talked Ruth through stitching him up. Since their brutal activities, Lane had parked their MRAP inside a highway salt warehouse and secured the sliding metal door with a padlock. The added security measure wasn't really necessary. On the way into town, a massive grave had been dug by the roadside that was filled with what looked like the entire town's population. The bodies had been hastily buried, and the various flocks of carrion birds were still dining.

They'd located an inn conveniently located across the street. Lane and Ruth carried their packs and went inside a room where they could see the Roadworks building. Beth opened the door with the key she'd taken from the clerk's desk drawer. Inside were two full-sized beds covered with generic blue comforters that matched the decor of the room. Beth removed a pack of baby wipes and her headlamp, then disappeared inside the bathroom.

"I'm going to clean up too. Don't come out until I say so," Robert announced. Quickly, he stripped to his birthday suit, literally. He'd noticed the date on his watch; he turned twenty-three today. He mimicked Beth, removed a pack of baby wipes, and quickly but thoroughly wiped himself clean from his toes to his nose. He removed a less-than-fresh pair of boxer briefs and a Grunt Style T-shirt with a red, white, and blue skull on the front. "Okay, I'm done," he called out, satisfied that he was a little fresher.

He and Beth had gotten closer and were now comfortable enough with each other to routinely sleep with each other in their underwear. Nothing sexual had happened yet, but the tension was always there. He had remained a gentleman and controlled the urges that plagued him nearly every second of the day. It was okay to him though; he could control himself. It wasn't like sixteen anymore. Their room had the same view as Lane and Ruth's. He peered through the curtains, causing a small cloud of dust to fall. There was nothing to see. He sat on the bed and opened the nightstand drawer. He removed a pamphlet advertising local restaurants and bars; it was four pages in all. He returned the pamphlet, closed his eyes, and gingerly touched his wounded shoulder. He heard the bathroom door open, then felt the bed move. He turned to look at the girl he was in love with.

"Happy birthday," Beth said in a sultry voice.

Robert went rigid as he took in her attire. He had no idea where she'd gotten it, but he was thankful that she had. She now wore a white lace bra and panties. Dark patches were visible in the places that drew a man's attention. She noticed his lingering eyes and inched closer until she could feel his warm breath on her breasts. His heart rate was climbing, as was his breathing. She knew how he'd restrained himself for so long, and today she was going to be his birthday present. She gently reached down and pulled his T-shirt over his head. This act resulted in him finally touching her and allowing his hands to explore her body. Then, in an explosion of carnal desire, they were naked and only aware of each other. The rest of the world faded away as minutes turned into hours.

Lane's chubby appearance was nearly gone now, save for the perpetual jelly roll that lingered at his waistline. Ironically, he, too, was using his headlamp to clean himself up. His gunshot wound was still pink, but his shoulder no longer hurt when he used it. When he emerged, Ruth was lying on her side wearing nothing but his T-shirt. He sat on the bed, removed his leg, then set it by the nightstand and rolled onto his back, letting out a sigh of relief. The adrenaline fatigue from the fight seemed to be rebuilding his combat stamina, but he was tired, and after a few deep breaths, he fell asleep.

When he woke, it was still light out, but the sun was starting to set. He rose and leaned against the headboard. He took a cigarette from his pack, then smirked at the No Smoking sign that was placarded on the opposite wall. After the third puff, a small hand reached over and took it from him. A single puff later, it was returned. Ruth rolled from the bed and went to the window. Seeing nothing, she disappeared into the bathroom to relieve herself. She emerged, standing in the doorway, watching Lane smoke. After a few seconds passed, she walked over to him and removed the T-shirt, letting it fall to the floor, revealing that she was completely naked. She climbed onto Lane's lap as he crushed out the cigarette on the surface of the nightstand.

It had been years since he'd been with a woman, but he was positive he still knew how to do it.

FEBRUARY 20, 2024

THE INN HAD A FIREPIT FILLED WITH lava rocks in the outside courtyard. Luckily, there was still some propane beneath the pit that immediately caught flame as soon as Beth stuck a lighter to the rocks. She started the percolator to warm as Robert removed the lid of a canned ham that he'd found underneath a cashier's counter inside a ransacked convenience store. She smiled to herself as he woke, smiling, and could not erase it from his face. He set the ham near the fire to warm and removed a stack of cloth-covered cornbread cakes they'd made a few days ago.

Beth walked by him and swatted him on the ass. He immediately turned to her as if he was expecting a replay of the previous night. She winked at him and sat in an all-weather plastic chair. While they waited for the breakfast to warm, they whispered about their encounter and remarked on how much they enjoyed this thing or that thing.

When Lane and Ruth joined them, they looked refreshed. Ruth noticed Beth staring at her and blushed bright red. So, like all girls, they made an excuse to look for something and exchanged girl talk. Lane noticed the stupid grin on Robert's face, to which he immediately looked away, rolling his eyes. He knew exactly what had transpired the previous evening. Deep inside the hotel lobby, he could hear the girls giggling, and that confirmed it.

When the ladies returned, Beth gave him a shit-eating grin that made him immediately blush, causing his Irish complexion to look clownish.

Beth removed the padlock, and they were soon back on the road heading to Denver. They planned to take I-25 into Wyoming, then take I-90 into Montana, and that would take them all the way to Washington. Once inside Washington, I-5 would take them into Canada.

Compared to everywhere else, Denver seemed to be thriving. There were hundreds of people here, and it unnerved them all. They were stopped at a roadblock almost immediately once they entered the city limits, which mainly consisted of Humvees parked bumper to bumper. A master sergeant approached them with caution. Lane immediately presented the pass that Captain Wallace had given him. The senior NCO took it and went to a radio to verify its authenticity. He seemed disappointed when he handed it back to him and motioned for two Humvees to back away and clear the road. As they passed through, he spied gangland markings in spray paint underneath an overpass. In flamboyant letters, it read Uno Raza.

As they made their way out of Denver, he stopped quickly and exchanged positions with Robert. Taking one of the rear seats, Lane took out the road atlas and began examining it.

"What are you doing?" Ruth asked.

"Looking for plan Bs and Cs," he answered.

They saw more and more signs for Uno Raza but surprisingly no personnel to go with them. They stopped in Casper three hours after leaving Denver to scavenge for fuel. They pulled into a truck stop that catered almost exclusively to the trucking industry but had installed a few gasoline pumps for the wayward travelers. There was a service bay at the far end, and Robert expertly turned in front of it and backed in. They all grabbed their weapons and packs and got out. They covered the one hundred yards between them and the main building and discovered it was padlocked from the inside. They walked the perimeter of the building, all taking turns rapping on the window front with their knuckles, but no one appeared.

Convinced nobody was home, Lane took a metal umbrella stand that was sitting by the entrance and smashed a side entrance door. It took four strikes for him to make a hole big enough that he could use the stand to knock loose random shards that hung from the edges. They all backed away as the stench of death escaped the interior. The smell was strong enough that they all backed away immediately, causing Ruth to empty her stomach convulsively. Lane motioned them back, and after he gained entry, he opened both doors and used jugs of windshield wiper fluid to hold them open. After an hour, the smell of decay had lessened but still hung in the air. With the doors open, flies had found the city of gold and almost seemed to pour in. There were no dead to be seen. After several minutes, with everyone holding their shirts over their noses, which did nothing to stifle the smell, Lane found a door marked Employees Only.

He knew he'd regret it but cracked open the door, and a fresh wash of putrid hit him square in the face. He motioned others back and took only a few seconds to examine the scene. A severely obese man and woman were huddled together on the floor when they died, their bodies blackened. Three empty insulin bottles and as many syringes lay beside her. Beside the man was a snub-nosed, hammerless .38. It was clear how he'd died. He found a janitor's wide mop in a closet along with a jug of bleach. He wedged the mop against the door and generously dripped bleach on it until it spread beneath the crack of the door.

He escorted them into the shopping mart, where a good bit of things were still on shelves. Beth quickly found the air freshener display and grabbed an assortment of sprays, little cardboard trees, and fruits that could be suspended from a small loop. Robert grabbed three displays of beef jerky and dropped the contents into a reusable shopping bag. Lane didn't find anything of use until he found a lip balm dispenser that was labeled as a one-shot pepper spray. He smiled to himself and put it in his pocket.

Ruth rounded a corner and handed him a clipboard. He quickly examined it and saw that it was an inventory list of remaining fuel. She then handed him a cap tool that made it possible to access the underground fuel stores. Discovering this, they quickly found themselves outside looking for the access caps. It was Robert who held his hand up and whistled. They all joined him, then Lane used the tool to twist the green metal disc free. With a cursory inspection, he could make out that there was diesel remaining in the tank. He quickly removed the plastic hand pump from the MRAP, and after lengthening the feed tube with a piece of PVC, he stuck it in and started pumping the accordion plastic until fuel started spilling into one of the 5-gallon jerry cans.

Robert drove the MRAP over so that they wouldn't have to fill the MRAP with the jerry cans. Once they were filled, the accordion hose proved to be just long enough that two inches fit into the opening. It was a laborious process, and finally, after forty minutes, they were refueled and on their way.

Just as they were about to get back on the interstate, two men on horses rode in front of them. The horses wore modern cattlemen saddles, but the riders were something different. Their facial features were hard and angular, typical of Native American men. But the appearance was mottled by what he could guess was war paint. The man on the left wore shiny black circles all over his face, while the man on the right wore several vertical lines of red. He imagined the lines might have come from lipstick. What they both had in common were AK-74s, and neither looked happy at their presence.

Robert was driving, so Lane popped open the top hatch and waved an oil rag above in a half-pitched attempt at a peaceful greeting. "They doing anything?" he asked Robert.

"No, just looking pissed off like before."

Lane emerged high enough that his saddle seat put him at waist level above the opening. "What can I do for you, gentlemen?" Lane asked them.

"Leave," said the man on the right.

"And don't come back," said the man on the left.

"That's not a problem. We're just passing through." He started to lower himself back down, but the man on the left stopped him.

"Wait," he pleaded. "You're not part of the Group, are you?"

Lane resettled himself in the seat. "No, I'm not part of those fuckers, nor is anyone else in here. I'm going to Alaska to find my son." He cursed himself for giving away information needlessly.

"We can give you information for safe passage as far as Washington. That's as far as our people's network goes. We belong to the Eastern Shoshone. We maintain contact with the other reservations. We can provide safe passage, but we need things to barter with.

What you choose to trade with us for this information and passage is up to you. We will not steal from you," he finished.

Damn right you won't steal. All I gotta do is spin this .50 at you and this conversation is over. The thought vanished as he considered what their people might be going through. "How about 100 ounces in junk silver?"

They both looked at each other for a minute, then the man on the right spoke. "Have you got any ibuprofen?"

Lane disappeared, and a moment later, he popped out the rear hatch and walked over to the men. Beth jumped up in the rear hatch in case they decided to change their minds.

Lane handed the man on the left a bank sack full of silver and handed the man on the right a 500-count bottle of generic ibuprofen 500 mg. The man on the left handed Lane a bundle of feathers bound in a leather strip with muticolored beads on it. "That's your subway token. I'll pass along that you're heading their way. Bring me a map."

Lane yelled at Ruth to hand him his atlas. She handed it down to him, and he walked back. The man on the left took it, and after removing a red pen from inside his coat, he marked out a new route for them to follow.

"Wait, how will you be able to let them know?" Lane asked suspiciously.

"Smoke signals, of course," the man said without any hint of humor.

"Are you serious?" Lane asked in surprise.

"Nah, I'm just fucking with you. We got ham radios and repeaters that work. They'll all know within minutes. One other thing, those fat people, they dead?" he asked.

"Dead like the president," Lane replied and got back in the MRAP.

MARCH 3, 2025

ROBERT SAT CRADLED BEHIND THE .50, ITS barrel smoking. Lane was prone on the ground thirty yards ahead, four men lay dead in front of him with the last remnants of their lifeforce staining I-5 crimson in Custer, Washington, a little over five miles away from the Canadian border. Beth had been answering nature's call when the thugs, concealed by cargo vans that blocked the interstate, caught a glimpse of her bare ass hidden behind a Volkswagen Jetta. They were drunk and immediately started whistling and offering their carnal services. That's when Lane got out of the MRAP and walked toward the blockade. Robert opened the hatch, climbed in the saddle, and manned the .50. Lane warned them one at a time when they emerged from the corner of a U-Haul truck. Then he told them collectively just how bad it was going to end for them if they started anything.

They were all armed and passing a very large blunt around. Lane opted to approach them with his .44 holstered and nothing else, hoping that it would ease any anxiety they might have. The truth of the matter was they could have shown up with an entire battalion of pissed-off Rangers, and it would have done nothing to dampen the thugs' bravado. The lead thug raised his weapon, and that's when Lane dropped to the ground and Robert opened fire. There was no time for them to evade the hellish munitions that cut them down. Lane stood up and disappeared behind the moving truck, then came back around and waved all clear.

Ruth drove the MRAP up close and exited the vehicle. Beth and Robert got out of the rear and joined Lane and Ruth. Ruth held out a canvas bag while Lane deposited the pistols. Robert briefly examined the long guns and, after unloading them, broke them against the ground and threw the pieces into a flooded ditch. Lane went to the rear of the MRAP and came back with a heavy chain. He looped the chain around the rear tire of the truck and attached it to a hauling bolt. Ruth climbed back in and put it in reverse. The chain went tight, and after a brief moment of doubt, the tires started leaving rubber tracks as they inched away from the blockade. After a few moments more, Ruth deftly maneuvered the truck away until there was an opening wide enough for them to pass through. Lane disconnected the chain, and they all got back inside.

Fifteen minutes later, they were passing through South Surrey, Canada. There was nothing remarkable about the little town. In fact, as they passed through greater Surrey, it was much like any large town they had passed through. The roads were littered with derelict vehicles, and here and there, corpses were left to the crows and the ever-increasing appearance of rats. They crossed over Fraser River and were soon entering Burnaby. Ruth was telling Lane about a dog she had when she was a little girl after seeing a street sign named Basset Hound Boulevard. The story she told lasted until they passed through Vancouver and crossed over the bridge out of Stanley Park.

They were all laughing at the story when Ruth stopped laughing and slowed the MRAP to a stop. Blocking their path were six vintage Jeep Wagoneers, all painted powder blue with red maple leaves and RCMP decals on the doors. A dozen men stood vigil armed with a mix of ARs and hunting rifles. They were also uniformed and wearing badges.

One man slung his AR and approached them. He was a tall, heavyset man who looked as if he'd spent a lot of years in the gym. He wasn't young or old, but his skin was weathered from time spent outside, and the way he carried himself screamed confidence. He lifted a tortière to his mouth and took a bite. He was all smiles and chewing when he came to the door.

Ruth lowered the window and made a point of visibly returning her hands to the driving wheel. Lane put his pistol on the dash, holding it by the barrel.

"Thanks, folks. I appreciate the courtesy. Passports?" he announced like nothing had changed since D-Day.

"Say again," Lane piped up.

The man's grin vanished, and several seconds passed before he broke out in a snicker. "I'm just razzin' you, eh."

Lane and Ruth visibly relaxed. "You had me there," Lane mumbled.

"Where you guys heading in the war wagon?" the officer asked.

"Alaska, to find my son. He's above the Artic Circle in Noatak," Lane admitted.

"You're in for a journey. You've got about 1,350 miles of road and snow before you cross the border again. You're also gonna have to get through native gangs from here on out. They aren't the Group, but they're damn close enough. So I'm gonna let you folks pass through. I am going to need a toll. Me and my boys are shacked up close to here, but we don't exactly have a lot of supplies. I'm not going to search your vehicle, but if you have food to spare, it will really help." The Mountie put on his best sad face.

"I'll be right back," Lane said and disappeared in the back.

Five minutes later, Lane got out carrying a box. He approached the officer and handed him the box. They had been fruitful during their journey and scavenged enough food to last them through the entire trip. The box contained coffee, sugar, canned meats, freeze-dried fruits, dry beans, ramen, salt, pepper, saltines, mustard, hard candies, cocoa mix, and cigarettes. The man smiled at the contents and genuinely looked surprised. Lane handed him the box and walked beside him until they reached the rest of the men. Lane lit a cigarette and passed them out to the smokers. The men looked through the box and patted Lane on the back in appreciation. He shook hands with everyone and turned to leave. That's when the smiling man set down the box and hit Lane in the back of the head with the butt of his AR. He crumpled to the ground, and two men grabbed him by the ankles and started pulling him behind one of the Jeeps. Before he disappeared behind the vehicle, his prosthetic came free in the hands of an abductor. They all laughed and raised their rifles at the MRAP.

EPILOGUE

NEW YEAR
JANUARY 1, 2025

EIGHT MEN SAT AROUND A LARGE DINING room table. They were heavily tattooed in jailhouse ink, and their shaved heads were equally adorned with tattoos that the worst of mothers would never have approved of. They were eating a breakfast that would make Jeff Bezos blush. A buffet of meats, eggs, cheeses, fruits, pastries, and potatoes filled the table, along with orange juice, coffee, and pints of Guinness. Three scantily clad women serviced the table and the men. The women displayed their own ink; they all had tags inked on their necks identifying their owners. The youngest of the three had a black eye that had started to yellow at the edge of the bruising. She picked up a carafe of orange juice and filled the largest man's glass. He thanked her by slapping her on the ass so hard that she yelped out loud. She rubbed her ass, wincing; a red handprint could be seen that disappeared beneath her white cotton panties.

Chuma was a captain and enjoyed the benefits of being an enforcer. He'd been born into crime at an early age, apprenticing at the heel of his father's motorcycle gang. Once he was old enough to ride, he'd learned quickly that power was the most valuable thing any man could possess. When his father's leadership was usurped, he stood by and supported the man who succeeded him. He waited for two more years, proving himself, before he broke the neck of his father's usurper and leader in front of the whole population of Swan Sharks. It had been at an annual gathering of the club, an opportunity for anyone in the club to challenge the leader for his crown. So at the age of twenty, Chuma Borofski became the leader of the Sioux Falls chapter of Swan Sharks. He learned shortly after that day that a Russian mafia organization was the gang's support and benefactor. The Bratva stayed in the shadows and kept them fueled with methamphetamine and guns, issuing orders to the gang leader through an intermediary. They, in turn, did the Bratva's bidding whenever asked.

The girl pulled her panties away to view the handprint and gently returned the elastic band to her waist. Chuma grinned at her, thinking he would put more handprints on her ass after breakfast. She noticed him watching her and faked a smile.

He was a hulking figure at 6'8", his body displayed dedicated years of prison yard muscle. Like many idiots, prison was the result of poor decisions and stupidity; his was not. At the age of thirty-three, he ran seventeen chapters of the South Dakota Swan Sharks. By thirty-five, he was president over South and North Dakota chapters and was one of the three biker presidents who sat at the table with Bratva leadership to conduct business. It was around this time that Bratva needed him to take one for the team. Chuma gave himself up as a sacrificial lamb. He was caught on camera selling three hundred AK-47s to a native gang from a nearby reservation. The haul was large enough for the ATF to put him away for sixty years without parole, along with several of his sergeants. While all the heat was going down with Swan Sharks, the Bratva started partnering with a small trucking company, trafficking everything from drugs and guns to technology and humans. The business became so lucrative that the trucking company branched out to Canada. By accident, the trucking company started competing with legitimate national brands. Soon, their fleet was so large that hubs were being constructed around the country, and because they had so much cash to launder, they were able to pad their profit margins and outbid two of their competitors into financial ruin and bankruptcy.

Soon, the political machines started soliciting their support in Washington. This is where Moscow started pulling strings with the Bratva. By the end of 2022, nearly 70 percent of the Democratic Party was bought and paid for, and with their cooperation, Moscow made sure they were reelected. Six weeks before D-Day, the seeds of an extended friendship with Russia and China were firmly planted. After D-Day, Moscow had had enough of the Bratva running things and used their inexhaustible resources to put someone into play whom they could trust.

The warden of the federal prison that held Chuma and his fellow Swan Sharks was paid handsomely to provide a loving home for their newest residents. They were given special food and privileges and a steady stream of women that kept Chuma and the Swan Sharks happy. Once a week, the warden would meet with Chuma in his office to make sure everything was to their liking. This was when inmate 811 first noticed Chuma. It wasn't the food and women that caught his attention but the one-on-one meetings. The warden used counselors for all meetings with inmates without exception, but not this man.

Inmate 811 paid closer attention to the large bald man and his cohorts. He was amused by how the transition was easy enough for Chuma and how soon he became the boss of all the Aryan gangs inside all the prisons in the Dakotas. By the time he was forty, he ran all Aryan activities in the northwest. Nothing happened unless it went through him first. It was around this time that inmate 811 broke his silence and introduced himself when Chuma became Kiril Viktor's puppet.

The girl rubbed her ass again as bruising started to take the place of the red handprint. He laughed watching her, motioned for her to come to him, and she did. He pulled her into his lap, cuddled her, and kissed her on the neck. She seemed to soften a little and was about to relax when he bent her over his lap and bit her on the butt cheek hard until tears filled her eyes. He let her up, and before she could scamper away, he slapped her on the ass again. All the men laughed, and Chuma filled his mouth with eggs and potatoes.

Kiril Viktor walked into the dining room carrying a mug of tea. He looked nothing like the men who sat at the table. The men wore the warmest clothes they could scavenge, and nearly all of their garments were mismatched. Viktor was the complete opposite. His body was void of any markings. His silver hair was neatly groomed and combed with a part on the side. He wore pleated black dress pants, a cream-colored linen button-down shirt, and gray Italian leather loafers. The only piece of jewelry he wore was a Russian Vostok wind-up watch. The men noticed him immediately and grew quiet. He walked to the fireplace and stared at the fire. He bent over, placed a piece of wood into the flames, then turned to the men.

"Do you all know how control can be measured like a fire?" he asked and made eye contact with each of them.

They all looked at each other in puzzlement, then answered no or shook their heads. Chuma started to say something but wisely remained silent.

"You see, once you have built a fire, you can do many things with it. You can provide warmth. You can create sustenance. You can forge steel and harden it. Above all things, you can keep predators at bay." Kiril paused for effect and was glad to see he had their undivided attention; even the girls were listening intently. He went on. "Now if the fire grows too big, you exhaust very precious fuel and the fire dies…so does the asset that was keeping you alive. If you let the fire burn down to embers, you must tend it carefully so that the embers can be rekindled when you need it. A good camp still requires time to tend a fire when it burns to embers. Right now, we have a struggling fire and not yet embers. Our other camps, however, are close to embers. Why is that?" He paused for effect again because he knew they didn't have the answer.

"I'll tell you why. There aren't enough capable people to tend the fire. That's why on this New Year's Day, I am changing the scope of leadership and bringing in family that I know will not only tend the fires but build new ones. You see, that's the other part of fire. Fire can be used as a weapon if it's big enough and hot enough. You bunch are not big enough or hot enough," he said, turning his back to them and warming his hands by the fire.

Chuma began to squirm uncomfortably in his chair; the rest of the men betrayed themselves with similar body language. The swinging door to the kitchen opened and swung back and forth as two men clad in black fatigues entered the dining area. They were tall, hard-looking men; their faces were expressionless, clean-shaven, and marked with scars. They each held HK45 tactical pistols with suppressors that were comically large enough to double as Pringles cans. All of the men seated at the table averted their eyes; they'd never seen these men before.

"Chuma, isn't your team in charge of Indiana?" Kiril asked the man.

"Yeah, boss," he answered quickly.

"I thought so," Kiril replied and imperceptibly nodded toward the hard-looking men.

One of the hard-looking men nodded to a shadow in the room, and the girl with the sore ass strode in and stood behind Chuma. He didn't notice the girl as his attention was locked on the men and their suppressed pistols.

"You have value, Chuma, you always have. But you're like an old bull. You're the meanest and biggest bull in the pasture. You fuck every cow that crosses your path. The problem with that is all the other bulls begin to stray because the pasture isn't big enough for them. They look for other pastures, and that, my very large friend, is something I can't allow. Your bulls are disappearing, looking for larger pastures. Like this scout team you sent into Tennessee without my knowledge. We've tipped our hats, as they say. And we lost vehicles, guns, and men," Kiril told him, still facing the fireplace.

The girl with the sore ass moved so fast that Chuma could only touch the surface of the wire garrote that circled his neck. He tried to squirm his fingers beneath the wire, but it was too tight.

"Here's the thing, though. Those bulls did not have adequate supervision. The good part is my former Spetsnaz friends were able to keep an eye on those bulls. They also saw who eliminated the team in Tennessee. Their bulls are currently on the way to deal with that inconvenience. Their fire is carefully built. Their bulls aren't looking for new pastures." He finished by nodding at the men in black.

They moved quickly with practiced and professional proclivity with the pistols. Chuma watched as a single round was placed into each of the men's heads at the table. In as little as three seconds, all of the bald men at the table wore ghastly wounds. As blood pooled on the table and floor, Ms. Sore Ass released the garrote and stepped away. Chuma touched his throat, his fingertips coming away covered in blood. He turned and looked at the girl in disbelief as she turned on her heels and left the room.

"The next time…well, there won't be a next time. Tend your fires, Chuma. Changes are coming soon, and I need all of my fires tended. Suffice to say, I haven't been home in nearly four decades. However, they also say home is where the heart is. And my heart is about to be warmed by the fires of home. So make sure you find some bulls that won't leave the pasture. And if you touch my niece ever again, I'll have her use that garrote so that the old bull will no longer be useful to a cow." Kiril turned and left through the kitchen door, swinging back and forth. Chuma could hear him say something in Russian from behind the door.

"Wait, I don't speak Russian. What does that mean?" Chuma asked, staring at the door.

The two men in black turned and followed after him. The last of the men paused in the doorway and looked back at him. In heavily accented English, he replied to Chuma's question.

"It means, go do my bidding." He smiled barely enough that a scar raised over his lip, and then he disappeared behind the door bouncing on its hinges.

The two women stood motionless in the corner, cowering. Chuma stood up and looked at them. "Go to your room."

He then walked to the mantle of the fireplace and spoke into a radio. A few minutes passed before a young man entered the room with six men on his heels.

"You're all taking over these men's territories. Call together your sergeants, and get the word out ASAP. Do what you're told, and make sure you do it right. Take these bodies and bury them in the sand trap by the fourteenth hole. Meet me back after that's done. We have fires to tend."

ABOUT THE AUTHOR

J. T. WHITE IS A US ARMY infantry veteran and patriot who descended from wartime veterans on both sides of his family. He spent his young adult life in northeast Tennessee. When he wasn't working in various industries, he spent his time studying martial arts, fishing, hunting, and hiking the woods and mountains of his home.

As a youth, he spent his time prowling libraries and being inspired by the likes of Stephen King, Anne Rice, and Clive Cussler. After relocating to central Georgia, he began writing countless volumes of work until he found a fascination with dystopian fiction. It was this fascination that inspired him to complete his first book and start developing a world that he could shape into his own.

Upon completion of this book, he announced that two other books are already in the works, and the second is close to completion. He explained that his other books will remain in the same universe, and at some point, many of the characters will cross paths.